T0328506

BOUNDLESS

BOUNDLESS

Kefen Budji

SPEARS MEDIA PRESS
BAMENDA

Published in 2015
Copyright © Kefen Budji 2015

All rights reserved.
No part of this publication may be reproduced, distributed, or transmitted in any form
or by any means, including photocopying, recording, or other electronic or mechanical
methods, without the prior written permission of the publisher, except in the case of
brief quotations embodied in critical reviews and certain other noncommercial uses
permitted by copyright law. For permission requests, write to the publisher, addressed
"Attention: Permissions Coordinator," at the address below.

Spears Media Press
P O Box 1151
Bamenda, NWR,
Cameroon
www.spearsmedia.com
Email: info@spearsmedia.com

Ordering Information:
Quantity sales. Special discounts are available on quantity purchases by corporations,
associations, and others. For details, contact the publisher at the address above.

ISBN: 978-1-942876-02-1 [Paperback]
ISBN: 978-1-942876-03-8 [Ebook]

To Mum and Dad, thank you

PART ONE

Chapter One

1910

"Wake up Samarah, child wake up!" The young girl barely heard her mother's voice through the fog of sleep. She was dreaming of herself and some play mates, Bintum included, making catapults in the courtyard of the palace. She rolled over and pulled the hand-knitted quilt over her head, but her mother's voice would not fade away.

"Please, Samarah, don't sleep. This is not time to sleep!" Samarah stirred, forced her eyes open and focused them on her mother. The next second, she sprang from the grass bed and watched in growing alarm as her mother flung things here and there, picking bits of cloth up, and discarding them without so much as a glance. She could hear the *'Tum, Tum, Tum'* sound of the *Kinton,* the talking drum, as it went on and on. Something was very wrong. Nobody played that drum. Not even the Chief himself could order the playing of this particular drum, except in dire situations.

"Bwan, what is wrong?" Samarah had never seen her mother this frantic. Her mother turned to face her. Samarah could just about make out her mother's face in the dim light emanating from the fireplace, but weren't those tears glistening in her eyes? Her mother never cried. She always said tears were for the weak.

"The white men, child!" Samarah's eyes opened wider.

"Where? Here?"

"Just hurry. Don't stand there so! There isn't time. Here, tie your loincloth. Hurry!" Her mother finally put a small bundle together, and she assisted Samarah to tie her loincloth over her budding breasts so that it went right down to her knees. Then with the bundle in one hand and Samarah's palm in the other, she rushed out of the hut. Samarah had never seen so much commotion before. People ran helter-skelter. Panic filled the air. Mothers sobbed as they held their screaming babies to their breasts and gathered their other children around them. Very few men could be seen.

"Where is Baa?" Samarah asked. Her mother pulled her through the confused crowd till they passed through the courtyard, and reached the reception hut – the biggest of all the huts, which was built in front of the other five huts that formed a cluster, and made up the palace. Two *Nchindas* with their dark colour glistening in the moonlight, quickly made way for mother and child to pass.

A fire burnt brightly in the fireplace of the hut, illuminating the bamboo chairs and the ten or so sub chiefs occupying them. A tall man who wore the skin of a monkey on his back and a short loin cloth around his waist had his back to them. Samarah's hand shook in her mother's. She knew that under normal circumstances, no woman was allowed into the hut if the men (and not just men, sub chiefs!) had a meeting, except she had been summoned. It did not matter if the queen and princess wanted to see the Chief. They would just have to wait.

"Bwan, Baa will be very angry with us." The man who stood by the fire place heard Samarah's whisper and turned round, his arms opening wide. Samarah ran across and over the mats on the floor to him. He bent down to wrap her in his arms, as his eyes sought his wife's.

"Listen, my child, you must leave at once with your mother." The sub chiefs averted their eyes. Samarah's eyes met her father's.

"Why, Baa? What is happening? Is it true that the white men

are coming?"

"Yes, child. The Jaman people are on their way here."

"What do they want?"

"You won't understand." She buried her face in his chest.

"Then we'll stay with you, Baa." The Chief used his forefinger on Samarah's chin to tilt her head upward so that he could look directly into her eyes.

"No, go with your mother and protect her."

"*Bo Ntow* (My Lord)." Samarah's mother murmured. At once, the sub chiefs stood up and trooped out of the hut. The Chief rose to his full height and looked at his young wife.

"Take care of our child." He said as the reflection of the fire blazed in his eyes. She ran into his arms and clung to her husband, with their only child between them.

"*Bo Ntow*, please, come with us." She pleaded as she buried her face in the crook of his neck.

"You know Yenla that I cannot do this thing you are asking. The Chefwa people are known for their courage, and it would be wrong for me to abandon my people. Our people say it is a coward who hides underneath his wife's loincloth." Yenla sobbed into his neck. His hand came up to cradle her hair. "Where is my tigress, my daring and fearless woman? What happened to my enchantress who stood firm in the face of any adversity?"

"She fell in love." The queen sobbed. She leaned back to see his face. "You are the first person they should protect. You are the Chief."

"Woman! Would I be worthy of that title if I deserted my people in their time of need? Listen, Yenla, do as I say. Take this child to safety." As he spoke his hand touched her stomach, "He will grow up strong like his sister and mother." He concluded.

"On the condition that you promise to come back to me. Promise me!" The Chief held his weeping wife away from him.

"I am but a man. Giving or taking of life depends on the gods."
He looked at her for a second longer and then engulfed her and
Samarah in a warm embrace.

"Ahem. May we come in?" A voice called from outside. Samarah's
mother stepped away as the Chief asked the sub chiefs to come in.
The two *Nchindas* accompanied them. The Chief gave orders for
them to take all the women and children as far from Chefwa as
they could. Samarah's mother removed a bead-and-cowry necklace
necklace from around her neck and fastened it around his.

"This was the first gift you gave me when you began courting me.
It is my wish that you give it to me again when we meet." Samarah was surprised to hear her mother's voice so firm, and was still
more shocked to see that no tears flowed from her eyes any more.
She however sensed that this was probably a painful moment for
Yenla. The Chief embraced both of them again, and then stepped
back and gave his back to them.

"Now go." Heaving a sigh as quietly as she could, Yenla, queen of
the Chefwa people took her daughter's hand and without looking
back, walked out of the hut.

The commotion had reduced considerably. The women and
children had already formed a small group, with about twenty men
who would protect them. As Samarah and her mother headed
towards them, Samarah heard someone calling her name. She
stopped and turned round. Her face softened into a smile as Bintum
came to her. He was three years older than she was. He was the
son of one of the sub chief who happened to be her father's best
friend. Samarah knew that she had been betrothed to him at birth,
even though she hardly ever thought of marriage. At this moment,
all she knew was that he was her best friend, and would one day
be her husband, whatever the second part meant. She pulled her
hand from her mother's and ran to him.

"Are you going with us?" She asked.

"Shh, not so loud." He whispered. "Father says I should go because he thinks that I am a child, but I am not a child. I am fifteen. See how tall I am."

Samarah, who was a lot shorter, nodded solemnly.

"What will you do?"

"I'll pretend to leave with you. Then I'll find a way to sneak back and fight for our people."

"Spoken like a true prince." Samarah had heard that expression used by her mother before and she thought it would be a good reply to what Bintum had said. Following her mother's example, she removed a much simpler necklace, made of twine and one cowry, and wore it around Bintum's neck. Then she ran to join the others before he could say anything.

The group left the palace through a bamboo side-gate, and took a path which passed through the little forest. The undergrowth loomed in the dark like some fence or hedge which could slow them down, or protect them, depending on how one decided to look at it. The men asked everyone to be quiet. From time to time, a baby cried.

As she trudged along with the others, Samarah could hear the hooting of owls and the chirping of crickets. These were familiar sounds, sounds she had heard ever since she was born. They were comfortable sounds. She could relate to them, could understand that there was still some level of 'normality' around. She made a mental note to tell Bintum when they came back where they both could hunt for crickets. Occasionally, she heard some rustling in the bushes and imagined snakes crawling all over the place and at such moments she shivered and felt the goose flesh erupt along her arms. She completely, totally, loathed and feared snakes.

"Bwan, what do the Jamans want with us?" She asked to get her mind off the rustling.

"They want our land. Your father told them he had no more land to give. He has already given them so much farmland, but they are not satisfied. They are never satisfied. Give them a handshake, and next they want an embrace!"

"Bwan, Baa will be fine. The men will fight, just like they did in Nso." Nso was a bigger community just about two days' trek from Chefwa. These people had been popular because four years before, in 1906, they had rebelled against German rule. Even though the Germans had ultimately dealt mercilessly with them, their names had been woven into songs, their courage and fearless deeds recited at gatherings.

They walked most of the night. At some point when Samarah had stumbled for about the fifth time, one of the *Nchindas* picked her up and lifted her unto his shoulders. Shortly before dawn, they came to the entrance of a cave. Many of the adults knew of this cave. It had served in the past as a haven from the rain or other unpleasant weather for many a weary traveler. One of the men lit a fire torch and went in. Almost immediately Samarah heard a commotion which made her jump and cling to her mother's hand, and out of the mouth of the cave flew bats. They flapped their wings and screeched and she imagined she understood how they felt, being rudely awakened from their sleep and ousted from their home by the threat of aliens, just as she had been by the threat of the Germans.

The man came out of the hut and reported that it was safe inside. Everyone trooped in. The first thing Samarah noticed was the cold which swept over her body. It was like she had stepped into the house of the god of hailstones and water. It was damp. She felt water under her feet leaking from the stones that made up the floor. She was pretty sure the walls were leaking too. The cave was much larger than she had imagined. It grew bigger and colder as they went deeper inside. Samarah rubbed the back of her neck with her palm. Her feet ached, her eyes felt heavy with sleep, her mouth felt parched and her body felt like it had been soaked in the stream all evening. She heaved a sigh and wished that they had come to the end of their journey.

Finally they came to the rear of the cave. It was the widest they had seen and felt less damp under her feet. The *Nchindas* lit more torches. Samarah's view was much clearer. She noticed water oozing from some spots in the cave wall. The floor felt less damp than in the rest of the cave. The green slime on parts of the cave gave a moldy odour which reminded her of the smell of rotting corn in the barn during harvest time in the rainy season. It was cold, so cold she could hardly keep her teeth from chattering. Her mother opened one of the bundles she had managed to tie together, and brought out two loincloths. She laid one down on the floor and asked Samarah to lie on it. Then she used the other to spread it over Samarah's body so Samarah would feel warmer. The other women were doing the same. Yenla gave the order. They would spend what was left of the night here and then see about food when the sun rose. While the others lay down and tried to make their exhausted bodies as comfortable as one could on a hard, damp floor, the queen sobbed quietly. Only Samarah could hear her. She had never seen her mother like this. She decided to stay awake to keep her mother company, but she was so tired, she soon dozed off.

They stayed in the cave for days without any news from those they had left behind. A few men went hunting during the day and some women went around the cave gathering as much fruit that they came across as possible. If the men happened to catch any game, it was roasted in the evening and shared to everyone. If they were unlucky, then there was always some fruit. The meals were never quite filling but no one was starving either. The children were never allowed to leave the cave except when nature called and that was only when they would go in a group with at least three men for protection. In this way four days went by.

Yenla had noticed on the second day that Bintum was not with them and after asking questions, especially to Samarah, her sorrow had increased. Nobody seemed to know where he was, not even Samarah. Yenla was distraught, but she hid it well. Bintum, as Samarah's husband to be, might very well have to be the next Chief if the men who had stayed back to fight did not survive. What if something happened to him?

On the fifth night, one of the sentries came in earlier than usual, supporting a young boy who was covered with blood. He brought the boy to the queen, who ordered that he be cleaned up as everyone gathered round. When the blood was washed away, both Yenla and Samarah gasped. It was Bintum. At once, the queen asked that he be given food and attended to but he wouldn't hear of it. She was dying to know what had happened but she thought what Bintum needed first was rest.

"We were defeated, Highness." He croaked as he was stretched out on a loincloth. "There were too many of them, and they had weapons we did not know – they even had the sticks that spit fire."

"And the Chief, Bintum, what about him, and the Council of Elders?" At her question, the lad bent his head and said nothing, but he struggled to remove something he had tied to his loincloth.

"*Bo Ntow* asked me to give you this." Yenla took what was in his hand with a pounding heart and a sense of foreboding. The world stopped moving for her when she glanced into her palms and recognized her necklace.

"No," She whispered, clutching it to her chest. "No, he was supposed to return this to me himself… the gods have killed me." She raised one hand to her head and squeezed her eyes shut.

"What is it, Bwan? Bintum, where is my father? What about your father and the others?" Samarah was confused as she looked from her mother to Bintum. Neither of them seemed to notice that she had spoken. The queen retreated to an isolated part of the cave. Some of the elderly women went to her.

"Bo Ntow noh laa, Bo Ntow noh laa (the Chief is lost)." People whispered to each other. Chiefs did not die. They simply got lost and disappeared from this life to that of the ancestors.

"The Jamans have done it. They have killed me!" And for the first time, Yenla broke down and cried in front of everybody. The women joined her in shedding tears and most of the older women ululated; while the men shrugged, shook their heads from side to side, and muttered in low tones,

"The sun has set on our land; the lion is no more. Emeh! Rot does not spare even the cocoyam, Emeh!"

As the mourning was going on, another man burst into the cave. His loin cloth was torn and his feet were bleeding. At once, men went toward him, but he limped past them as he cried,

"Bo Ntow noh laa! Quick, Highness, it is time to leave this place. They are coming." Yenla did not hear a word he said. She sat frozen staring into space. The men rallied the group together and they started to move out.

"Bwan, let us go." Samarah's hand slipped into her mother's. Yenla was not crying anymore. She just stared into space. One of the *Nchindas*, after apologizing for what he was about to do, bent, wound one hand around her waist, pulled her up and supported her as they started to walk towards the others. No one was supposed to touch royalty, except royalty itself, but these were desperate times, and what had to be done had to be done. Two others supported Bintum on both sides.

The group had not walked ten minutes from the cave when a sentry at the back saw torches of fire coming toward them.

"We must go faster. They are almost here." He shouted. No sooner had he said that than a shot was heard and one of the women went down. Chaos broke loose. Everyone scattered in all directions. Yenla immediately pushed Samarah in front of her and turned to see about Bintum as more shots were heard. One of the men supporting Bintum went down too. Yenla took his place and shouted orders as they sped along.

"Run people, save yourselves. Let it not be that our men sacrificed themselves in vain! You, Kontai, carry the princess. Wangaa, we need to carry Bintum."

The two *Nchindas* carried their charges and ran on with the queen behind them. Another shot and a man behind the queen fell down, pushing the queen down too, his body trapping her. The two men turned back to aid her stand up.

"No, forget about me." She screamed. "Take my daughter to safety. Will I lose a husband and a daughter at the same time?" The guard carrying Bintum ran on but Samarah's cry of "Bwan, Bwan" caused her own guard to turn back and try to pull the queen up with one hand, the other holding Samarah on his back. They heard men's shouts in the distance. Next thing they heard was a shot. A bullet went through the guard's forehead. One moment, Samarah was fine. The next, she felt herself flying through the air, from a great height all the way down to the ground.

"Bwan!" she screamed as she felt someone fall on top of her.

"My daughter, my baby." Yenla tried to pull her from under the dead man's body. Someone grabbed her from behind just as she succeeded in pulling Samarah free.

"I have two," the man who grabbed her shouted.

"Bwan!" Samarah cried as she clung to her mother, her arms wrapped around her waist. The man spun Yenla to face him, and she stared in horror into the eyes of a black man.

*

A majority of the people were captured that night. The prisoners, most of them women and children, were taken back to the cave and made to sit on the damp floor. Samarah sat beside her mother and leaned against her. Her body ached and she longed to sleep but whenever she closed her eyes she saw either her father's face or Bintum's and then she would open them again. Finally she realized that she had managed to doze off only when she opened her eyes to find the faint light of dawn seeping in. She felt arms holding her tight. Where was she? Was this a dream?

"Mmmm." She murmured.

"Shh. I am right here, child," Yenla murmured as she wrapped her arms more tightly around Samarah.

"Where are we?" Samarah whispered.

"Back in the cave."

As more light filtered in, Samarah looked around her. All the captives were sitting on the wet floor. There were some other people in the cave too: two black men, whom she had never seen before (obviously, they were not Chefwa people), and three white men slept to one side of the cave, as far away from the rest of the people as possible.

She must have nodded off again because she jumped awake when a voice boomed, "March out!" in one of the dialects of the area. Her eyes flew open and she was surprised to see light cascading into the cave. She saw the captives struggling to stand. Her mother stood up and pulled her up too. As she stood up she noticed a red stain on her mother's leg. Blood. Was it her blood or her mother's or one of the *Nchindas'*?

"Bwan, where is Bintum?"

"I looked around last night and stayed awake to see the new arrivals. He was not brought in."

"Does that mean that he got away?"

"I hope so. Ye gods, I really pray so."

Just then one of the black men surged forward, grabbed Yenla's arm and pushed her to join the others who were already trooping out of the cave. Samarah ran to help Yenla get her balance. Her mother held her with one hand and flattened the other against her belly. They went out with the others. They were made to stand in a long line.

The men told them not to talk and with whips, they forced them to walk in the opposite direction of the road they had taken the night before. Towards evening, exhausted, hungry, thirsty and full of pain, the group finally entered a clearing in the forest. They could hear the sound of running water nearby. Samarah complained that she was very tired and her throat was parched. Yenla squeezed her daughter's hand but said nothing. What did one say to a ten year old who had in less than a week witnessed death, suffering, pain and anguish, especially when these had never been part of her world?

Some more white men were at the clearing. It seemed they had been waiting there for some time. The captives were asked to sit down. Most of them were thankful for the rays of the sun that succeeded in penetrating the intertwined leaves overhead. It was much better than the damp and chilly cave.

Samarah watched as the white men who had been waiting talked with the other three who had been in the cave. Then they all walked towards the group, and stood looking at them. Presently, one of the new arrivals spoke to a German and Samarah gasped and pointed at him as she said to her mother, "that man is an Englishman. He speaks English."

Samarah's father had decided to send her to a school, opened by the Basel Mission since 1885, under the protection of the Germans. Though the chief had had nothing to do with their religion, he had let his daughter attend their school and even their service. Chief Kintashe had not been a fool. He had known that the old ways were fast dying out as the oracle had foretold to his fathers before him. So when his gaze had fallen on his baby girl for the first time, he had wanted to equip her to face the future and find a place in the fast changing times. Thus, six years after her birth, he had taken her to the missionaries to teach her their ways. Though they were mainly Swiss, missionaries from other countries joined them. Father Clement had been an Englishman who was of the Basel faith and had been sent to the hinterlands to spread the Good News, along with some German and Swiss missionaries. Samarah had been a part of his congregation, and had consequently learnt to speak English and German.

The queen tried to push Samarah's hand down. "Don't point, Samarah!" Too late though. The man had seen them and he headed their way. Samarah's heart beat fast in her chest, as she whispered to her mother, "what is he doing with the Germans? Father Clement told us they were enemies."

"Then he must be a sell out," Yenla said.

The man looked at mother and child for a while and muttered to himself, "I wonder if Lucy will want this gift. I wish I'd find a bloody native who could at least articulate sounds in the queen's language."

"I speak English," Samarah said before her mother clapped her palm over Samarah's mouth, but the man had already heard. His bushy brows knotted in a frown.

"You, stand up," he said. Samarah obeyed, but Yenla remained seated. Even though she understood a little English because Samarah had been trying to teach her a word or two in the language, no man – white or otherwise- would order her about. She was a queen.

"So you do understand English."

"Yes," Samarah said. The man slapped her across her cheek. At this, Yenla sprang to her feet to shield her daughter with her arms. Samarah clutched her mother's loin cloth and began to cry.

"You say 'sir' when you talk to a white man, little girl." He ground out, his face growing red. He raked a hand through his short, brown hair, and muttered to himself, as he walked back to the other white man. Yenla and Samarah watched the two men, and saw the British man hand over some money to the German. A hefty black man was sent their way. He came towards mother and daughter, tied their hands with ropes and led them away. Yenla bore all this with silent dignity. She did not protest and did not slump in the least, but held her head high as she and her daughter were led out of the clearing to a wagon, pulled by two horses, which stood out of sight of the clearing. There were some other people from another village in the wagon –two men and one woman who was probably in her sixties. Yenla sat down with a vacant look in her eyes. Samarah clutched her hand and smiled at them in greeting and they smiled back. . Then Samarah looked towards the clearing and saw other white men leading the captives in several directions. She glanced up at Yenla, who, after following Samarah's gaze, nodded and told her that their people were being bought and taken to work for the white men, just like she and Samarah had been bought.

But how can you buy a human being? Samarah mused as the black man who had brought them there got on to the cart too, and with a whip, caused the horses to pull the cart. The cart jolted and rattled down a path, through trees, jerking its passengers as it passed over roots, sticks, and stones. The passengers had to grip the sides of the wood they sat on as the cart bumped along the dusty road. Samarah's whole body ached and her head felt like a thousand sharp-pointed sticks had been stuck into it. She glanced behind and saw the man who had slapped her following in a jeep. That was the second jeep she had ever seen in her life. The first had been brought by a visiting missionary when she was six years old.

At noon they stopped by a stream and were allowed to bathe in the water. As Samarah followed her mother to the stream she noticed a brownish-reddish stain on Yenla's loincloth.

"Bwan, there is something wet on your loincloth." She said. Yenla stopped so suddenly that Samarah bumped into her. Yenla's hand came back to touch her loincloth where it covered her behind. She touched something sticky.

"No, please no!" Yenla muttered as she plunged into the water and whipped the loincloth from her body to look at it. Blood. More of it flowed from her into the stream. Yenla gripped the loincloth to her and would have sunk into the water but the woman who had been in the cart with them came to her aid, and assisted her to the banks of the stream. Yenla cried, shaking with the force of her sobs as the woman cradled her and told her the gods knew why, and it was probably best for the child. Child? What child? Samarah wondered. She felt an urge to ask her mother what that woman meant, but seeing Yenla so broken she did not utter a word. Instead she went to them and slipped her smaller palm into her mother's. She felt Yenla exert pressure unto her fingers as she tried to stop her sobs, which gradually reduced to whimpers. Finally Yenla wiped her face, got up, waded into the stream, and set to washing the loincloth, denying the woman's offer to do it for her. Samarah kept silent. She had never seen her mother look this stony. She was scared.

When they rejoined the others they were given some fruits and nuts to eat. Everyone ate but for Yenla. She still had that faraway look like she had been frozen in time. They journey for eight days on the wagon. Samarah knew that they must have travelled a very long way from home. Every day she noticed how the vegetation grew more and more different. First the grass disappeared, then the soil looked redder, next the soil became rockier, and then more trees appeared, and finally they passed through forests, scary sometimes, silent other times, but always very different from what she had known. This was a different land. This was a strange place they were going to. Where would it all lead? When would their journey come to an end? She sometimes sniffed herself and wrinkled her nose. She smelled vile! She needed a bath!

Yenla spoke very little throughout the journey. She would just sit and stare into space, and then sob at night when she thought Samarah was sleeping. Most times she had her palms cradled over her belly as if she was trying to protect something or someone there.

On the ninth day, they finally left the forest behind and the road opened up from just a trifle bigger than a path to a whole lane where two carts could bypass. Now they saw more people than they had seen in the past eight days. Samarah looked at the people they passed with interest. They would have passed for Chefwa people if she hadn't been so sure that Chefwa was a long way away. There were dark-skinned people, brown ones, and much fairer ones. However there was a marked difference in the way they dressed. Back in Chefwa, the women wore loincloths tied over their breasts so that it went down to their knees or sometimes ankles. Here, most of the people wore fragments of skirts and shirts just like the few white men she had seen before. In contrast though, some of the men had loincloths tied around their waist so that it bulged before going right down to their ankles, and wore hardly anything to cover their chests. The women also wore loin cloths around their breasts, and then around their hips too. Their hair was generally braided and there were white markings on some of their faces. These were a different people, but black nonetheless, and Samarah was greatly relieved that it was not the white man's land. She had not seen a single white man here.

At about noon, they pulled in front of the tallest wooden gate Samarah had ever seen. The gate was thrown open and the wagon entered a compound so large that Samarah was sure twenty huts could have been built on it, with large courtyards. The house directly ahead of them had two floors with about nine windows facing the front. It had a large veranda with five big steps leading up to it. Like the gate, it was painted white. Towards the back, Samarah was relieved to see a cluster of huts with thatched roofs almost like the ones built by her people.

The main door of the big white house flew open and a white white girl ran out of the house. Samarah watched as she gave a delighted squeal, ran down the steps towards the man who had come out of the jeep and flung herself into his arms. Samarah thought the girl looked like the picture of an angel she had once seen in Father Clement's chapel. This girl had curly blond hair, which framed her face. Her skin was white while her cheeks were a little pink. She wore a knee - length yellow dress and platform shoes. Samarah thought what was missing were the wings. The child's voice, when she spoke sounded so soft and musical that Samarah couldn't help but listen.

"Father! What did you get me? Nanny said you'd gone to get me a gift."

"Dearest Lucy, I've got a gift for you alright. I got you a personal servant. See that little girl over there?" He pointed at Samarah. Lucy looked in her direction and nodded. "Well, there she is," the man finished. With her hand in her father's, Lucy walked towards Samarah and Yenla. She looked at Samarah from the hair of her head to the soles of her bare feet. Samarah had the uneasy feeling that she was being inspected like a little boy would examine a rare insect. Lucy's eyes met Samarah's and they stared at each other. Then slowly Lucy raised her head to look at her father and raised her eyebrows with a tiny frown.

"And she can speak English too." Lucy's father continued. Lucy's face brightened at that.

"Really? Great. The people here always speak a chattering language I don't understand. That really makes me angry."

"I've noticed, my dear. That's why I got her and her mother."

"Hmmm. They must have cost a lot."

"Lucy Wakerman!" Lucy's smile was sheepish.

"Sorry Father. I just figured you'd bought them, like they bought slaves in England in the past."

"Slave trade was abolished in 1772, young lady. We are in the twentieth century." To hide his discomfort, Mr. Wakerman pulled his daughter toward the house.

"Well, I'll consider her my personal slave." Lucy giggled.

"I am not a slave!" Samarah exploded. Father and daughter turned to stare at her. The bushy eye brows knotted over eyes as blue as his daughter's.

"You will say 'miss' when you address my daughter... what is your name?"

"It's Samarah... Sir."

"From today onward, you do whatever Miss Lucy tells you to do. Is that clear?"

"It is, Sir."

Mr. Wakerman turned to the man who still held the ropes attached to their hands.

"Take them to the empty hut. That will be their home. The old woman can join those in hut five, while the two men of course go into the barn."

"Yes Sah." The man answered, and pulled Samarah and Yenla away.

Their hut at the back of the house had a straw bed and two stools with a fire place. As soon as the man untied them and left, four women came in to the hut. They brought water to drink and some *Sese-planti* to eat. Samarah and her mother accepted the food and drink and thanked them. When they had been left to themselves, Yenla looked at her daughter

"This is our life now, Samarah. We have to make the most of it."

The next morning, they were awakened by the sound of a bell ringing.

"Inzpection!" A voice yelled. They heard doors opening. On

opening theirs they saw lots of black people running to the courtyard at the back of the house, and standing in two lines – men
and boys in one, women and girls in another. A white man with a
beard and a cap was inspecting the lines. There were at least thirty
people there. Samarah and her mother fell in line. After the man
had gone round, he stood at the front of the group.

"Vho here iz Zamarah?" the man bellowed. Samarah raised up
her hand. He looked her up and down.

"Hm. After your bath, go to Miz Lucy in ze mazter'z house.
Iz zat clear?"

"Yes, Sir." She replied, then whispered to her mother,

"He has a funny accent. He is probably German."

"Verdammt Wilder! (Damned savage)," the man cursed, as a
boy ran into the line.

"He definitely is German." Samarah confirmed with a nod.

"German or not, he is white." Yenla replied.

Yenla was assigned to assist the women in the kitchen, and
clean the house.

That evening, Samarah returned to her mother in their hut. Yenla
had already started a fire and she was heating up water to cook fufu.

"How did today go?" She asked her daughter.

"Terrible. That Lucy is lazy and spoilt. She made me fetch every
single thing she needed, and she called me a slave. She looks like
Father Clement's angel, but she does not behave the way Father
Clement told us angels behave."

"Shh. This child! You will put me in trouble."

"Sorry Bwan. Today, when Lucy's teacher was teaching, I knew
the answers to all the questions, but she answered only a few and
refused to answer others."

"Does that mean that you have to stay there even when she has
her lessons?" Yenla asked.

"Yes."

"Thank the gods. Now your father can rest in peace because you will continue your studies. Listen, Samarah, pay close attention to what Lucy's teacher says, but please, don't talk and get into trouble. I have already lost one of you. I don't want to lose the other."

"I hear you Bwan, and now I can continue to teach you English and all the things I learn." Yenla smiled but made no comment while Samarah wondered if her mother was referring to her father or someone else. She decided it most definitely was her father.

That night, after Samarah had said her bedtime prayers just like Faather Clement had taught them, she climbed into the narrow bed she shared with her mother and scampered to the back.

"Bwan."

"Hm?"

"What happened during the slave trade? Was it that period our people refer to as the Time of Dread?"

Her mother was silent for a while. Then she said,

"Yes. Those were strange times. Many, many years ago, before your father's father was even born, white men came to our land. They caught our ancestors and took them far, far away across the great waters to the white man's land. Those who escaped came back with frightful stories of how cruelly they were treated, and how they were sold to other white men. These people were taken away to work for the white man. Later, some black men helped them. Often these men's families were threatened and if they did not do what the white people said, their own families would be sold into slavery. There were some wicked black people too who helped the white men to catch their own brothers. They provoked tribal wars and got captives. Those were dangerous days, when one couldn't trust anyone else, not even his brother."

"Why did our people not fight back?" Samarah wondered. Yenla's laugh was short.

"Fight the white man? What with – sticks, spears and bows and arrows? Hah! No, my child. They had weapons we did not even think existed. See what happened to our village… to your father…" Yenla could not bring herself to go on and Samarah felt her hand shift to rest over her belly again. Even though Yenla did not make a sound as minutes went by, Samarah knew that she was crying. She wrapped her arms around her mother and held her tight. Yenla tried to stop the crying.

"Any way, those days are gone," Yenla muttered.

"No Bwan, they are back. See what happened to our people. I am truly a slave." At this, Yenla stiffened and said,

"Listen to me, Samarah. No one has the right to call you a slave. You are a freeborn, you are a princess. No matter what happens to you in this life, never forget that. Do you hear?"

"Yes, Bwan."

"Now go to sleep. We have a busy day tomorrow." Samarah tried to sleep, but sleep would not come. She tossed, and turned and finally spoke again.

"Bwan!" She called.

"Hm?"

"Where could Bintum be now?" her mother heaved a sigh.

"I do not know, Samarah. I wish I did." There was silence.

"Why did you marry Baa?"

"Bo Nyo! (Ye gods). Because I loved him and I was betrothed to him."

"So you gave birth to me four years later, when you were eighteen." Samarah yawned.

"Sleep well, Bwan."

"Sleep well, my child." When Samarah finally slept, Yenla stayed awake. Her mind traveled back in time, far, far back…

Kintashe was a tall and very handsome prince. He would bring her flowers, and berries, and sometimes firewood, or even game he had

*hunted. She was the envy of her peers. She still remembered the best gift
he had given when he was courting her – her bead-and-cowry necklace.
In those days, courting was done in the presence of one's parents according to tradition, but Kintashe managed to lure her behind the main hut
(her father's hut), in their compound.*

*"I have something for you." He untied the necklace from his loin
cloth tied firmly around the waist. She screamed in delight and flung
her arms around his neck, while his hand lifted her up. That was the
first time they embraced.*

*Two markets later, Kintashe's father (who was the chief then), with
some of the male members of his family brought palm wine to Yenla's
father's compound. This first palm wine was always a deciding factor
when it came to marriage in Chefwa. It didn't matter whether the parties were betrothed to each other or not. If the girl's family wanted to,
they could refuse to drink the wine and 'buy' it with a couple of cowries.
This meant that the boy's family would bring drinks again and again,
until they were finally drunk without being 'bought'. Only after this
drinking without 'buying' would the marriage take place. So, when
Kintashe and his people brought the palm wine, and it was drunk,
there was a general sigh of relief from the family, especially the young
prince, who could not wait to make Yenla his wife.*

*The bride price was set at five goats, ten chickens, camwood, two
tins of palm oil, and cloth. These were the items that had been given on
Yenla's mother's head. One could give the exact quantity of items as that
given on a woman's mother's head, or more, but never less. If Kintashe
had been from any family other than the royal family, he would have
provided the Finchi – the cloth worn by the common people, but since he
was the crown prince, his family gave the Kilanglang, which was worn
only by the royal family and the Fais or sub chiefs. His family gave ten
goats, fifteen chickens, five tins of oil, and of course the Kilanglang to
Yenla, her mother, step-mothers and aunts. However, if Yenla ever had
a daughter, and a man wanted to marry her, then he would be obliged*

to give just what was agreed on as the bride price and not the excesses, except he wanted to add.

On the wedding day, the Chief, his son, and all the members of their family who could be there —wives, grandparents, uncles, aunts, brothers, sisters, and in-laws, came to Yenla's father's compound, where her own family was gathered. The men of both families went into Yenla's father's hut. When it was full, the others sat outside on wooden stools. The women and girls joined the other women in their huts as they cooked food for the occasion.

In Yenla's father's hut, the guests were entertained with palm wine he had tapped. After chitchatting for a few minutes about the happenings in the village, it was time for the ceremony to begin. The women were summoned and they crowded around the window, while a majority stood in the courtyard. However, Yenla's grandaunt, eldest female cousin, eldest stepmother, and mother were given space inside.

At her father's call, Yenla emerged from her mother's hut dressed in a Kilanglang tied as a loincloth. Her waist was covered with waist beads. Camwood was smeared on her body and her dark hair was braided and covered with cowries. On her neck was her bead and cowry necklace. The men ogled her beauty while the women admired her plump form as she walked into the hut and stood in the middle. Kintashe could hardly take his eyes off her, and she imagined he felt his heart almost burst with pride at the thought of being this girl's husband.

Her father cleared his throat and spoke,

"My daughter, these people say they have come here because of you. They have brought palm wine, the drink of the gods, to ask for your hand in marriage. Should we drink or should we let them go?" Yenla smiled at his words and glanced at Kintashe. She was amused at the anxiety in his eyes. It was a known fact that if the woman said they should not drink, then the marriage would not take place. It would just have to be postponed till she was ready. However if she kept on refusing then she would eventually be forced into it. This was very rare though.

Yenla's face broke into a grin as she replied,

"Drink it, my fathers." At her words, the women began ululating and clapping, while the men nodded and smiled, slapping their palms against their thighs. The drinks were drunk. Yenla was officially Kintashe's wife. He was free to take her home. The feasting began. People ate, drank, danced and made merry, and all the while, Kintashe held Yenla's hand, and gazed into her eyes, forgetting everyone else...

Yenla realized that she was twirling the necklace around her neck with her fingers as tears flowed from her eyes.

"How could you do this to me?" she whispered into the darkness. "How could you go on ahead and leave our children for me to bring up alone? I lost your son Kintashe, and now I don't know what will become of your daughter. How am I going to go on without you? Who will be my strength now?"

CHAPTER TWO

1913

A group of about twenty-five black people tied to each other arrived at Mr. Wakerman's compound. On this day Lucy was not feeling well and had gone to sleep, while Samarah hid behind one of the huts working on some sums. When Samarah raised her head and saw the men walking towards the back of the main house in single file, she ran to the kitchen to get her mother.

Both of them stood in the shade of a large mango tree watching the ten or so people who were at the rear of the line. Mr. Wakerman and his German foreman, Von Grausam followed behind.

"This reminds me of when we first arrived here," Yenla said.

"Bwan, will we ever leave this place?" Samarah wondered.

"Of course. One day, my child, we will leave. We will return to our land, where you will take your place as princess and who knows, one day you may be required to take the weight of our people upon your shoulders."

"But Bwan, how can that be? I am a girl and Baa often remarked that the throne would have to pass to his brother or his brother's sons unless you bore him a son." Yenla nodded.

"That's true, but your father was working on changing some of those laws. Besides if there is no one of royal blood left to rule, then the princess's husband will. Men may rule the people, but a wise woman knows how to rule a man and make him think he is ruling her." Yenla smiled, and continued pensively, "Bintum would make a good ruler with you by his side."

That night, Samarah sat on the narrow bed one of the workmen had made for her, so that she would not have to share her mother's. She was crouched over a few notes she had managed to scribble from Lucy's class room. The light from the fire illuminated the parchment she held in front of her. Yenla was adding palm oil into the pot of beans she was cooking and the food's sweet, spicy aroma filled the air.

There was a knock on the door and Samarah stood up and opened it. The person standing outside had his back to the moonlight so Samarah saw just the silhouette of a male, tall and lean.

"May I come in?" He asked. Samarah at once guessed that he was one of the arrivals, but there was something vaguely familiar about the way he stood – tall and erect – and about his voice. She made way for him to enter and turned to lock the door as he greeted her mother, not in Pidgin or the dialect all the workers on the plantation used, but in the language of the Chefwa people. Mother and daughter looked at him in surprise.

"Bwan, my queen, don't you recognize me?" The young man stooped in front of the fire place so that the light reflected on his face. Yenla's spoon clattered into the pot, while Samarah squealed.

Both women ran to Bintum and engulfed him in a tight embrace.

"My son! How we've worried about you. The gods are indeed kind!" Yenla exclaimed.

"I can't believe it. I just can't believe it." Samarah murmured over and over. Bintum laughed as he continued to hug her.

"It's really me."

"But how? Come closer, Bintum. Here, sit beside me, and tell us how you found us." She pulled him to her bed, while her mother pulled her stool closer to the bed.

Bintum told them how he had awakened a few days later to find himself in a hunter's hut. The Germans had left him for dead, but after they had gone, the hunter, who had been hiding nearby came to see if there were any survivors. He had found Bintum breathing, even though unconscious, and nursed him back to health. It had been a long and slow process, but finally, about a year later, Bintum was fully recovered. He had thanked the hunter, and gone in search of Samarah and her mother. He came to many villages, and had to stay, sometimes longer than a month, before he got any information, or left disappointed. Finally, he had come across an old woman who remembered seeing a woman and a child who fit their description in a wagon. She said they had gone to the 'Big White man's house' at the top of the great hill.

Bintum had asked more natives who lived not far from Mr. Wakerman's plantation, and they had confirmed that it was rumored that a little girl who could speak the white man's language lived there. He knew it had to be Samarah. So when Von Grausam had gone looking for more workers for the plantation, he had offered his services.

"Finally, my quest is at an end, for I have found the woman and her little girl with the white man's tongue," he finished and grinned at Samarah, who punched him in the chest.

"I am not, Sir, a little girl! For your information, father began courting mother when she was about my age. Apologise."

"What? To a woman?" Bintum teased.

"Not just any woman, your future wife and queen – ehm – princess of Chefwa."

"Could you two stop your bantering? Ye gods, what will I do with two weaverbirds? Pray tell, Bintum, did you go to our land, to Chefwa?" Yenla asked. He nodded.

"It was a sad sight. The Germans burnt down the whole village." All three were silent, each lost in thought. Yenla heaved a sigh, "*Bo Ntow* always said, 'we will die and our age group will learn from our actions'. Emeh! Was it really worth it? What could be worth a whole village?" She asked, her eyes downcast.

"Freedom Bwan." Samarah's answer was a near whisper. After a few more minutes of silence, Yenla forced a laugh, "let's not spoil today. We have seen Bintum again. Why don't you two go outside and talk? I'll call you when the food is ready."

The two young people went outside and after spreading some plantain leaves on the ground, Samarah adjusted her loin cloth over her breasts and sat down beside Bintum. They reminisced about their lives before the attack by the Germans.

"Remember the day you put a beetle on Father Clement's chair?" Samarah asked amid giggles.

"The poor man's face went from white to red when he sat down!" Bintum howled with laughter at the memory, and Samarah joined him. She soon noticed that he had stopped laughing and when she turned to face him, she saw him staring at her with an expression in his eyes that she had never seen before. It made her feel nervous and anxious at the same time. Her heart seemed to turn over in her chest, and her stomach seemed to be tied into knots. She shivered. He must have noticed because he put an arm around her shoulder and gently pulled her so that she went closer and half-leaned her back against his chest.

"Cold?" he asked. She nodded, then laughed,

"I'll manage." They watched the sky.

"You've grown up and you are still as beautiful as I remember," he whispered into her ear. *What does one say to that?* she wondered. For the first time in her life, Samarah ran out of words. Her throat felt parched like the land was at that time of the year.

"I'm so glad we are betrothed. I can't wait to be your husband." At his words, Samarah cleared her throat and bent her head.

"You've become more handsome too," she whispered. She felt him throw back his head and heard his laugh. His voice had changed.

Now it was deeper, and made the knots in her stomach tighten.

"As soon as we leave this plantation, I'll take you both back home, and then we'll get married. However, if we are still here in three years, we will marry if that is alright with you."

"Oh, Bintum." She raised her head to look into his eyes and realized he was very serious.

"Promise you'll never leave me," he said.

"Bintum, I am going to be your wife. Where could I possibly go if I left you? Marrying you will make me a very happy woman."

"Girl."

"Woman!"

They would have continued arguing if Yenla had not called them to come in and eat.

*

"Lucy, I've asked you a question," Lucy's teacher yelled. Lucy looked at him and continued tapping her fingers on the table.

"Look here, missy, I'm paid to teach you. That's a very easy question. Anybody can answer it."

"Hah, not everyone, Mr. Novelle. Try Samarah. Go ahead and ask her, let's see if everybody can answer." Lucy spat out. Samarah's head snapped up from a corner where she was trying to be invisible.

"I'll do just that." Mr. Novelle turned to look at Samarah. "When did the French revolution take place?"

"From 1789 to 1795, Sir."

"Good. Which writers contributed to its ideas?"

"Rousseau, Voltaire and many others, Sir."

"Excellent. Lastly what principles or ideals did the revolution stand for?" Samarah glanced in Lucy's direction and saw her face turn a shade of pink. This meant she was furious, but that only egged Samarah on. She was totally enjoying this.

"Equality, Liberty, and Fraternity, Sir." Mr. Novelle turned with a wide smile and raised eyebrows back to Lucy.

"See? That shows that I've not been wasting my time here. At least someone has been listening. This girl has been paying attention."

"I'm sick and tired of listening to how wonderful Samarah is. Samarah this, Samarah that! Why don't you teach her instead? Know something? No matter what she does, Father says she will always be a common black slave." With that, Lucy stomped out of the room.

A quiet but smiling Samarah went out of the house. She should feel remorseful, she thought. Bwan always warned her about upsetting Lucy, but sometimes the desire was just too strong. Like the white man would say, at such times the spirit was willing but the body was weak. Right now Lucy did not look like an angel anymore. Her hair had grown longer, her color more tanned, but (some part of Samarah had to admit), she was still stunningly beautiful. Samarah could not count the number of times she had seen the young male labourers staring at Lucy with a vacant and longing look in their eyes as she walked by. Lucy never even spared them a glance but their eyes always trailed after her until she went out of the gate much to Samarah's disgust. Bintum was very lucky she had never caught him staring at Lucy with that adoring puppy dog look in his eyes which she had seen in most of the other boys' eyes.

"Samarah, report here immediately," Lucy's voice cut into Samarah's thoughts. She sighed. What did the spoilt brat want this time? She dragged herself behind the barn from where Lucy's voice had come. As she went around the corner, she saw Lucy holding one of Von Grausam's whips.

"On your knees slave." Lucy tried to imitate Von Grausam's gestures before he flogged a worker. Samarah stared at her. This only helped to incense Lucy, who screamed, "Are you deaf as well as stupid? I said on your knees!"

"Why?"

"You dare to question me? There is only one Miss here and it's me. You do what I tell you."

"What did I do?"

"You'll know soon enough. Down!"

"No." Lucy's mouth hung open at that one word. Samarah had not raised her voice but the word came out all icy, menacing in its calmness. There was no anger, or hurt, but it sounded cold. Lucy shivered and then she frowned.

"No? Then have this slave." Lucy struck Samarah with the whip. It got her on the left shoulder. Samarah cried out but did not take a step back.

"Don't do that again, Lucy, or I swear you will be sorry."

"You dare to threaten me? You coarse black slave. You dare to answer back?" Lucy struck again, but Samarah caught the whip and pulled it out of Lucy's hands.

"You land thieves, you murderers!" She shouted. "Your people are evil, Lucy. You make us pay taxes and you insult us on our own land. When will you people leave us alone? Isn't your god supposed to be a just and loving one? Then why are you all so greedy and heartless? I hate you."

"You bastard! You good-for-nothing! I'll teach you a lesson!" Lucy screamed again, and the two went for each other's throats.

Lucy who was not getting the better of the fight screamed at the top of her voice. Von Grausam and some workmen appeared on the scene, drawn by Lucy's shouts. Most workers were around because it was their break time. They pulled the two girls apart as Mr. Wakerman, who had been wakened from his afternoon nap by the disturbance, reached them. Samarah was satisfied to see that she had done a good job of scratching Lucy's face.

Lucy ran to her father. "She started it, Father. I did nothing to her. She attacked me."

"Lucy, for once speak the truth," Samarah spat out.

"Shut up! I'll teach you to fight white people! You useless bag of filth." Mr. Wakerman ordered two men to take Samarah to the spot where public punishment was usually administered. All the way there, Samarah kept struggling to free herself.

"Leave me alone. I am not, and will never be a slave," she yelled at the top of her voice. Out of the corner of her eye, she saw some women restraining her mother.

At the spot of punishment, Samarah's hands were tied together and then attached to a stake. Mr. Wakerman seized Von Grausam's whip and flexed it in the air. The first lash caused Samarah's loin-cloth to slide down her back to her waist. A red line cut across her back. She cried out.

"NO!" her mother wailed and tried to break loose, but the women held her back. The second lash caused her feet to sag beneath her.

"Baa, give me strength." She whispered. The third had her so dizzy she did not know where she was any more. "I can't take any more. I am going to die. Oh God, help me." Then she felt some-one's arms wrap around her and a voice pleaded "please, beat me instead, please." Then everything went black.

When she came to that night, she found herself in bed. Both Yenla and Bintum were sitting on either side of her. Her mother was sobbing.

"Bwan," she whispered.

"You are awake! Thank the gods." Her mother leaned forward and took her hand in hers.

"What happened?" Samarah croaked.

"You lost consciousness. How are you feeling? Let me get you something to eat."

"My back aches."

"I'll get the medicinal herbs we brewed for you from Ma Fomba."

Yenla stood up and hurried out. Bintum took Samarah's hand in his.

"Thank you for standing up for me," she said. "Did they beat you too?" He nodded.

"I'd take any beating for you, my princess. I am so proud of you." Samarah's eyes misted over at his words.

"Lucy lied Bintum. She started it. She called me a slave."

"Shh. Don't think about it. Now, we must focus on making you well again. Wait till my children hear the stories about their brave mother." Samarah looked directly into his eyes.

"And their braver father... what about Lucy?"

"In bed too. You can scratch! I will be very careful in future. I would not want you to scratch my eyes out," he said.

*

Two weeks later, Samarah was almost healed, even though the scars of the beating still remained. Lucy was still in her sick bed and Samarah had to help in the kitchen. One day as she went to fetch water from the well a little distance from the compound, she saw Von Grausam. He beckoned to her to come.

"Woher iz your mama?"

"In the kitchen Sir." He smiled and walked towards the back door of the house just as Yenla came out. There was no one else in sight. Samarah would have gone on, but just then she saw him grab her mother's arm. She started to walk back and hid herself behind a hut near enough to hear what they were saying.

"Hello, mai beauty, vant some vine?" He held up a flask with liquor in it. Yenla took a step backward.

"Please Sir, I have work to do."

"Ow, c'mon, beauty, vi got ze know each ozer!" Samarah saw her mother shake her head from left to right.

"Please Sir, please, leave me alone."

"Not mai fault you are sehr attraktiv. Come here." He grabbed her arm, pulled her closer, and tried to cover her mouth with his, but she struggled to break free. Samarah ran out of her hiding place.

"Bwan, come quickly." Von Grausam let Yenla go as he cursed in German, and walked away.

"What did he want?" Samarah asked Yenla.

"Nothing. Let's go."

Mr. Wakerman had decided that Samarah should help in cleaning the surrounding and go to the market with other girls to sell some of the produce. He did not want her any where near his daughter or in his house. He knew everyone would assume it was because of what she had done to Lucy's face but then there was something else too. He'd be damned if the girl didn't grow more desirable everyday. What was it about these native women that made them so attractive, even a little girl Lucy's age? Finally he sent her to work in the fields most days. Samarah was happy with the change because now, she could be with Bintum all day, and he never let her work, unless she insisted, and then only for a few minutes.

CHAPTER THREE

1915

"Do you think the British and the French will defeat the Germans?" Samarah asked Bintum as they sat arm in arm in front of her mother's hut. News had spread among the natives that the English and the French were coming to send away the Germans.

"They form a double force. I think they will be successful. Besides, the Germans won't get much help from our people. You know they have not treated us fairly at all. Remember how King Bell was hanged for plotting against them? And this was a man who had signed the document giving our land to them." Bintum's tone was bitter, "a clear case of biting the hand that fed you." He concluded. Samarah sighed, "I know what you mean. Then there is also the forced labour we are subjected to, and the fact that we have no rights and are treated as slaves. They have no regard whatsoever for our traditions and customs… I hope the English win. If they turn out to be like Father Clement, maybe they will leave us and go back to their land."

"After that, we can return to our homeland and I can finally make you my bride." Bintum smiled as Samarah moved close to him.

"I wait impatiently for the time when I can become yours forever. There is a small matter we have to thrash though."

"What is it, my love?"

"Bintum, I know that my father was pressured to take other

wives. I also know that our tradition makes allowance for a man to marry as many women as he can provide for."

"Samarah, look at me. There's no other woman for me but you. You are the one I want, the only woman I have ever loved, the one I want to be with in the next life. I will never love any woman like I love you. I will never let you go. You are the only woman I will marry." For Samarah, it was not just the words. She could feel his sincerity right in her heart. She smiled at him and rested her head against his neck.

"Tell me something Bintum. Do you think the Anglo-French will leave our land if they succeed to defeat the Germans?"

"I really can't tell. White people seem to me to be very much alike. Maybe it will just be a change in the dancing style while the tune remains the same."

"I suppose by that you mean white authority on black land." Samarah groaned.

"And what do you think will be done to sell outs like Mr. Wakerman, who have all these years connived with the Germans?" Bintum asked. A smile spread over Samarah's face.

"I hope they grind them to dust!"

"Samarah!"

"Joke. I am afraid that the Germans may come back for more soldiers. I still remember last year when you had to go into hiding. What I don't understand is why they keep taking our young men and enlisting them to fight a war which concerns us in no way." Bintum's arms tightened around her.

"They won't come again. Even if they do, have no fear. I won't let them take me away from you and your mother. I found you again, and I can't afford to lose you a second time."

"Well spoken Bintum." Bintum glanced at the sky and sighed.

"It's late now, and you must get some rest. I will see you tomorrow." He stood up and pulled her to her feet. She embraced him.

"I will wait for tomorrow breathlessly. Sleep well, Bintum."

"Sleep well my Samarah. May the gods protect you." He kissed her forehead and they went into their separate huts.

Upstairs in the main house, Lucy Wakerman shut the curtains, and turned away from the window with a smile on her lips.

Days later, when Samarah and some other girls had left for the market, a jeep pulled up in front of the house, and three German officials got out. Yenla was in the kitchen when she glanced through the half-open door and saw Mr. Wakerman ushering them in, nodding. Why had these men returned? Then she saw Lucy, her long hair tied back by a ribbon, her yellow gown flowing, as she descended the stairs. Lucy listened to the conversation in the sitting room, and then spoke in English to her father,

"Oh I know someone who would make a very fine soldier. I think he is in the fields right now. Papa, I have heard the natives complain that he's a lousy worker."

"Who could that be?" her father wondered.

"The chap who is always with Samarah. He should be about nineteen. I'll accompany you to the fields, so that I can single him out. Just give me a minute to change into my riding outfit."

As four white men admired the slender beauty as she ran up the stairs, Yenla did some running of her own. As fast as her feet could take her, she went in search of Bintum. When she found him, she begged him to run away that minute.

"I'll tell Samarah where to find you when she returns. Just hide where you hid before. Go now, there's no time!"

Lucy led the men through the banana plantation. Her father also owned a rubber plantation but she knew that Bintum had been assigned to work in the banana plantation. They passed by men with the sweat glistening on their backs and faces. The workers stopped to stare at the party, and several said, "Sah" in greeting to Mr. Wakerman, which he acknowledged with a nod. Lucy searched

Bintum among the workers but could not find him. Then fearful of what the officials might do if they thought she was pulling a stunt, she picked out someone else. The boy was caught, tied and dragged away.

That evening, Samarah sat on her bed with tears in her eyes, which she refused to shed. *I am a princess, and we don't cry that easily... why does Lucy hate me that much? What did I do to deserve her hatred? Why are white people so heartless? They kill each other in the war, and now they want to kill us too.*

The next morning, Samarah took some food and put in a basket. Then she left for the market with the other girls. Among the wares they carried were pineapples, kola, and tea leaves. Mr. Wakerman cultivated these too, but on a much smaller scale, not for export to Europe like the cocoa and bananas, but for consumption and selling in the local markets.

On their way back in the evening, after having sold almost all of their wares, the other girls teased Samarah about Bintum.

"When are you two going to do it?" one asked.

"Do what?" Samarah quirked an eyebrow. The others giggled.

"Start having babies," another said. They already knew she would branch off to see him.

"Give him our love, and say we all envy you!" they screamed as she went off. She waved and then took a short cut through the bush. There was no doubt in her mind that she was the envy of most of the girls for real. Bintum grew more arresting each passing day and she was very proud when he singled her out among the girls for an embrace. She still had a smile on her lips when she reached the mouth of a cave and whistled twice. Bintum's head popped out of the cave. Samarah flew into his arms and they held unto each other. She gave him the food and stayed with him till it was dark. Bintum guided her through the path till they came to the main road. He walked in the darkness with her until they saw the gate ahead.

"I shall wait for you tomorrow. I carry you in my heart," he whispered as he held her to him once more.

When Samarah entered their hut, she noticed a third person with a hood over the head, sitting on a stool.

"Bwan?" Her eyes darted from her mother to the stranger and back. Her mother shrugged as the hood fell back to reveal in the glow of the fire's light shiny blond hair. Samarah's eyes almost popped out of her head and her mouth hung open.

"Samarah, come, here is your supper"

"What is she doing here, Bwan?" Samarah glared in Lucy's direction as she snapped in the Chefwa language. Her mother sat up straighter and looked directly into her daughter's eyes, so like her own.

"She will be living with us for some time."

"What?! Why? How?"

"The master says the English and French people are fast approaching. He wants to look for a way to get her out of the land. He asked me to hide her in case they reach here before."

"We can't. Not after everything they have done to us."

"We really don't have a choice. And besides, your father would expect us to be hospitable."

"Not when we receive cruelty in return." Samarah spun on her heels and went out, banging the door behind her. She leaned against the mud wall, trying to work out her anger. Yenla found her there a few minutes later.

"My child, I know you are upset, and I know Miss Lucy has not been very good to you." Samarah's snort made her pause, but she went on, "look, when she made her father beat you up, she was only sixteen."

"So was I, Bwan. That's not all. She just had to make Bintum run away, and I'll never forgive her for that, NEVER!"

"Don't talk so, Samarah! This is out of our hands."

"Where will she sleep?"

"I was thinking your bed." Yenla's words dropped and her voice sounded just above a whisper.

"A slave's bed for princess Lucy? Haha, no way."

"Then she'll have mine," Yenla sighed.

"Bwan, don't try to make me feel guilty because it won't work," Samarah pouted and wrapped both arms over her chest. Both were silent.

"Now it will be difficult for me to sneak food out to Bintum," Samarah pointed out.

"I've already thought about that. I'll wake up earlier than usual to pack it."

"See what I mean? She has not been here two seconds and our lives are already more uncomfortable," Samarah grumbled as she walked past her mother into the hut.

All night, she did not say a word. Finally, she crept into the space behind her mother on her mother's bed and fell asleep, but not before she smiled as she heard Lucy tossing and turning on her straw bed.

The next day, Samarah left her friends in the morning so that she could have a whole day with Bintum. They were supposed to get her on their way back. As she wound her way through the bush, she heard hissing sound in the thick undergrowth. Fear gripped her and cold descended into her bones. Lying across her path was a huge snake. It was black and slithery. Its tiny eyes shone like beads in the morning sun. If there was one animal Samarah feared with all her heart, it was a snake. She felt sweat running down her back and moistening her nose. She tried to scream, or even move, but her voice stuck in her throat, and her feet were rooted to the spot. All she could do was whimper. *Oh God, I am going to die, and I will never see Bwan or Bintum again!* She thought as she shut her eyes tight.

"Shh, nicht bewegen. Ich werde dir helfen." (Don't move. I will help you)," a voice whispered from behind her in German. Samarah's heart almost jumped out of her chest in surprise and fright, but her mind told her to obey. Then she heard a gunshot and the snake writhed and finally lay still. Samarah took a step back with another moan, and her back rested against the trunk of a tree. Her heart was still racing, but she forced her eyes to dart around to see who her savior was, with so strange an accent. Perchance it had been an angel of the white man's god sent to help her.

Her wandering gaze fell on a boy. The first thing Samarah noticed about him was that he was white. She jerked away from the tree and stood staring at him. She had never seen a white boy before, even though she had seen lots of middle aged and old white men and a few women. This boy looked about Bintum's age. Her eyes looked him up and down, much like one scrutinized a strange animal. He was tall – almost as tall as Bintum. He had dark hair which went right down to his shoulders, parted to the left side and curly at the tips. He was wearing a khaki shirt and a pair of khaki trousers, with a pair of rangers on his feet. The first three buttons of his shirt were undone and this gave him a roguish appearance. She raised her head, and was startled to see that his dark eyes were perusing her much the same way as she had watched him.

Her fear turned to anxiety and just a trace of panic. Who was this boy? What was he doing here? Had he been sent to hunt Bintum down? She felt the fear returning, only this time, it was for Bintum. She must not let them find him. She must protect him. However, part of her thought the boy looked harmless. He looked so… well so… handsome! Yes, he was! She was sure he was the most handsome white she had ever seen. *Looks can mislead.* She mentally told herself. *When I saw Lucy for the first time, I thought she was an angel. See what she turned out to be.*

The two stared at each other for a while longer, and then the boy smiled, and took a step forward. Instinctively Samarah took a step back. He must have noticed her fear, because he said,

"Hallo, verstehst du Deutsch (Do you understand German)?" Even though Samarah understood what he said, she did not say a word. The boy frowned when she did not speak and then said,

"Don't be afraid, I am not gonna hurt you. Do you speak English?" Samarah still did not reply, but just continued staring at him. The boy tucked his shotgun into his back pocket.

"Damn! I wish I knew what language she spoke." She heard him mutter to himself. Then he looked at her and spoke again,

"Uh, I don't know if I am making any sense. See, I have put my gun away. I want to help." He gesticulated as he spoke. Samarah frowned. Help? Did that mean that he didn't want to hurt Bintum? Could she trust him?

"Now I have made her frown. How ever am I gonna ask her if she has seen Ayuk and my other friends?" Samarah's eyes widened slightly at his muttering. He had called a native's name, and referred to him as a friend. Maybe this white boy was lost.

"I… I understand, sir." Her voice was low. He jerked his head up to look at her again and his face broke into a grin, revealing a dimple in his left cheek.

"Well, what do ya know? She can talk after all. You live near here?" She nodded. "And what's a cute gal like you doing all alone in the woods, or are you a nymph?" Samarah noticed that his accent was different from any white man's she had heard before. Clearly, he wasn't from these parts. She mustered up courage and spoke.

"Thank you for killing the snake, sir."

"Pleasure's mine, babe." He grinned. *Babe?* Why did he call her that? She had heard stories of white men who forced their attention on black girls. Could this boy be planning something like that? The fear returned. She had to get away.

"Good bye." She said, and turning, she jumped over the dead snake and ran away as she heard him call,

"Hey wait! I just wanna talk. Didn't mean to scare you; please, wait." But she ran on. No white man would have his way with her. She hated them. She would not let him make a slave of her.

Samarah did not mention what had happened to Bintum, for fear that he would stop her from coming to see him. She found herself comparing Bintum to the white boy. Both were about the same height, but Bintum was attractive in a totally different way. He had an oval face with eyes that tilted upwards and outwards. He was dark brown in complexion and his hair was short – actually cropped almost to the scalp. When he smiled, Samarah felt hot and cold at the same time and all she wanted to do was hold him.

Four days later, on their way back from the market, Samarah again went to see Bintum, and she took one of the girls with her. When he saw them off, he hugged them and told Samarah he would be waiting for her the next day.

"When are you two going to get married?" her friend asked, as they continued together.

"As soon as we can go back to our land. It is not safe now, because the Germans are still forcing people to fight."

As they approached the gate, Samarah had a feeling that all was not well. She saw lots of natives running into the compound. Both of them started running too. When they went into the gate, she saw lots of people crowded in front of their hut, which was on fire.

"No, Bwan!" She rushed to the spot, and forced her way through the crowd to the front. On the ground, she saw Lucy sitting on a bamboo chair looking ill, but there was no sign of her mother.

"Bwan! Please have you seen my mother? Where is she?" she screamed. No one would meet her gaze. Two women stepped forward and tried to hold her. "No, Bwan! Bwan!" She tried to run into the flames but they held her back. Just then, a man burst out of the hut with fire burning on his clothes. People rushed to cover him with plantain and cocoyam leaves. Samarah could make out the form of her mother in his arms.

"Bwan." She cried and squatted beside her mother's unmoving form when the man laid her on the grass. She did not care who saw her crying. Princesses needed to cry sometimes. They were first of all human.

Mr. Wakerman arrived in a jeep and Von Grausam helped him to put Lucy in it. As he started to drive away, Samarah ran after them screaming.

"My mama, please take her to the hospital too. Don't leave her behind master, please, sir! She'll die if you leave her here. Please, master, please!" The jeep did not slow down. Samarah would have continued running after them but two men caught up with her, and held her back.

"It's no use, my child. No matter how much the grasshopper tries, it can never become a bird," one of them said, as they led her back to the scene.

More men helped to carry Yenla into a neighbour's hut. owner was already brewing a concoction of fever grass and guava leaves to ease Yenla's pains. Samarah sat by the side of the bed on which her mother lay, and said all the prayers she could think of for her mother. As she looked down at her mother's burnt and swollen face, tears ran down her eyes.

"Bwan, who did this to you?" she asked in a whisper.

That night, Samarah did not sleep. In the early hours of the morning, her mother stirred "S… Sam," she called weakly.

"Bwan, you are awake. Thank God! Oh Bwan, the herbs worked." Her mother tried to move her body. "Lie still Bwan. I will get you something to eat."

"No child… I am going."

"What are you saying Bwan?" Yenla spoke in gasps.

"To see your... father."

"No, Bwan." Tears ran down Samarah's cheeks. "You can't leave me here alone. Who did this to you, Bwan, who?"

"Grausam... this afternoon... He came when Lucy... was asleep. He wanted to ...I said no, but he... got angry and he... and closed his palm over my mouth... I fought him...he slapped me... and tried to force himself on me... but he didn't Sam... I bit him... and he slapped me... And burnt the hut... but he remembered... Miss Lucy. He ... carried her out... but locked me in. I couldn't ... get out."

" Oh Bwan," Samarah sobbed and squeezed her mother's charred hands in hers. "Don't worry Bwan. I'll make him pay, I promise you," Samarah swore. Her mother coughed.

"No, my child... leave vengeance to... to the gods... Take my necklace... Did I ever tell you... it was the first gift your father gave me? I am going home... I am going to him...and to your baby brother... Be strong my baby... I will always... be with you. I love you."

"Bwan, please stay with me. Bwan." Yenla breathed her last. Samarah's screams woke the others. They immediately came and tried to console her, but she would not be consoled. She clung to her mother's body as her mind tried to comprehend what had just happened. Her mother has just gone and left her alone. How could this happen? What would she do without Yenla?

At dawn, Yenla was buried behind one of the huts. Samarah stood at the grave long after everybody had left. She clasped her mother's necklace in both hands as she sobbed. It was raining, but she did not even realize that she was soaking wet. The rain finally subsided to a drizzle and still she stood there. She could not believe that her mother was truly gone. As she stood there, someone touched her from behind. She turned round, and saw Bintum looking at her with red, puffy eyes.

"I just got the news. I am so sorry." She leaned into his arms and looked at the grave. *I'll always remember you, Bwan. My first daughter will be named after you. And this necklace... this necklace will never depart from us.* She vowed in her mind.

"Come with me," Bintum said after a moment. "There's nothing left for us here. We'll run away."

"Where will we go?"

"Back to our land. We will get the people back together, and then we will fulfill our destiny." She nodded.

"Let's go."

"Not so fast, young people," a voice said from behind. Bintum turned round and pushed Samarah behind him. Mr. Wakerman and Von Grausam stood there. Mr. Wakerman pointed a shotgun at them.

"Nobody tries to kill my daughter and goes free."

"Who tried to kill your child?" Bintum asked.

"Know what I really hate? When half-wits act like they can really understand. Who would have thought that Yenla's plans would misfire? She tried to burn Lucy, and got burnt. Grausam told me." Samarah had never before thought that she could hate any one the way she hated the two white men in front of her at that moment. She jumped out from behind Bintum.

"That's a fat lie! He set fire to the hut because my mother would not let him defile her. Don't mock my mother's memory."

"You were always a loudmouth," Wakerman remarked. As he was talking, some of his hired hands, the same black men who had first brought Yenla and Samarah to the plantation, and who generally acted as overseers on the plantation except when they were away helping to capture more people, joined them. Wakerman ordered them to tie Bintum and Samarah up.

"My dear boy, you're going straight to the army. One can't have the British on one's heels. So you and a few others will be my ticket out of a tight situation. Once I get you registered in the West African Expeditionary Force, the Anglo-French will see that I am on their side and everyone wins… As for you, girl, you have already been asked for."

"I don't understand," Samarah mused. Wakerman ignored her, and ordered the men to bundle the two into the back of his jeep. Von Grausam and Wakerman drove off.

They came to a crossroads and Von Grausam jumped down and reached for Bintum.

"No! Don't take him away from me too. He's all I've got, please." Samarah wept. No one paid her any heed.

"I'll find you again, my Samarah. I promise. I'll carry you in my heart," Bintum told her in the Chefwa tongue as he was dragged off, and Wakerman drove off. Samarah felt like someone had taken a sharp knife and carved her heart out of her chest, leaving behind a hollow nothing could fill. She kept looking back until they were far away and Bintum and Grausam were just specks to the eye. Then the jeep rounded a corner and they were gone. *Oh God let me die,* she prayed.

In the late afternoon, they arrived at an estate. It was fenced with brown sticks. The main house like Wakerman's was extremely large. However, it was painted cream white and golden brown. Although it was like Mr. Wakerman's two storeys, what looked like a turret could be seen at the right corner.

A white man, about Wakerman's age, or older, was sitting on the front porch reading a book. When the jeep pulled up in front of the house, the man laid his book on the table near a set of wooden chairs and descended the steps.

"Hiya old chap," he grinned at Wakerman who grinned back.

"Hey old man. I see you are doing fine. See here she is, just like I promised." The man's eyes rested on Samarah for a few seconds and she returned the look.

"Was it really necessary to tie her up? I hope she doesn't gimme any headache," the man remarked.

"I assure you she won't. What's more, she speaks and writes really good English." At this information, the man looked at Samarah with renewed interest.

"She does, does she? Well, we'll see about that."

The man returned to the porch and rang a small bell on the table. Immediately a black man who looked about thirty years ran to them from the back of the house. Samarah guessed he was a servant.

"Massa call?" asked the man.

Mr. Wakerman's friend instructed the man to take Samarah behind to her room and then ask the housekeeper to bring them some juice. Next he addressed Samarah.

"Your duty will be to serve me and my guests. Also, you will always make sure the house is clean, and you will assist in the kitchen. Is that clear?" The black man assisted Samarah from the jeep, and untied the ropes around her hand.

"It is clear, Sir," she replied. She followed the man to the back of the house. Behind were simpler houses which looked like barns with many doors. Each door led to a room. All were painted white. Samarah was shown to one of the rooms. It contained a small bed as well as a table and chair.

She sat on the bed and burst into tears. She could not stop crying. She cried for her father, her mother, her brother who never even got to see the light of day, her betrothed, and her race. What would life be like without support from her mother and Bintum? The tears stopped flowing from her eyes but she wondered when they would stop flowing from her heart.

PART TWO

CHAPTER FOUR

1916

Mayne Patterson stood along the harbour of the Port of London along the River Thames and stared at the water He watched the approaching vessels as he let his thoughts wander. It was sunset. He loved to watch the sun set over the sea. It gave him an insight into the world of the mysterious. He was sure that no artist could do justice to the sight that met his eyes. His mind moved to thoughts of God. He had to admit that it rarely did so, but when faced with such magnificent beauty, how could one not wonder about the Creator? A cool breeze blew the salty air into his nostrils and he inhaled deeply. The shore always in this foreign land, gave him a sense of freedom and longing to return to the place he had known as home since he was four years old.

It was a whole year now since he had left Cameroon. Bhe was an American but he had spent seventeen of his twenty-two years in Cameroon. His father had moved to Africa a few months after his mother had passed away. A friend of his had told him about the little West African territory and the profits he could make there with the presence of so much fertile land. Being an agricultural-ist, Patterson Senior had decided to change place and in so doing, get over his wife's death. Although Cameroon was a German colony, his friend had assured him that he could buy land from the Germans without any problem, as long as he had the money.

So Patterson had moved with his four year old son, whom he had adamantly refused to leave behind with his parents, to a land he would not have thought of, if Isabella were still alive. Isabella had been British, but he had refused to send Mayne over to Britain to stay with her parents, even though they had begged him to do so.

Mayne smiled as he remembered when their vessel had docked at the port last year. That year the first aerial bombing raid on London was carried out by the German zeppelin airships on the 31st of May. The zeppelin had dropped high explosives over the East End and the dock, killing seven people. Since then there had been over six airship raids. London had not been very safe ever since. Mayne had been surprised and a little uncomfortable when at his arrival, he had seen so many white faces and hardly any black face. How ironical, seeing as he was white! While he was growing up in Cameroon the only time he saw white children about his age was when one of the white landowners would throw a party. These parties usually lasted the whole week end and guests arrived from all over Cameroon. Some traveled for days to make it. Most of these families were German and as a result, Mayne grew up to speak German as fluently as he spoke English.

He had grown up an only child. He would have given his arm to join the labourers' children when they played but his father had warned him not to 'mix' with them. One day, he had been so tempted that he had disobeyed and gone swimming in one of the streams with a black child his age. That was the one and only time his father had used a whip on him. The boy had not understood why his father had been so angry.

"I told you never to hang out with these natives!" Mayne had been surprised to see his father's face livid with rage.

"But Father, they are my friends."

"They are not your class! They are inferior to you." Mayne did not really known what inferior meant at the time but from his father's intonation, it had to be something really terrible. He had burst into tears.

"Ayuk is really friendly Father, he is not inferior."

"Listen young man, the white man does not cultivate any friendly relationship with the black. Blacks are second class. Whites should be their masters, not their friends. That's how it has been in the past, that's how it is today, and how it will be. We have to maintain the status quo." *Status quo?* Another word he did not understand but he had not dared to ask. His father had been almost spluttering with anger.

"Father..."

"You shut up!" his father had yelled and ordered him not to be friends with the natives again. Mayne had tearfully promised to obey, but in secret, he had met his friends in the bushes whenever he had the chance.

As the years went by, his father ceased to dictate most things to him and allowed him more freedom. Those were glorious days for the teenager. He had gone hunting, and swimming and fishing with his friends, eaten with them, and slept with them when his father traveled to the coast on business. Why, his first crush had been a pretty, buxom, chocolate brown coloured girl. All his friends had had a crush on her and he had been elated when she had fallen for him. At seventeen he had his first sexual encounter with her, and promised to marry her. After a few months though, they broke up because her father had wanted her to be third wife to a man twice her age. Mayne had cornered her just before the wedding and asked her to run away with him. She had been too scared to comply and Mayne was left brokenhearted.

But his heart had mended rather quickly and well too. There had been other girls, both black and white. Mayne seldom went to the house parties, but the few times that he had attended, there was always a willing German girl who found him irresistible. Most of them had been older than him but he hadn't been bothered. He had always maintained that age was just a number. However he had been careful not to let his heart become involved again. This time, he would date for the fun of it.

"I'm a rogue at heart," he used to boast to his friends when they were out camping.

"Yes, fine white boy, fine pikin," they would tease him back.

Those days of sheer bliss had not lasted though. Over a year ago, his father had walked in on him and a pretty black maiden. He had not been trying to seduce her – at least not yet. He had only been trying to teach her to read in the barn. Maybe, he had been sitting closer to her than he needed to and caressing her back while pointing out the letters to her, but his underlying motive had been good. Anyway one look at them and his father had screamed, "that's it! You are going to university in England. I'm sending you to your grandparents."

For two months, Mayne had pleaded with his father to let him stay but to no avail. Three days before his departure, when his father had traveled to the coast to make final preparations for his journey, Mayne had packed a small bag and accompanied Ayuk and their other friends into the hills, so that they could camp for the last time.

That was when he had met the girl. Once again, he wondered who she had been. He had helped her and when he had looked into her eyes, his heart had constricted at the fear he had seen in them. It was as if she had been more afraid of him than of the snake. Till this day, Mayne just had to close his eyes to picture her face. He had almost been struck dumb by how striking she was. Her hair was braided into 'Bakala' and her loincloth had reached just below her knees. Even though she wore animal skin slippers, Mayne had thought her feet were simply gorgeous. He could tell from her slenderness that they were long and as round and shapely as her calves. Just the memory of her face made his heart lurch again.

Damn! That's how the people react to us in Cameroon. I can't say I blame them. We give them enough reason. Mayne's gaze followed the ship which was almost on shore now. He did not know how much time he stood there watching, but he noticed a young girl and a man walking away from the docks. He was pretty sure that they had come out of the vessel. The people were tanned almost like Mayne had been when he had come to England for the first time. He thought they had probably come from India, or Africa.

Glancing at his watch, Mayne frowned. It was time to go home. Since the German raids had begun, times had become hard, and being outdoors late into the night was putting oneself at risk. Following the passing of the Defence of the Realm Act in 1914, it was now illegal for people to loiter under railway bridges, consume more than two courses if they were eating at a public place, or whistle for a cab between 10 p.m. and 7 a.m. Alcoholic beverages were hardly available anymore and if you were caught feeding birds or stray animals, you paid a fine.

Mayne decided not to hail a cab. He lived a walking distance from the central Port of London. As he walked he saw some of the posters that had been put up to encourage young men to enlist in the army. One of the posters showed an airship hovering over the city of London and the caption read, "It is far better to face the bullets than to be killed at home by a bomb. Join the army at once and help to stop an air raid. God save the King." This poster had been in circulation since the German attacks had started in 1915 when they had raided Yarmouth. Another poster showed a man with two children – a boy and a girl. While the boy sat at the man's feet playing with tin soldiers in red uniforms, the girl sat on her father's lap, reading a history book. The caption of the poster read, "Daddy, what did YOU do in the Great War?"

Mayne smiled at the posters as he walked along, thinking of all the propaganda that was going on to coerce young men to enlist in the army. He would have loved to fight in a war to protect the people he cared about but this world war just did not make sense to him. He did not understand how a war would usher in peace. He guessed that was one of the paradoxes of life.

Mayne reached his lodgings. When he had first arrived, his grandparents had been only too glad to accommodate him in their house in Westminster, but he had insisted on having his own quarters. With their help he had secured the flat he lived in now. It was situated around Clare Market, not far from where his school was. His grandparents had gone on to employ a manservant for him. There were so many people out of work and looking for a job, any kind of job.

Mayne came in just as the man was preparing to depart for the day.

"I trust your walk was to your liking, Sir."

"Oh yes, John, thank you. Did you get *The Times*?"

"Right next to your plate. Will you be needing anything more, Sir?"

"Nothing, John, thanks."

"Then I'll bid you a good night, Sir."

"Good night, John." Mayne smiled as he made his way to the dining section. He had tried over and over again to get John to stop the Sir, but the old man wouldn't hear of it. Mayne had finally realized that it was much better just to let him say it, but it never ceased to amuse him.

He grabbed the newspaper as he made his way to his bedroom. He collapsed unto the bed and glanced through the paper. There had been an increase in the sales of newspapers since the war had begun, even when the papers inflated their prices. Mayne searched for England's exploits in the colonies. Since Cameroon had fallen to the Allies and Germany had been ousted from the territory, he was eager for news. The major development that had been reported after that was that the Milner-Simon agreement had been signed by the French and British. The document endorsed the partition of Cameroon between the two colonial powers to be ruled as two separate entities. As he looked through the paper, there was hardly anything new in Cameroon. Now he thought, 'there's hope yet for Cameroon. They will get their complete freedom soon.' Mayne believed that the freedom of a people was right and important. He found his thoughts reverting to Cameroon again. He did not fear for his father. Being an American, he knew the British would let him stay on. However, he felt sorry for the German families he had known in Cameroon. Some of them had been good people, just trying to make a living in this part of the world. And the Germans had invested a lot in trade. Why, way before 1884 they had established over sixty factories mostly in the coastal areas, and by the time they had annexed the territory they had control of the ivory trade, exporting over 20,000kgs each year. They had also traded in palm oil which they got from the hinterlands. Prominent among them had been the Woermann and Thormahlen firms. But who did these firms really benefit? Mayne knew they got raw materials at give-away prices and exported these to Germany. The finished products, however, when they made their way to Cameroon, were sold to the people at exorbitant prices. That was trade for you, making profit whatever the cost.

*

Two weeks later, Mayne put on a well-tailored long-tail black suit and struggled in front of the mirror to comb his unruly hair. He still wore it long, but not as long as in Cameroon. Now, it barely touched the nape of his neck. Finally satisfied with his appearance, he winked at his image. "You are one exotic dude!" he chuckled.

He was on his way to a party thrown by one of his father's friends – the one who had told him about Cameroon. The party was in honour of the man's brother and niece who had just arrived from Cameroon. Mayne looked forward to meeting them and getting a chance to chat with 'fellow country men'.

This time, Mayne took a cab. As he sat in it, he wondered at the gaiety that had infected the population as the war raged. It was like people were defying fate to be happy. Maybe it was because of the shortage of young men, or maybe it was the reality that a person's life could end at any time and so they ought to make the best of it. Mayne thought that one of the ways of maybe coping with the devastation of the war was to organize parties. It wasn't just parties, films had come up too. A month earlier, *The Times* edition of 22nd of August, has reported on how when the film about war called *The Battle of the Somme* was released, crowded audiences had been thrilled and interested to see the reality of what was happening in the war. Even if some women had had to shut their eyes from time to time to avoid the horrors in the film, it was declared a great success.

Also there were songs that accompanied the requests and supplications for people to enlist in the army like *Pack Up your troubles in your old Kit-bag*.

When Mayne arrived, he handed his overall to a butler who stood at the door and went in. The large room was glowing especially as candle light reflected on the women's colourful gowns and jewelry and on the men's watches. After exchanging greetings with the few people he knew and smiling politely at those he did not know, he looked around for the host. Mayne spotted him talking with another man who looked just like him – the same bushy eyebrows, knotted over deep blue eyes, the same brown hair receding from the forehead, and the same moustache. Mayne made his way to them and bowed low as they exchanged greetings. On closer look, he realized that this was the man he had seen at the docks two weeks earlier.

The host, Mr. Sheldon Wakerman, gripped Mayne's hand and after shaking it introduced his brother.

"Mayne, meet William, and dear brother, this is Arnold's son, Mayne." They shook hands.

"Pleased to meet you my boy. Your father speaks very highly of you, and seems so proud of you too. He wrote you a letter which I have somewhere in this coat." As he spoke, Mr. Wakerman rummaged in his coat pocket and finally pulled out a twisted envelope.

"Aha! There you are. When my brother told me you would be coming today, I decided to take it along. I gather you have been here a year," Mayne replied that indeed he had. Then he received the letter, thanked Mr. Wakerman and excused himself. He just had to find a quiet place to read it. He had to read it immediately! He made his way to the terrace, at the back of the house and almost tore open the envelope in his anxiety to get to the letter. It usually took months to get mail across the seas and most times, the mail got lost. He was glad to hear that the plantation was thriving and his father was in good health.

Several minutes later, after Mayne had read it over and over again, he folded it, put it in his pocket, and went back into the hall to talk some more with Mr. Wakerman.

"I hear that Cameroon is under the control of the Allies now." Mayne observed. Mr. Wakerman nodded.

"When I left the Germans had already departed."

"Will you be here long, Sir?"

"Only a couple of weeks. There is no one to take care of my plantation. My foreman had to leave the country in a hurry, since he is German."

"Papa, I do love London. It's great!" An excited female voice cut in. Turning towards the sound, Mayne's eyes widened, his breath caught in his throat and he was pretty sure his mouth hung open too. In front of him was the kind of beauty poets mooned over. At first sight, he thought he was looking at an enchantress! The girl was about 5ft 5inches, with long, blond hair, which cascaded over her shoulders and Mayne was certain, all the way down her slender back. Her eyes were blue, as blue as the sky in spring, and her lips looked like rose petals caressed by the morning dew. Mayne's eyes traveled down her body, and he couldn't help but draw in his breath again. She was slim, shaped like a perfect number eight, and bronzed to an even tan. She was wearing a blue ball gown, which emphasized the blue of her eyes. When his eyes came back to her face, he realized that she was looking straight at him with a half-smile playing on her lips. He could barely hear Mr. Wakerman saying,

"Allow me to introduce my daughter to you. Lucy, this is Mayne Patterson."

"Pleasure," Mayne drawled as he took her hand in his and kissed it, his eyes never leaving hers. Lucy giggled, and the light seemed to dance in her eyes.

"Patterson? Papa, that's your friend's name, isn't it? Were you in Cameroon? Did we meet?"

"I would certainly remember if Aphrodite graced any occasion I attended in Cameroon," Mayne replied with a dimpled smile. "I left Cameroon last year. Your father tells me he will be returning soon. Will you go back with him?"

"No, she won't. She's staying right here. That territory is not very stable right now." Mr. Wakerman answered for her.

"It's really boring in Cameroon," her voice came out all throaty and seductive, and Mayne suddenly thought of her waking up in his bed all ruffled and rested, and with an effort, tried to concentrate on her words as she went on, "I don't get to see any people."

"There are people everywhere in Cameroon. Didn't you have any

workers, or did your father build a tower to keep Rapunzel away?"
Mayne teased. Funny how fairy tales could stick in one's head from
childhood. His lips stretched into a smile again when he noticed
the pink spots appearing on her cheeks. Her blush made her more
beautiful, he decided.

"I mean people, not the natives," she said. A part of Mayne took
offence at this. He felt the old anger he had always felt in Cameroon
when anyone referred to the blacks as lesser beings, but the anger
was gone as soon as it had come. He was completely wrapped up
under her spell.

"We were just talking about the Anglo-French administration
in Cameroon," he said in an attempt to sail on to safer waters.
His eyes left Lucy's to involve the other two men, whom he had
totally forgotten about for a few seconds, in the conversation. "I'm
glad Cameroon has been placed under the Anglo – French. I'm
positive that means they'll have their independence soon." The
others exchanged glances.

"Do you think the natives can handle power and freedom right
now? Besides, that would mean losing all our wealth," Mr. Wakerman commented.

"Their wealth you mean. It's their land. There is nothing more
important to a people than their freedom." His companions said
nothing. Mayne heard music filtering in from the dance room. He
again gave a dimpled smile and glanced at Lucy, "would the lady
care to join me for a dance?" He quirked an eyebrow. Lucy giggled
and took his outstretched arm.

"Excuse us," Mayne said to the men, and led Lucy into the dance
room and unto the dance floor.

Lucy had been fascinated by Mayne as soon as she had seen him.
It wasn't just that he was so handsome. No, there was something
else. Maybe it was his eyes, so dark and sensual that a girl could
drown in their depths, or maybe it was his nose, which was aquiline,

or maybe it was his beautiful mouth, full and firm, or his almost stubborn chin. Even though they might view things differently, and she suspected that they did, she rejoiced and her heart sang as they swirled around the room. After two dances of no talking, Mayne bent low and whispered into her ear about it being hot and would she do him the honour of walking her to the terrace? Her skin tingled and she nodded. He led her out and to a loveseat. Then he leaned against the balcony and looked at her.

"You are so beautiful," he marveled. "I imagine a beauty like you would have a host of servants back in Cameroon, because your father would definitely treat you like a princess."

"My father did have lots of servants. What about you? Did you have servants in Cameroon?"

"My father insisted that I should, but I'd rather have done things by myself," he answered. Lucy shrugged. She did not see any reason why she should do things for herself if others could do them for her.

"I had one servant all to myself. She was a naughty one!" Lucy said.

"Care to explain what you mean?" Mayne came to sit beside her. Frankly he was tired of the small talk and could think of a thousand more interesting things he could do with her, and none of them involved talking, even though most of them involved the mouth. She scooted over to make space for him. The loveseat was a trifle small. He didn't mind. It suited his intentions just fine.

"That's what happens when a native gets any kind of education. She thought she was my equal. She did not know her place as a servant. Why when we were sixteen, I decided to teach her a lesson." Mayne was barely listening to her. He was enthralled by the tendrils around her ear and wondered whether she would object if he decided to trace them with his tongue.

"Hmm," he murmured as he leaned closer to her. She nodded.

"We fought, and Papa beat her until she went unconscious. That sure taught her her place." When Mayne made no comment, Lucy's inquiring gaze shot up to meet his and she noticed the slight frown on his face and his stricken look. All thoughts of getting his lips on her fled from his mind as he listened to Lucy's words.

"You are not serious are you?" Mayne's eyes opened wide. "Your father beat a sixteen year old till she lost consciousness? Good God, did she try to kill you or something? Were you punished?" Lucy still couldn't comprehend his shock as she answered, "of course not! I was carried to my room and a doctor was sent for. Why do you look so surprised? You grew up in Cameroon. You should understand these things."

"I see." With an effort, Mayne composed himself and flashed his best devil-may-care smile. "It's cold out here. How thoughtless of me to keep you in this cold, especially as you are from the tropics. You will find the weather here can be pretty chilly. Come on, let's go in." He rose up, held both of her hands in his and pulled her to her feet. Then he offered her his hand and they walked back in.

Once he had escorted her over to her father, he quickly took his leave. As he sat in a cab on his way home, a pair of dark, frightened eyes came to his mind.

I deserved that look. My race has caused them so much suffering! Beat up a child to a pulp? Mayne shook his head from side to side. at the thought. He had thought that his father was hard on his workers. Now, he realized that his father had been relatively kind. Patterson Senior would never allow flogging on his Estate. Instead, if a worker had to be punished, then some amount was deducted from his wages. *God forgive us.* Mayne prayed with all his heart.

That night, as he lay on his bed, he tried to recall Lucy's face and how much he was attracted to her, but his mind kept on straying to the girl he had met in the forest. When she had run away, he had finally traced his friends and they had returned to the camping site. For the remaining two days they had spent there, he had come to that spot everyday hoping to see her again, but each time, he had been disappointed. She had intrigued him, she still did, and Mayne hated to let a mystery go unsolved. Somehow, he wished he could see her again, talk to her again, and maybe this obsession with her would finally be laid to rest.

*

The London School of Economics and Political Science was situated in Westminster, Central London. Founded in 1895 by some Fabian Society members, the school had joined the federal University of London in 1900. As the years had gone by, its popularity had increased to the extent that they were thinking of moving it to a new site – 10 Adelphi Terrace.

As Mayne walked through the long halls, past other students with similar intentions of getting to their lectures in time, he pondered the events of the day before.

When he entered the lecture hall, he glanced around and a big smile lit his face as he walked down the aisle, tapped his best friend on the back, and slipped into the seat next to him.

"My, my, you sure look pale today. Didn't you sleep well last night? Had a chick with ya?" Carl's eyes twinkled.

"Nah, no such luck. You don't sleep when you hear the horrible things I heard last night. Whenever I closed my eyes, I saw whips and heard sixteen year olds crying."

"Huh?" Carl scratched his head and gave Mayne the are-you-sure-you-are-alright look. Mayne recounted his talk with Lucy.

"And of course, you couldn't stop thinking of that fantasy girl of yours," Carl smiled. "How many times do I have to tell you to forget it? There's really nothing we can do about it. That's the kind of treatment our black skin beckons almost everywhere, from slave trade to present day."

"This is not the eighteenth century! "Men have evolved. Look, you are a black American and here you are in a British university. That's what I am talking about, man. This is not the eighteenth century, Mr. Carlton White!"

Carl burst out laughing and said, "My surname always makes me laugh. Imagine a black boy called White! The irony is hilarious. Hahaha, but I take consolation in the fact that my name is a popular one." Mayne rolled his eyes at Carl's words.

Carl went on, "no, really. In the United States, George Henry White got elected into Congress as a Republican. He was the only black member of Congress from 1897 to 1901. I like to think that I am a distant relative of his!" Carl finished with a wink. Mayne snorted, "how do you know so much?" Carl's smile spread as he responded, "I try to know my history. Seriously though, colour is a dividing factor among humans. What about the 'dirty South'? Check out Memphis, man! I tell you this colour struggle is on everywhere - in America, in Asia, in Africa, and you must admit here too. You and I both know how some people are aghast when they see us together. What they do not understand is that you are more African than I!" Carl laughed and patted Mayne on the back.

"To lighter pursuits, my friend. Tell me about this Lucy girl." Mayne complied, and described Lucy in detail. After listening to Mayne for a while, Carl whistled. "She's really had you. That's a relief. Now you can lavish your emotions on the living, not some figment of your imagination. Miss Fantasy has been replaced by a solid flesh and blood blond," Mayne heaved a sigh.

"Miss Fantasy as you call her is just an unsolved mystery to me." At his words, Carl rolled his eyes,

"Is she? If I didn't know better, I'd say you'd fallen hard for her."

"Me? Goodness, Carl, you know me – player for life. Besides, I couldn't possibly fall for someone I met once, and whom I'll likely never meet again, could I?"

Carl shrugged, "it's been known to happen."

*

Mayne and Lucy grew closer. He spent almost all of his free time with her. He realized that she was witty and funny and had a love for adventure and life as a whole. She never bored him. Each day with her left him wanting more. He made up excuses to call on her, and with her uncle's permission took her out to dinner a couple of times. One day, it was almost midnight when he brought her back home. At the door he thanked her once again for accompanying him. Lucy asked him when she would see where he lived and he said he would take her there the coming week end.

"Promise?" Lucy whispered.

"Promise." Mayne folded her in his arms and drew her closer to him. She wrapped her arms around his neck. At her touch, he pulled her still closer and bent to whisper into her ear,

"You've cast a spell on me."

As his breath grazed her earlobe, Lucy shuddered and stared directly into his eyes, relishing the expression she saw in them. This was the first time Mayne had done more than take her hand and she felt powerful, and beautiful. She smiled. He bent his head until his lips touched hers. At the contact, a flash jolted through him and he deepened the kiss. She clung to him and thought of nothing except these new sensations coursing through her body. When he finally pulled back, she gasped and opened her dreamy eyes to look at him.

"Week end then?" She whispered. He nodded and smiled.

CHAPTER FIVE

1917

After the Germans had left Cameroon in 1916, and the British and French had taken over, Anglo- French missionaries had once more come to settle in the land. When Samarah had come to Mr. Pattersnon's plantation she had joined the Catholic Church since she could not find any Basel churches in the area. The Basel mission had left Cameroon with the ousting of the Germans. The Catholic Church had been in Cameroon since 1884 but had mostly been along the coast specifically Bota. The Germans had not granted them permission to establish around the sea port of Douala, or go into the hinterlands as they had asked to do because they were French. However, with the expelling of the Germans, this church had finally been welcome. Samarah attended mass in a parish set up by the Sacred Heart Fathers from England. They had been in Cameroon from about 1912.

Samarah had just left mass. As she walked towards the branch to the estate, she contemplated just how deep Christianity ran for the colonial masters. During mass, the handful of white people who attended made sure they sat in a secluded area. If any native happened to sit nearby, they quickly changed their seats. She wondered what they thought when they read the book of Exodus. Did they think they were any different from the Egyptians of that time? There was one sentence she loved about that book: 'Let my people go!' Civilizations would not last forever. Oh no, where was the Egyptian civilization now? Where was the Roman civilization? One day her people would be free too, for like the Israelites, they would not be held captive forever.

Before she left the church premises, two workers' children ran to her with a Bible story book and begged her to read it to them. They said it had been given to them by the parish priest. Knowing that the master generally let his workers have time to themselves on Sundays, Samarah smiled and asked them to get her a stool. About four boys ran off to do that while the other children sat on the grass. When they brought the stool she sat down and started reading. "The tale of Moses, the man who defied a great king and freed his people." As she read to them, mimicking voices for the characters the children listened with glee. At the end, they cheered and as she raised her head to smile at them, she found the priest, Father Vincent, sitting on the grass behind them. He was smiling and clapping too. She grinned as he came to her.

"You read wonderfully, Miss Samarah." When she heard his words, she smiled back as she remembered how they had met.

When the Catholic priests had once more taken up residence, and set up a church and a community school in the area, she had kept her distance from them. Then one day, when she was going on an errand to the neighboring estate, she had passed by the churchyard. She noticed some native boys playing with a ball. She had been extremely astonished to see the priest playing with them. That had brought back memories of her childhood, when Father Clement had played games with them. These memories had brought a sharp pang to her heart and tears to her eyes. She would never be that free child again. She would never again know the love of a parent, or the companionship of a childhood friend. These simple, yet so very important things had been taken away from her.

While she had stood there, lost in her memories, the priest started walking toward her. Instinctively, she had turned and tried to rush away, but he had caught up with her.

"Good day, Miss. My name is Vincent. Do you understand English?" She had nodded. He was lanky, around middle age, with sandy, shoulder-length hair, and grey eyes.

"What is your name, Miss?"

"My name is Samarah, Father."

"Strange and exotic!" He grinned. A smile touched the corners of Samarah's lips at his words.

"Pleased to meet you, Miss Samarah." He smiled, waved and left.

As she had walked on, she had felt a bubble inside her. No one had ever called her 'Miss' before!

Now, Samarah saw his face light up as it usually did.

"Excellent reading, Samarah. I need to speak with you."

When the children had left, Father Vincent told her that the nuns were about to open a nursing school to train nurses to help in the hospitals and health centers they had started. He wanted to know if she would be interested. Samarah was almost bouncing up and down with happiness. Now she had a chance to continue going to school. However she told him that she did not know if Mr. Patterson would let her attend. The priest said he would talk to him.

A week later, Mr. Patterson called Samarah and told her that she would be needed in the mission in the afternoons because the priests needed her services. When an excited Samarah later on asked Father Vincent what he had said to get Mr. Patterson to agree to send her to school, he smiled and replied, "God takes care of his own."

As she walked back home after her first lesson Samarah thought of her parents. She knew they would be proud of her. She wished Bintum was with her now, so she could share her joy with him.

How she missed talking to him! Where could he be now? Was he still fighting somewhere? Was he still alive, or – no, she wouldn't think about it. Bintum had to be alive, he just had to be!

When she went into the gate, she saw the other workers crowded at the foot of the steps which led to the main house. She wondered what was going on as she adjusted her loincloth over her breasts and quickened her pace. The foreman – a big, black man of about fifty – was speaking to them in pidgin.

"Massa di sick. Any person de here weh e fit write n'grish? (The master is not well. Can any one here write English?)" Samarah said she could and the man asked her to follow him. She cleaned the soles of her woven slippers on a door mat outside and went up the steps. At the door, the foreman stooped to take off his shoes made of goat hide.

They both went upstairs and followed the long corridor till they reached the master bedroom. Even though Samarah cleaned the house almost on a daily basis, she had never been into this room. The master's manservant usually cleaned it. The foreman rapped on the door and the manservant opened it. Samarah followed the foreman in.

The room was large and airy, a little larger than all the other rooms in the house. It had in addition to the family size Iroko bed, a set of cane chairs and a table, two carpets, a wardrobe which almost covered all of one wall and two windows which covered almost half of one side of the 6 x 6m walls. Mr. Patterson was lying among the gold coloured sheets, with a face as pale and white as a sheet of paper, Samarah thought.

"Massa, this girl fit write," the foreman said as he bowed slightly. Mr. Patterson coughed.

"Leave us alone," he croaked. As the men left Samarah examined the master. He looked thinner than the previous day. She was certain that he had had another heart attack, because the foreman had mentioned as they walked up the stairs that the doctor had just left. She supposed this man had once been good-looking. He had an oval shaped face and beneath his not-so-bushy eyebrows were eyes a trifle grey. His long, straight nose gave him the look of an aristocrat, while his receding hair made him look more frail. His beard was not very long, but well-kempt.

Samarah preferred her life here a hundred times to that at Mr. Wakerman's plantation. True, Mr. Patterson hardly ever noticed her and had seldom spoken to her in the past, but he did not have his workers flogged, and he even paid them some wages. Yes, he still acted like he was royalty itself and no black people were allowed into the house except the cleaners and the cooks and since she fit into both roles, she was one of the very few who ever walked along "*His Highness's*" corridors.

"Come closer, girl. Don't stand there daydreaming. I assume you can write readable English." She should be used to it by now, she thought as she walked closer, but she still felt her temper flare at his words. She gripped her hands into fists and took a deep breath to calm down, then she replied,

"I can Sir."

"Hmmph, we'll see. As you can see, I am too weak to write. I need to let my son know what's happening... You will write about my heart attacks. Tell him to come home. I want to see him before... is that clear?"

"It is, Sir."

"You will find his address on that table. Be fast girl, I haven't got all day." Samarah almost retorted that he had nowhere to go, because illness had stuck him to that bed, so he indeed had more than all day. However, she sat down and composed the letter. When she had finished, she showed it to him to read. After reading, he raised his eyes to her in astonishment.

"Goodness, where did you learn to write like that? Not one

wrong spelling!" Samarah fought hard to hide her triumphant smile. She knew that she had shocked him, and for some ridiculous reason, that made her feel elated. She sealed it and Mr. Patterson sent it to be posted at the Parish house.

As the days and later weeks went by, Mr. Patterson grew worse. Most mornings, landowners from neighboring plantations would drive up in their jeeps to see him. Most afternoons, he slept and Samarah had more time to go to nursing school. The doctor came more often and finally said Mr. Patterson should stay in bed. At his command, Samarah attended to the sick man. She was in charge of giving him his medicine on time and reading to him. Many times she wondered why she did not just go away, but she knew she could not, not when the old man was so sick. True, white people just weren't worth the trouble, so why did she stay? She had no answer to that question except that she had nowhere else to go.

*

Mayne Patterson wondered what kind of relationship he had with Lucy Wakerman. On one hand he felt this strong pull towards her. She had become almost an obsession to him. On the other hand, there were times when he didn't think he liked her much. As he talked with her more and more, he was not sure he liked the way her mind worked especially in relation to nonwhite people.

"And she keeps saying we are better than others, simply because our skin is white," he complained to Carl once.

"You have to understand her Mayne. It's not really her fault. She is just a victim of circumstances. She was brought up to think that way and she had no choice."

"Everybody has a choice, Carl. I grew up in much the same condition, but I chose not to let it influence me. Sometimes, when I listen to Lucy, I can't help thinking of that girl in the forest."

"Ah, Miss fantasy again. Don't you think it's high time you concentrated on the living, not some ghost in your head? You hang out with Lucy, you always talk about her. I think you are falling in love with her." Mayne's head snapped up at Carl's words but then he saw that his friend was grinning and he relaxed. Carl went on, "At least part of you must feel something for her."

"Feel is an understatement." Mayne smiled.

That night when he got home and tried to slot his key into the lock, the door swung open. Frowning Mayne glanced at his watch. It was too late for John to still be around. Had John forgotten to lock the door or had someone broken into his house? Keeping his eyes wide open, he edged into the room, melting into the shadows as his eyes became accustomed to the darkness. Everything looked alright, but then the room was dark. What if the intruder was still around? It always paid to be careful. He locked the door and tip-toed towards the bedroom. Light was struggling to force its way out through the crevice between the door and the jamb. If there was an intruder in the house, then the person was obviously in his bedroom. He peeped in through the key hole. His eyes widened with surprise, and then his muscles relaxed. He turned the door handle and swung the door wide open.

"Lucy? What escapade is this?" He drawled as his eyes raked down her body. Lucy rolled over on his bed to look at him, and smiled. She was wearing the skimpiest black nightgown he had ever seen on a girl. The contrast emphasized her milk-white skin.

"John let me in. I wanted to see you." He was only half listening to what she was saying. His eyes were busy exploring her body slowly and then they finally fastened on her bosom, and he drew in his breath at the reaction of his body at the sight of her skin. With an effort, he forced his eyes up to meet hers.

"What is the meaning of this?" He realized that he was almost tripping over his tongue. Lucy smiled. Her blond hair cascaded over to cup her face, and then over her shoulders as she leaned forward. Mayne felt his heartbeat quicken as she slid off the bed and walked towards him. She stood close to him, reached up, and looped her arms around his neck.

"Mayne, I'm in love with you." Mayne felt his heart jump at her words – from fear or joy? He couldn't decide which. His gaze never left hers as he replied,

"Don't say that Lucy. Come on, I'll take you home." Even to his ears his voice sounded hollow with very little conviction. One of Lucy's hands slid down to undo the first button on his shirt, and she leaned towards his neck.

"Don't worry, Mayne. They think I'm sleeping over at Amy Wilson's." She purred. Her breath caressed his neck and Mayne thought he'd simply die from wanting her. He bit his lower lip.

"Are you sure about this, Lucy? You're a child."

"Tsk, tsk, Mayne, I am no child and you know it. No one would react to a child the way you react to me, the way your pupils dilate when I touch you like this." As she whispered, her fingers traced a path down his chest and undid the rest of his buttons, and then both hands slid into his shirt to caress his skin. Mayne thought he had to do something while he could still muster a little control, because having her so close, inhaling her perfume, was jumbling his thought processes.

"Love is a big word." He whispered back as he leaned in to inhale more of her scent, "One I try never to misuse. I don't know what my feelings for you are, but they are so strong." Lucy leaned away from him to look into his eyes. They stared at each other for some time and then her eyes glinted with determination.

"Ok, I accept." Mayne was at a loss.

"Excuse me?"

"I accept the condition."

"What condition?"

"We'll start from wanting each other." She reached up to kiss his neck.

"Lucy please," he pleaded as his hands moved to put her away from him but only succeeded to wrap around her waist.

"Just this night, Mayne. I want you to make me a woman. I want to be with you just this once." What was she saying? Mayne wondered. All he could think of was the fragrance of her perfume and the feel of her lips on his skin. He leaned forward, and placed his lips on hers. She was as hungry for him as he was for her and his last coherent thought was to carry her to his family size bed.

*

"You look like you got hit over the head by a truck," Carl commented as he sat in his flat with Mayne. "It's not that Miss Fantasy again, is it?" Mayne said no, and Carl peered at him and then burst into laughter. "Aha, you done it with Lucy, haven't you?" At Mayne's look, his laughter increased. "I wondered how long it'd take you. And what's got you upset about that? Didn't you like it?"

"Like? Oh no, I loved it! It was great and swell and all I can think of now is doing it again with her... but I can't help feeling that it wasn't supposed to happen."

"You're not making much sense. These things have never worried you before."

"I know. I've never thought about it like this, but you know, after last night, it feels like... well, like... a sin. Like I took something from her you know."

"Sin! Now you've really lost it. You've been doing this stuff for the past four years at least and it's been okay. What's up with it now? And Lucy, how does she feel?"

"Over the moon!"

"Ah, I assume you were her first." At Mayne's nod, Carl went on, "well, you know what they say about first love. She will want you all the more, and I suspect you care about her more than you are willing to admit to yourself."

"Look, I know she's attractive, but that's all I thought I felt for her… attraction."

"And would you know the difference between attraction and love?"

"Carl, trust me, I don't even *like* her sometimes."

"You sure had a funny way of showing your loathing last night." Mayne shot Carl a piercing look. Carl laughed again and went on, "Sometimes love creeps up upon us and we do not realize it till we are swept up by its tide and all we can do is let it carry us along, because sailing against the current would not only be exhaustive, but might lead to our doom." When Carl was done talking, Mayne whistled.

"Who would have thought you'd be the type to spout words of wisdom?" Carl shrugged with a grin.

"I have my moments. At least it's a relief to hear you moaning about some real woman and not that Miss Fantasy of yours." Mayne refrained from telling him that just before he had fallen asleep with Lucy in his arms, a pair of dark eyes had flashed in his mind and somehow he had felt guilty.

A week later, Mayne received a letter from Cameroon informing him about his father's illness, and advising him to come home. Mayne made plans to travel that same weekend. As Carl saw him off at the sea port, he commented, "I still can't believe you haven't told Lucy. Have you been avoiding her?"

"Of course not. It's just that with my studies and all, I've been too busy, and she has been busy with school too. Don't forget to give her the letter, Carl, and tell her I miss her."

*

It was a few days after Easter. The land was so dry that it was cracked in places and the smell of dust filled the air. The rains were late in coming. The sun beat down upon the defenseless earth and what was left of the grass had turned brown. People did not know what to think. Whenever the rains were late, it meant the gods were angry. It was a long time since this kind of dryness had been experienced and people wondered what it meant. The rains were supposed to have fallen three markets ago!

Samarah reached the estate from school and walked into a lot of hustle and bustle. She wondered what was amiss as she went into the kitchen to ask her fellow cook and friend on the estate, Bessem, what all the excitement was about. Bessem had practically grown up on the estate. Her parents had worked for Mr. Patterson until they were too old to do so. Even though they lived a few miles from the estate, Bessem lived at the manor house, and had done so for the past ten years. She always told Samarah stories of how the master's son had got into trouble with her brother who had been his best friend. Now Samarah saw a bright light shining in Bessem's eyes.

"Mayne is back! He has arrived!" Bessem screamed. Samarah raised an eyebrow.

"Really? I was beginning to think his father did not matter to him. With their kind, anything is possible." Bessem shook her head from side to side at Samarah's words.

"Mayne is not your typical white man, Samarah. You'll see for yourself. By the way, the master asked me to tell you to come and see him as soon as you returned."

"I'll go now. Where is the young master?"

"I just got back from the market and heard he's taking a bath. I haven't even seen him yet. Hah, young master indeed," Bessem chuckled.

Shaking her head in mock exasperation at Bessem's obviously

excited tone, Samarah made her way up the stairs to Mr. Patterson's room. When she knocked on the door and went in, Mr. Patterson's wrinkled face broke into a smile.

"I thought you were never coming." Samarah narrowed her eyes at his teasing tone, her disbelief growing. He was propped up in bed, with his back against a pillow leaning on the top part of the bed. The sheets reached up to his waist, but somehow he looked younger and better than he had in days. The arrival of his son seemed to have worked a miracle.

"My son is here, Samarah, he has finally come home and I have you to thank for this." Samarah smiled and her eyebrows knotted over her eyes. He chuckled.

"I deserve that look, don't I? Sit down, Samarah. Pull your chair closer, good… When a man gets old, he thinks about his life and tries to make reparations for his shortcomings. By the way, Father Vincent says you are a very promising student." Samarah stared at him. He chuckled again. "Oh yes Samarah, your nursing classes have been of interest to me for a long time now… you know, many times in life we give priority to things which aren't that important… things like status… or wealth… or colour." Samarah's bent head shot up at the last word and she discovered that his eyes were on her, and all the laughter had gone out of them. "My son has grown up to be a fine man. I'm sorry your parents did not get the chance to see you grow up too… I used to think… actually I'd been taught to think that my race was better than the others, and it was our divine role to guide the less fortunate and teach them civilization and manners. I still think that we do have a lot to offer the world and our generosity should know no bounds. However, knowing you, seeing how you have taken care of me all these months, listening to the glowing reports Father Vincent gives of you, have got me rethinking… maybe we have been going about this in a way that's not quite right. I believe you think my race is evil and wicked, but what if you tried to see things from our own angle? We are just the result of years of training, and you have to admit, most populations are better off for knowing us." Samarah wondered whether things would have been better if she and Bwan had been brought to Mr. Patterson's estate instead of Mr. Wakerman's. Maybe things would have been different and they would still be together.

"Sir," she began, trying to quell her emotions, "my memories are too painful. It's hard, it's just too hard losing what you treasure most in the world."

Mr. Patterson nodded and heaved a sigh. "I understand. Why don't you go to your room and get some rest?" Samarah nodded, thanked him and went out. Truly, the master was a man of many facades. You never knew what to expect when it came to him. One minute he was kind and understanding, and the next he was cold and aloof, or raging like his heart was on fire. She met Bessem in the kitchen and commented that the master had changed and looked much healthier all of a sudden. Bessem commented that it was all Mayne's doing, and Mayne was the kindest soul on earth.

"Kind? Can a white man who's not a priest be kind?" Samarah was disgusted at the other girl's adoring tone.

"Mayne was sent to England because his father caught him teaching one of my friends how to read. Before that, he'd been caught working, actually doing the manual work with the other workers, in the plantation many times."

"I am pretty sure I have an idea why he was teaching a *girl*. He sounds like a rule breaker," Samarah remarked.

"He has always had a mind of his own. No one can make him do what he doesn't want to do."

"Thank you Bess, it feels good to hear that," a deep voice drawled from behind. Both girls spun round to see who was talking. The next second, Samarah saw Bessem picked up and raised high up in the air in a joyful hug.

"Mayne, put me down!" Bessem exclaimed but both she and the white boy, who had his back to Samarah, were howling with laughter. Samarah looked on, fascinated. Finally he put her down, but kept his arms around her.

"How are you? How is Ayuk? What about your parents? Gosh, I can't wait to see everyone. I have missed YOU and I brought a present just for you!" He pulled her to him and hugged her. Bessem embraced him back as she answered.

"Everybody is fine. We've missed you too. Ayuk got married and now invests in trade. He buys things from the coast and sells in the hinterlands, then he gets things from there as well and brings them to us here. He travelled just last week. He will be gone two months. It is really wonderful to see you Mayne." Then she spun him round as she added, "there's someone behind you I'd like you to meet."

Mayne flashed a polite smile for Bessem's friend. When he looked her full in the face, the smile froze on his lips, and his heart did a flip. Those eyes! He had dreamed of those eyes everyday for over a year. This could not be happening! But it had to be her. She was looking at him with the same expression of disbelief and wonder. Both of them stared at each other, oblivious to Bessem's introductions.

"You?" Samarah whispered. Mayne couldn't keep his heart from racing. It was her, his Miss Fantasy right here in his father's kitchen. Bessem looked from one to the other and back. She touched Mayne's hand.

"You know each other?" It was like he had been called back from a far away place. He looked at Bessem and nodded.

"We've met before." *For less than a minute, yet I've thought of her for over a year now*, his mind added.

Still spellbound, Samarah wondered if this was real. A couple of times in the past year, she had found herself wondering who he had been, and wishing she had talked to him a while longer. She had felt then that he had not looked at all like a dangerous person. But then looks could be misleading. As she looked at him, it dawned on her that the day she had met him was the last time she had been with Bintum for hours. Pain welled up inside her at these memories. A curse be on the white man for all he had done to her kind! Tears welled up in her eyes as she turned to walk out.

Mayne had once again watched the play of emotions in her eyes, as he had that day, many months ago, and when she turned to go out, he instinctively took a few steps closer, reached out and touched her arm to hold her back. She spun round and the fury in her eyes made him take a step back, and drop his hand.

"Don't run away from me again." He said so softly that only Samarah heard. "Where are you going?"

"To lie down, Sir. I have your father's permission to do so, Sir." She replied. Mayne glanced over his shoulder at Bessem, who shrugged, then returned his gaze to Samarah.

"Sir?" He grinned. "Call me Mayne, everyone does."

"That will be difficult, *Sir*. You see, it was a lesson I learnt when I was ten, a lesson I learnt the hard way. Black people must always say Sir when they talk to others of superior quality!" With these words, she walked out of the kitchen. A thoroughly confused Mayne turned back to Bessem, who looked just as confused.

"I've never seen her like that. I know she has some internal issues but she hardly ever snaps at anyone. What happened when you both met?"

"Nothing that would warrant this I guess...any way, I'm dying to know what I've missed, so pray tell, what's new?"

*

A week later, Samarah and Bessem were in the kitchen when another servant came in to say two white boys had come to see Mayne. They were brothers from one of the neighbouring plantations. They had learned that Old Patterson's son had come from London. Since their family had moved to Cameroon from Britain after the Anglo-French had ousted the Germans, they had hardly heard news of home. Now was a good chance to do that and hopefully get acquainted with the son of Mr. Patterson. The servant told the two girls that Mayne had asked if some fruit juice could be brought so that he could entertain his visitors. The servant informed the two girls that Mayne had requested for some fruit juice to be brought so that he could entertain his visitors. "Tell them I'll bring it soon," Bessem said.

"He said he wanted Samarah to serve them," the servant replied. Samarah fumed as she put a jar of orange juice and three glasses unto a tray. "I am so tempted to spit into his glass right now," she told Bessem who burst out laughing. She fastened her loincloth over her breasts and then walked out into the morning sun. She made sure she kept her eyes down as she murmured a 'good morning' and placed the tray on the table where they were sitting. She felt Mayne's eyes on her the whole time she poured the juice into the glasses and walked away.

When she went back into the kitchen, she burst out, "is that how your friend goes around staring at every 17 year old black girl he meets?" Bessem shrugged.

"You started it. Why are you so hostile towards him? What did he ever do to you?" She glanced from where she was stirring the egusi soup on the stove to Samarah and then back again. Samarah was standing akimbo and glaring into space.

"Actually he saved me from a snake… but that's not the point. It is just that he reminds me of Bintum."

Bessem looked at her again and she could see in this second look that she did not need to say any more. Bessem understood. She had told Bessem all about Bintum. Deep down however, Samarah knew it was more than that. And that frightened her. How could she tell Bessem that she had thought of Mayne the whole of the previous evening? How could she say that every time she tried to think of Bintum, Mayne's face would also be conjured up? She really wished she could talk with her mother. If she was truthful to herself, (and she thought she was) she would acknowledge that the white boy had invaded her thoughts, but that had to end. She had much better things to think about.

Soon, both girls heard Mr. Patterson's jeep start.

"Mayne's probably driving them back," Bessem commented. Samarah continued to slice the green beans for lunch and made no comment, Bessem said,

"Why don't you get to know him? You'll like him." At those words, Samarah rolled her eyes.

"I don't have that much time, Bess. Come on, let's finish this so that I can go to school."

*

It was about a quarter after six p.m. two weeks later when Samarah began her homeward journey from the church premises. She was thinking about the master's son, as she was prone to do these days. They had hardly exchanged words other than greetings for these weeks and she knew it was her fault. She kept away, meeting him only when she could not avoid it, like when she had to attend to his father in his presence. Most times still, she had felt his eyes on her as she went about her chores in the house but whenever he tried to talk to her she had made up some excuse and walked quickly away. She heard the sound of an approaching jeep, and moved to the side of the road to make way for it to pass. However, she heard it slow down, and raised her eyes to see who was in it. Mayne smiled at her, and even she had to admit that his smile lit up his face. She felt her heart rate increase. *It's this fear he makes me feel. Maybe it's because whenever I see him, I think of Bintum.* She told herself, as she looked away and continued walking. Mayne kept abreast with her in the jeep.

"Through for the day?" he inquired. She nodded without taking her eyes off the road, and without missing a step. "Hop in, let's go." He continued.

"Thank you, Sir, but I will walk," she stared straight ahead.

"Don't be a fool. It's getting dark. Get in." Samarah took a deep breath, stopped walking, turned to face him and looked directly into his eyes.

"Is that an order, Sir?" she asked. His smile appeared again.

"No, I am sorry if it came out like one. It is a request. Let's go home."

"In that case, leave me alone," she said in a voice that was barely above a whisper. Then she walked on. Mayne heaved a sigh, and swerved the car to block her path. She was forced to stop and glower at him. He looked right back. The girl could try but there was no way he would let her intimidate him.

"Why do you hate me so much, Sam?"

"The name is Samarah, Mr. Patterson. I don't need an excuse to hate or like people, and what I think should not really matter to you... *Sir*." The last word was uttered with as much anger as she could muster. Without flinching, she walked round the jeep and away, down the road. Seconds later, the jeep sped past her leaving a whirl of dust behind it.

When Samarah entered the gate about twenty minutes later, she did not notice Mayne standing in front of his bedroom window on the second floor, watching her. He observed her as her loincloth's edge blew about, tossed by the dry harmattan wind. This young woman intrigued him and boy did she have a sharp tongue! This was the second chance life had thrown his way to solve the mystery of Miss Fantasy and there was no way he would let it slip by. Since seeing her the day before, he had hardly thought of anything else. What would her smile be like? He wondered. How would it feel to hold her close, and kiss her till he occupied her thoughts as she did his? Mayne's head jolted to one side. That was hardly likely to happen. She had made it clear there was no love lost between the two of them.

"It's rather unfortunate that I find you this captivating, my dear. I intend to find out just what makes you tick. So be ready, Sam, I will get to know you more," he swore to himself.

Two evenings later, Samarah stood alone in a clearing a few meters away from the house. She usually came here when she wanted to think. A stream flowed nearby. During the day, it was very busy. Many native women washed clothes there, and children splashed and swam in it too. At dusk however it was very quiet and the only sound one would normally get would be the sound of running water, accompanied by the croaking of frogs or chattering of a bird or two. Samarah made her way to one of the big stones that were near the stream, sat down, and fixed her eyes on the water.

'I wish you were here Bwan. I miss you and Baa so much. And I am so lonely. You left me with Bintum, but he has been gone for so long. Sometimes, I wonder if I will ever see him again. I wonder if he is still alive and if he will come for me. I need to see him really soon because… well, because the white boy frightens me. I don't know why. He is kind to everyone, but whenever he comes around me, I feel like there are ropes fastened really tight around my stomach… Oh Bwan, I don't know why that makes me sad… maybe I just need to feel you now.'

Tears ran down her face, but she did not bother to wipe them. She knew queens and princesses did not cry, but there was no one here to see her and she truly needed to let it all out. So she cried and cried. She sobbed for all what she had lost because of the white man. All had been snatched from her on her own land, and she had been powerless to stop the thieves.

A twig broke behind her, and her head jerked up and over her shoulder.

"What are you doing here, Sir?" she snapped, mortified that he of all people had seen her in her moment of weakness. Mayne squatted beside her, his eyes full of compassion.

"I saw you leave the house, and well, it grew darker and you didn't come back, so I got worried. Bessem suggested I might find you here."

"Since when do the masters care what happens to the dark – skinned servants?" She tried to keep her hands from shaking as she wiped the tears from her face with the back of her palm.

"Sam, I don't know what has happened in your life. Some white men have probably done despicable things to you; but you shouldn't condemn every other white –skinned man. Look, I am just trying to help."

"Why? Why do you care?" she demanded. He shrugged.

"I don't know. It's just… something about you tugs at my heart strings. Talk to me, Sam." Samarah maintained a stony stare at him. He edged closer and looked her straight in the eyes. "I really need to know you," he whispered. They maintained eye contact for a few seconds. Mayne saw her eyes soften just before she looked away.

"You don't understand." She returned her look to the water.

"Then help me understand. Tell me why you hate us so much. What did my kind do to you? Don't you think it is unfair to judge us all based on…"

"Unfair?" she cut in and her eyes blazed as she scowled at him. "I'll tell you what unfair is: do you know what white signifies to me? Death, pain, loss, fear! So when I look at you that is what

I feel. Do you know how it feels to lose a loving father in a war fought to protect what was rightfully his? Do you know what it means to first lose a sibling you never saw, because trauma made your mother lose her pregnancy, and then later lose that mother in a fire? " her voice rose and quivered as she jumped up to her feet. Mayne stood up too, " a fire started in her hut by a white man because she would not succumb to his carnal desires?"

"Sam, please..." Mayne started to say, but Samarah went on, too incensed to stop.

"Do you know how painful it is to lose someone you were tied to as children, your betrothed, and only friend, the last person who meant everything to you? Sent to fight in a stupid war which means nothing to us! I don't even know if he is alive or dead... Of course you can't know. You are the white, the master, the supreme. How can you understand?" Tears ran down her face unchecked, and then the anger went out of her just as suddenly as it had come and her back slumped. Without thinking, Mayne took a step closer and enfolded her in his arms as her shoulders sagged. She leaned into him, her head coming to rest just under his chin. He could feel her trembling as she sobbed into his shirt, and his arms tightened around her.

"I'm so sorry," he murmured, as one hand remained around her back and the other came up to touch her hair.

"How can you say you understand?" Her voice sounded muffled. "At ten, I had no father. My mother and I were sold as slaves. At sixteen I was flogged until I lost consciousness." Mayne stiffened. Could Samarah be the girl Lucy had talked about? "The worst days of my life were those I spent on Mr. Wakerman's plantation. Those people gave me so much pain." He felt the wetness on his chest again.

"I'm sorry," was all he could say. "I didn't know. I'm so sorry."

For how long they stood like that neither could tell. Sensing that she would not appreciate being held in his arms once she had calmed down, Mayne slowly edged away from her. He looked into her eyes and his heart tightened. She looked so fragile, and so lost.

"Listen Samarah, I want to be here for you. If you ever need a friend, you can count on me."

She looked at him and he could see how softened her eyes had become. This made him smile.

"Good, now could you please smile, Miss?" Samarah found herself responding to that dimpled smile with a smile of her own that barely touched her lips. The transformation was so sudden, Mayne's breath caught in his throat.

"You are stunning when you smile. You should do it more often." He looked at her as if mesmerized. The fingers of his right hand came up to cup her cheek. She didn't cringe or pull away as he had half-expected her to. Instead she looked at him as if in a daze.

"You are so beautiful," he whispered as he bent forward. As his face descended he felt his eye lids closing. after his lips lightly brushed hers, she made a choked sound and the next thing he knew, he was staggering backwards over stones and trying to keep his balance. His bewildered eyes stared into skeptical ones.

"What are you doing, Sir?" she demanded. He groaned.

"I thought we had gotten rid of the 'sir' thing." He walked back closer to her.

"Well, let's see, before I was so rudely interrupted with that push, I believe I was about to kiss you." His grin was back. She didn't smile back.

"So that is what you are really after!"

"Huh? Sorry, you lost me."

"I know about white men who force their attentions on black girls, but that won't happen with me," she retorted. Mayne rolled his eyes.

"Here we go again – the bad white man. Do you actually think

I would force myself on you? I could make you want me." He chuckled as he drew nearer and bent to whisper in her ear, "In fact I am positive it won't be that difficult. You have so much fire, or is it passion, bottled up in you, just waiting for me to unleash it." The last sentence was spoken like a caress and his eyes slowly swept down the length of her and back up.

"You are just like all the rest," she spat, angered that his mere look could make her stomach clench, like his closeness a few seconds before had.

"Gimme a break! Goodness! Girl, you've got issues! You could tempt the patience of a saint. What the heck is wrong with you?"

"Nothing! Leave me alone," she yelled, and turned to leave, but Mayne's hands on her arms spun her back.

"No Samarah. You will listen to me now, and damn, listen good!" He shook her. She felt fear grip her – fear and something else she could not quite name. "I tried to kiss you because I like you – I like you a whole lot more than you can ever guess. I am attracted to you and I feel the attraction is mutual. You've got two options: One, you can let go of all this hate and hurt and let me help you work through them and go on with your life, or two, you can imprison yourself in these destructive forces, get stuck in the past, and miss out on all the good stuff life has to offer. The choice is yours."

He let her go. Without so much as a glance at him, she fled towards the house, his words echoing in her ears.

*

Two weeks later, Mayne stood looking at the house with an expression of longing on his face. It was time for him to return to England. The day before, he had hoped that Samarah would come to see his father, so that he could at least talk to her. Since the day they had met by the stream, she had avoided him. Somehow she had gotten his father to send her to the market each day and she usually stayed in school till late. Mr. Patterson had taken up almost all of Mayne's time too because he knew Mayne would be leaving soon.

Mayne had hoped that morning that she would at least come to say good bye since he was sure everyone in the plantation knew he was leaving. She had not shown up. Proof of just how headstrong she was!

"Drat!" he exclaimed and stormed away.

Samarah sat on her small bed that morning. Bessem had told her that Mayne would be leaving and she told herself that she couldn't care less. Nevertheless, some part of her kept thinking about that day by the stream, not about their argument, but about that brief moment when she had felt his warm, soft lips on hers, smelled his male scent. She wondered if she had misjudged him. Would it have been alright for her to apologize to him? Well, now it was too late. He had already left.

Her thoughts were interrupted by a sharp knock on her door, and then it flew open. Mayne strode in, dressed in khaki trousers, ranger shoes and a shirt. Her eyes widened at this violation of personal space and her heart thudded. Both stared at each other.

"Won't you wish me good bye?" his voice was low. Samarah swallowed but said nothing. "I hate to leave without telling you how sorry I am about what I said to you. I had no right to do that." He paused and waited. She did not say a word.

He went on, "I am going now Sam, but not for long. I'll miss you. Day and night I'll think of you. One day, I'll come back for you." He looked at her for a while longer, as if to memorize her face, until they heard the hooting of the jeep. "Sam, I…" He did not finish his sentence. He gulped, spun on his heels, and was gone.

"I am sorry too," Samarah whispered as she heard the jeep pull away.

CHAPTER SIX

LATE 1917 - 1918

Carl hugged his friend as soon as he stepped down from the vessel. He helped him carry his hand luggage and hail a cab, all the while commenting on how different Mayne looked – how long his hair had grown, how tanned his skin had become and how refreshed he looked. As the cab sped along, Mayne glanced out of the window and was overwhelmed by what he saw. The streets were almost full with women and children who looked like urchins. He could see them approaching passersby and begging for money or even food.

"I didn't know it had become this bad," he commented. Carl followed his gaze and nodded,

"Ever since the Military Service Acts, you remember, two years ago, more and more men have been forcefully conscripted into the army. Now there is hardly any man left to take care of the women and children. It has worsened all this time you have been in Cameroon. Many more women have gone out to look for work. They have entered munitions factories, agricultural sectors, and taken over many other roles we have known men to play. You should see them on the move. Even Princess Mary is doing her part to help. She has been visiting hospitals and welfare organisations to help out." Mayne listened intently.

"The Royal Navy has been doing a lot too," Carl went on. "They have had some small victories against the Germans. They have played a major role in protecting the flow of food and munitions into Britain, and have defeated the Germans on the Atlantic twice. The number of soldiers in the Royal Navy has increased, especially following the imposition of conscription into the army. When I think of being forced to join the army, I cringe. I would rather wish to have the right to decide for myself. Aren't you glad we aren't British and so the Act did not apply to us?" Carl asked with a slight grin. "I could still have enlisted if I wanted but I can't. It is not that I fear dying. It is just that I don't see the reason for this war, for killing so many people and causing so much misery. I would rather a more peaceful way was found to handle conflict," Mayne said.

"I know what you mean. These days everyone looks so sad, one would kill for a bit of gaiety. Let's talk about something more jolly, shall we? Mayne, the way you look, I am willing to bet a whole meal, and you know how hard that is to come by these days, that it is the result of a woman!" Mayne threw back his head.

"It feels so good to be off the water. No more queasy feeling of being rocked and now my stomach can finally settle." Carl smiled at Mayne's comment and asked about Mayne's father. Mayne said Patterson Senior would outlive them all and see his grandchildren. At his words, Carl raised an eyebrow.

"Man you sure some girl didn't turn your head around? Why that sly smile on your face as if you're enjoying some private joke?"

"You wouldn't believe who I met and fell in love with in Cameroon," responded Mayne. Carl peered at his friend.

"Mayne Patterson, bachelor of all time in love! Is this girl the daughter of one of your father's friends in Cameroon?"

"Nope. She actually lives and works in our house."

"Headline! Master falls in love with servant, or better yet: Black and White in love!" Then Carl exploded into a fit of laughter.

"Laugh all you want. Just wait till you see her. Man is she fine!"

The cab reached their destination and they carried Mayne's two boxes into his flat. Mayne continued talking as he opened the door and they dragged the boxes inside. "She is just so beautiful, all chocolate – dark, rich, sweet, tempting… but she can be headstrong!"

"This is intriguing man. You know if I didn't think it was too much of a coincidence I'd say… but no, it can't be." Carl shook his head, deep in thought.

"Want a drink?" Mayne went toward the bar. "What were you going to say, Carl?"

"Well, this may sound funny. You speak of this girl with the same intensity as Miss Fantasy. This girl must be something to have replaced that image in your head." Mayne had on a big smile as he handed a glass of Sherry to Carl. They both sat down.

"Miss Fantasy has a name. She is called Samarah."

"Hah, and I am George V, ruler of Great Britain!"

"I'm serious, I finally found her again." Mayne narrated to Carl how he had met Samarah again and when he paused for breath, Carl whistled.

"You must be a very happy man."

"It's not that simple. I have the most rotten luck."

"How so?"

"I meet a girl in the woods, dream about her for a whole year, fall for another girl, get involved with girl number two, finally meet girl number one again thousands of miles away from girl number two, but it just so happens that out of the billions of girls on the earth's surface, these two girls not only know, but hate each other with a passion."

"Whoa, this gets more interesting. Fill me in."

After hearing all the details Mayne could provide, Carl asked Mayne about the situation in Cameroon since the Allies had taken over the territory.

"I'm guessing the news must have found its way into *The Times*. The politicians here must be gloating about it. The British and Germans have had a history of conflict over Cameroon since 1884 when the Germans annexed the territory right under the nose of the British. You know, in order to protect the interest of the people, Cameroonian coastal chiefs, Bell and Akwa had looked to the British for annexation. They had been in contact with British Protestant Missionaries who had settled on their land since 1843 and seen the humanitarian works these men of God did. England wasn't too keen back then to add Cameroon to their list of African colonies, but in 1884 they changed their minds and sent the English Consul Hewett to annex the territory."

"And I take it he arrived too late and the Germans had already snagged the territory by the time he got there, huh?" Carl asked.

Mayne nodded and went on, "anyway, ever since the West African Expeditionary Force commanded captured Douala from Zimmermann about three years ago, Cameroon has been undergoing a lot of changes. Now the territory has finally been partitioned between the Anglo-French."

"Why ever would the Allies do that?" Mayne shrugged at Carl's question, then said "The joint administration did not work, except in Douala. Probably they realized that they were too different to work together. We both know that Britain and France hardly see eye to eye when it comes to colonial administrative policies. Indirect Rule and Assimilation are as opposite as heat and cold. Now, four-fifth of the country belongs to the French and one-fifth to the British."

"Now how mixed up is that?" Carl exclaimed. "First the Germans, then the Allies, and now individual France and Britain! And where does your father's plantation fall?"

"The British section. My father's cocoa and banana plantation is actually located near Victoria, which is a beautiful town by the sea. However, we also have a coffee plantation in the hinterlands, near a town called Bamenda. His foreman runs the place and he visits it or I do from time to time."

"Boy! Cameroon sure has an interesting history." Carl commented.

"You mean a disturbing one. This Anglo-French agreement signed a year ago, in March I think, just partitions the territory without any consideration as to ethnicity, or tribes. This will have future repercussions and could be the seed for future strife in the country. It actually bothers me."

"Especially as you plan to live there with Miss Fantasy." Carl nodded solemnly but his eyes twinkled.

"Her name is Samarah, and yes, I plan to do just that."

"What about Lucy?"

"What about her?"

"She's in love with you, Mayne. You should have seen her face when I gave her your letter. A sad puppy never drew more pity!" Mayne heaved a sigh,

"I wouldn't want to hurt her, but she'll forget about me, especially when I return to Cameroon."

*

A week later, Mayne came home to find Lucy waiting for him in his sitting room. One look at her and he felt a strong desire to pull her into his arms. She was still as beautiful as ever, and it had been so many months since he had seen her. He realized that he had missed her enormously.

"Lu!" His smile increased and he half-expected her to run to him and fling herself into his arms as she always did, but she looked at him coolly and maintained her seat. As disappointment welled in him, he said, "I wasn't expecting you."

"No, you weren't. You left without saying a word to me," she pouted. Mayne sat opposite her.

"I'm sorry. I left in a hurry. But I did write a letter to you. Carl gave it to you, didn't he?"

"A letter, Mr. Patterson, was not enough for me. You could have come by the house and told me yourself!" She turned her head away but not before Mayne had seen the hurt in her eyes. He got up and went to sit next to her. He took both her hands in his and said,

"I'm sorry. It wasn't my intention to hurt you. I've missed you so much."

When she didn't speak, he raked a hand through his dark, shoulder-length hair. "Come on Lucy, I'm really trying here. Do you think you could meet me halfway?" She looked at him for a while, and then relaxed and leaned into him.

"I've missed you too."

She smiled as she looped her arms around his neck and gave him a peck on the lips. Mayne leaned into her and closed his eyes as he enfolded her in his arms. *Will Samarah ever let me near enough to kiss her like this?* The thought jolted him and he involuntarily pulled away. Lucy's eyes flew open in surprise.

"What's wrong?" Mayne forced a smile.

"I just thought I'd take you out to dinner, and then we could talk more about what's been happening to you all this while. I know lots must have been happening and," his voice sank to a whisper, "I want to know all the details."

Later when Mayne helped Lucy into a cab, there was no doubt in his mind that there was no future for them. All through dinner - which had been a one-course meal- he had found his thoughts reverting to Samarah especially as he had stirred the conversation to Lucy's days back in Cameroon, and somehow got her to talk about her 'obstinate servant girl'.

"Drat! I've got a Herculean task ahead of me if I'm going to get

Sam to care about me," he concluded.

1918

Lucy waited for days for Mayne to call round, but he did not. She came to his place and left lots of notes for him to see her, but he did not. In frustration, she waited at his doorstep till late one night.

"Good Heavens, Lu! What on earth are you doing outside at this time of the night? You know how risky it is!" he exclaimed as he tried to slot his key into the lock.

"Good evening, Mayne. I get the feeling that you are avoiding me and I want to know why."

Mayne pushed open the door, and stood to one side to let her go in first.

"Do you want some coffee?" he asked as he closed the door and followed her into the sitting room.

"No, I want some answers." She was not smiling one bit.

"I've just been busy with school. This is my last year and I have to concentrate, you see?"

"No, I don't see. Mayne, what's wrong? Have I done anything to upset you?"

"No, Lucy, come I'll take you home." Mayne made to take her arm but she pulled it away, her voice rising a fraction.

"I won't leave till I know what's happening."

"I'm not in the mood for a fight."

"Is there someone else?"

Mayne choked at her question. She went on, "we need to be frank and tell each other the truth if we want this thing to work." Mayne shut his eyes tight and tousled his hair. Then he sat down.

"You'd better sit," he said. With a wary look in her eyes, she complied.

"I think we should stop seeing each other," he said slowly. The room suddenly felt too quiet.

"You must be out of your mind!" Lucy exclaimed.

"Believe me, I haven't taken leave of my senses."

"Then you must have had an attack of dengue or some other tropical disease." She said calmly.

"Lu, we can be friends. It's just that this thing we have isn't working."

"It is for me. In fact it was working just fine before you traveled. What happened in Cameroon, Mayne?"

"You'll find someone else, someone who'll truly love and appreciate you."

"I take it by that you mean you have found somebody to love and appreciate and that person is not me." *Curse her alert mind and sharp intelligence*! Mayne thought.

"Look, I'm very much attracted to you Lu."

"Forget attraction! You don't love me, do you?" Tears welled up in Lucy's eyes.

"I'm really sorry," Mayne mumbled. The tears spilled unto Lucy's cheeks as Mayne went on, "you are young, and talented, and beautiful and fun to be with. You have dozens of men falling at your feet."

"Yes, well, they aren't you, are they Mayne? It's you I want. You weren't like this before. Did you meet someone else?"

"I did." Silence greeted his words. Lucy looked like she had been hit over the head by a moving train.

"How can't you love me any more? I gave you my virginity."

"Which you cared very little about. You told me so. Even though that's no excuse for the way I acted. You seduced me."

"So now it's my fault! You let yourself be seduced. You wanted me as much as I wanted you," she screamed.

"You could have stopped me."

"Easy for you to say. You're not a man."

"And do you think that's going to make me feel better?" She stood up and walked towards the door. Mayne followed her.

"Please, Lucy, let me get a cab for you. It's late."

"Don't bother. We are not together any more, remember? I am not your responsibility."

She pulled open the door, then turned back to look at him, "I love you Mayne, I want you and I'll have you, or no other girl will."

*

"Gather round children, it's time for the moonlight story." The children ran to squat at the feet of the old woman bent double with age, as she sat on the bamboo stool beside the hut. Their parents and some teenagers sat a little away on mats and big cocoyam leaves.

"Monga'an O!" She chanted.
"Shing O!" They chorused.

The moonlight bathed the environment, giving it an ethereal quality. The huts dotted here and there looked like giant mushrooms coated with silver. The old woman cleared her throat, and her voice, rusty with age croaked out.

"I am something. The man who made me does not use me. The man who uses me does not see me. What am I?" Most of the older people knew the answer to the riddle, but they played along, and thought for a few seconds with the others.

"We do not know, oh wise old one. Please may your wisdom pour out on us like the rains." Someone said. The old woman chuckled.

"You will know at the end of my tale. It is a tale of wonder, of birth and of growth. This is the story of our people. As a small child, I heard it from my mother, who had been told by her mother's mother." The old woman's voice grew stronger. "Two brothers came around the

Wanmuang River. They had traveled far and wide, looking for a place to settle, a place the gods would show them. When they saw how fertile the region was, they decided to consult the oracle to know if that was the land they would possess. At first, the oracle chanted, and sighed, and laughed and finally it wept. Then there came a message from the gods:

'You may have the land.
It will yield.
It will produce.
It will be fertile.

But be warned!
Troubles will be involved.
Beware the stranger who comes in a canoe!

Then will there be mourning
Your women will run
Your children will cry
Your men will die

But do not fear
For many come and go
Civilizations rise and fall
But the Wise Old Sun smiles!'

The brothers went ahead and settled there with their wives and children and livestock. They however forbade the building of canoes, and used rafts whenever they had to go fishing.

One day, a long time later, when they were both over a hundred and fifty years old, these brothers sat on the river banks, eating kola nuts, and drinking raffia wine, the wine of the gods, when suddenly, they saw a speck approaching in the distance, over the water. What could this speck be?" The woman's voice had sunken to a hoarse whisper and it grew *louder and stronger as she went on, "The brothers helped each other up and leaned forward as the speck grew bigger and bigger. It approached like some ominous beast, and the words of the oracle rang it their ears. What was that? A canoe, but unlike any canoe they had ever seen. This one was large, really big. A whole forest must have gone into building it. The brothers stared in awe and dread as the canoe approached ."*

The woman's story was interrupted by a cry. As everyone watched, four hefty men brought in a coffin, which they placed in the center of the courtyard. The old woman cried out in a voice which belied her years, "This is the answer to my riddle. A coffin! Oh dreadful night! Whose body does this coffin bear?" One of the women ran to the coffin and screamed.

"It is my husband! Last year they took our sons and not one came back! Now they have killed my husband!" A little girl ran to the woman. She looked at the man in the coffin, and then her mother who still had her arms around it, burst into flames.

"Bwan! Don't leave me. Noooooo!!!"

Samarah sprang up for the bed all drenched in sweat. Her eyes darted every where and her breath came out in gasps. As she became aware of her surroundings, she realized that she was in her room at the Patterson estate. She lay back against the sheets and stared into space. The dream had been so real. She had seen both her parents. She forced herself to stay awake, afraid to go back to sleep. She wondered where Bintum was. It was over two years since he had been taken away from her, and still it hurt like it had happened the day before. "I hate them." She sobbed, "I hate them so much!"

Samarah was surprised when it was announced in church that she had a letter. Who could it be from? Nobody knew her except the workers on the Patterson estate. Maybe it was Bintum! Her heart raced at the thought. She collected it from Father Vincent. Then as she walked away, she tore the envelope open and her hands trembled as she read.

Dear Samarah,
How are you and how is life in our country, Cameroon? I'm fine here,
only missing you lots.
I know it must be surprising reading from me. I just wanted you to
know how much I am looking forward to coming home. I hope this war
ends really soon, so that I can come home and be with you once again.
I can hardly wait.
When you pray, pray for me, that I may finish soon in school. Pray for
us and remember that I think about you always. Extend my greetings
to Bessem.
I remain yours,
Mayne.

Samarah was so puzzled that she read the letter again and again.
There had to be a mistake, but the letter was addressed to her,
signed by Mayne Patterson. Was the silly white boy mad? First of
all, it was spelt Kamerun – then she remembered that since the
Anglo-French had split the territory, the English called it Cameroon, while the French called it Cameroun. Secondly, it was HER
country, not THEIR country! Thirdly, he was joking if he thought
she would waste her prayers on him. How dare he write to her?

When she had overcome her initial shock, a smile crawled across
her lips. Why, he had thought of her! Her heartbeat quickened.
She frowned. What was the matter with her? She assured herself
that she was happy because if the war ended, as Mayne prayed
it would, then Bintum would come back, seek her out, and they
would finally be together, and return to their people. She willed
herself to tear up the letter, but she found herself tucking it into
her loincloth, near to her heart.

*

"Mayne Patterson, snap out of your reverie. The war is over!" Carl burst into Mayne's bedroom early on the morning of November 12, 1918. Mayne's eyes flew open and he groaned.

"Goodness, Carl, a curse be on the day I gave you my spare key. I should have given it to Lucy. At least she knew how to get a guy up with style. Now what are you ranting and raving about?" He stifled a yawn, threw off the sheets and stepped into his slippers. Carl was bubbling with excitement.

"Rejoice with me and everyone else in the world – that is every one except the Germans." Mayne looked at his friend.

"Everybody knows that Carl."

"Well, how you can afford to sleep on a day like today simply beats my imagination. You, my friend, are part of history, because at the eleventh hour of the eleventh day of the eleventh month, that is yesterday, the first war fought by the whole wide world came to an end, and we survived it."

"Yeah, that's great and now the victors are meeting in France, huh?"

"Yep. The Allied and Associated Powers trudge to France soon."

"Think how humiliating it's going to be for the Germans, seeing as they had disgraced France in the Hall of Mirrors, and now it's their turn."

"Mmhm, payback's a bitch, huh? However, sweet as revenge may be though, that's not the only reason why Paris was chosen. Not much destruction was done in the city." Mayne nodded. Then all of a sudden, he skipped up and down like a seven year old whose favorite toy had just been handed to him.

"This is great news. I can't wait to go home." Carl shook his head from side to side.

"I pour out the world's events to him and all he can think about is leaving me for a girl!"

"Stop complaining. You'll come visit and I promise to make it a worthwhile event for you."

"I can hardly wait. I'll finally get to visit exotic Africa, see where my ancestors came from, and fish and sunbathe all day long with my best buddy. There are fewer things which are better in life." Carl sighed with exaggerated ecstasy.

*

Mayne and Carl finally graduated from university. Mayne had majored in Economics, while Carl obtained a degree in Political Science. Carl's parents, Mr. and Mrs. White travelled from the United States of America to watch their son graduate. Mayne's proud grandparents attended the ceremony, and organized a reception party for him at their house. Many of their family friends attended. The war was over, and those who had survived it were caught in a spell of thanksgiving and freedom from fear. Mayne had sent an invitation to Lucy and her uncle but he showed up alone saying she was not feeling well.

Mayne spent the next couple of days making plans to return to Cameroon. Carl would be going back to the United States of America with his parents. It was a tearful good bye when Mayne saw them off at the docks in the Port of London. They were taking a ship from St. Katharine's Docks, not very far from the Tower of London. Once again Mayne made Carl promise to come and see him in Cameroon. Then the friends embraced each other, and after shaking hands with Mayne, Carl's parents accompanied him aboard the ship. Mayne went back to making his plans for the trip back.

On the eve of his departure, as he was packing the last of his clothes into his box, there was a knock on his door. When he opened it, he saw Lucy. She gave him a small smile and asked if she could come in. without a word, he stood to one side so that she could pass in. She did and he closed the door and followed her into the sitting room. She stood with her back to him, taking in the emptiness of the place. He stood with his head bent, not sure where to look or what to say or do. Finally she turned round to face him.

"Uncle told me you'd be leaving tomorrow." At her words, he nodded. She walked closer, took both of his hands in hers and went on, "what about us?"

Mayne drew in his breath and exhaled slowly, then his eyes met hers.

"Lucy, there is no us. Please forget me and find someone else. That will help."

"I've tried Mayne. All these months I've kept away, but to no avail... Won't you even give me a good bye kiss? Some token to remember you by?" she whispered.

"I... I can't. I'm sorry."

"What we had was good," she continued. Her fingers moved to her dress and unbuttoned her top button, her eyes never leaving his face. Mayne's eyes followed the movement of her fingers as if he was enthralled. As the second button came undone, he forced himself to look into her eyes.

"Lu, don't do this."

His hand came to rest on hers, stalling her action.

"There was a time when the sight of me drove you crazy," her voice sounded hollow to his ears.

"You still do, but we can't do this. It'll just hurt us both. This is not right anymore."

"We have now, Mayne. Tomorrow you'll be leaving and I may never see you again. Please, don't turn away from me now." His palm came up to caress her cheek. She leaned towards him but he gently put her away from him and stepped aside.

"I've hurt you once, Lu, I won't do it again. I owe this to you and to the woman I love. I'm really sorry we have to part this way." Lucy's eyes filled with tears and with a sob, she ran out of the flat.

CHAPTER SEVEN

1919

"But now I tell you: love your enemies and pray for those who persecute you, so that you may become sons of your Father in Heaven, for He makes His sun rise on the bad and good, and causes rain to fall on the just and the unjust. Matthew 5: 44 – 45." Father Vincent closed his Bible and smiled at Samarah, who scowled back. Both of them were sitting in the Confessional, after Samarah had just confessed her sins.

"I've tried father, but it's not that easy. I keep thinking of all I've lost and then I feel the pain all over again. Maybe I'm just not ready to let go, to move on. When I think of forgiving Mr. Wakerman and Lucy, I get physically sick! Sorry Father, but forgiveness is something I haven't mastered yet."

The priest cleared his throat.

"I am white, Samarah. Do you hate me?"

"Of course not. You are different and you remind me of Father Clement. I do like you a lot." A wisp of a smile touched her lips.

"I won't push you. You have to do this on your own when you are ready, but I want you to remember that God loves you and forgives whatever you do. You could do the same, and when you do, you'll find such peace only forgiveness can bring. When you forgive, you do it for yourself, and then for the other person, because you free yourself of hate and hurt and pain. In addition you recite the

'Our Father' and you know the sentence 'forgive us as we forgive' so I'd say you are telling God how to judge you," Father Vincent concluded with a cheeky smile. Samarah smiled back as she shook her head from side to side and rolled her eyes.

As Samarah walked home that evening, she thought of Mr. Patterson. He had once more lapsed into illness, and it was far more serious this time. When she entered the gate, everyone was in a great frenzy. She found Bessem in the kitchen and asked what was going on.

"Mayne is back to stay!" Bessem was stirring a pot of groundnut soup. Samarah did not know why, but her heart skipped a beat at the mention of his name. She forced herself to sound uninterested. When she did not reply, Bessem gave her a shrewd look.

"Hmmm, Mayne is not your regular white man, but I'm guessing you already know that, even if you are just too stubborn to admit it."

"A lion can never give birth to a dog, and no matter how much a leopard tries, it can never change its spots. The child of a White-man will always be a Whiteman."

"Well, Mayne is human and so are we. You have to learn to let go. Forgive and forget the past."

"Now you sound just like Father Vincent," Samarah laughed.

Mayne sat in his father's room. His father's pale face was lit up with joy. They talked about anything and everything, Patterson Senior filling Mayne in on what had gone on in his absence. Finally he told Mayne details about his plantations all over the country and the accounts they kept. Mayne tried to tell him that they had time to discuss all that and he needed to rest, but Patterson Senior was adamant. He told Mayne that nobody would live forever and those who planned to do so were idiots.

"Father, you'll outlive us all," Mayne commented and that made his father laugh.

"Now that's a pleasant thought," he chuckled. "However, we both know that won't happen... Mayne, I need to go, knowing that you are taking care of everything I've built all these years. Promise me you'll make it all prosper, that you'll put in your best."

"Father, you'll live to see your grandchildren."

Mayne was frightened by the intensity in his father's voice. Mr. Patterson's brows creased into a frown.

"That reminds me. What are you doing about a wife? I married your mother when I was twenty-two. You're almost twenty-five now. Mayne, I want heirs. I want my descendants to build this land, to finish what I started. Now, isn't there a girl who tickles your fancy? Didn't you meet someone in England who doesn't fancy herself too posh to live in the tropics?" Mayne thought of Lucy and shook his head from left to right.

"I didn't need to go all the way to England to find someone. I found her here." At his words, Mr. Patterson sat up straighter in bed.

"Here, did you say? Who could she possibly be?" he mused, "One of the little English or German girls you met at those live-in parties, when you were growing up?"

"Nope."

"Then tell me. The suspense is killing me."

Mayne watched the smile on his father's face and sighed inwardly. He was not so sure if he should tell him. What if his father blew his top? *Well, better now than later*. He cleared his throat and opened his mouth to speak, but his father beat him to it.

"Look Mayne, you don't need to look like you've seen my ghost before I'm even dead. Just go ahead and spill the beans," Mr. Patterson's mouth quirked at Mayne's obvious discomfort.

"Ok, just don't freak out," Mayne muttered.

Mr. Patterson leaned forward. "What was that?"

"Uh, nothing... Ok, Papa, it's Sam." Mr. Patterson's eyes registered no recognition.

"Sam? Who's Sam?" Then suddenly, his eyes widened as a thought flashed across his mind. "You didn't fall for a boy, did you?!"

"God, no Papa, nothing like that! I meant Samarah." For a moment, Mr. Patterson sat as still as a statue, while Mayne's heart throbbed in his chest. Patterson did not utter a word, but stared at his son. Then he fell back against his pillow and burst into laughter.

"Good gracious, Mayne, you will be the death of me! Now quit this stunt and tell me who your lady is." When Mayne kept quiet, Patterson sobered up and searched his son's eyes with his.

"No," he whispered.

"Father, please listen."

"Oh no!" Patterson's face was as white as the sheet draped around him. Then both hands flew to clutch the region of his heart and his face contorted into a grimace as he cried, "My heart, my poor heart!" Mayne jumped out of his seat and bent over his father.

"Oh God, I'm so sorry Father." His fingers closed around the bell at his father's bedside and he began ringing it. The Reverend Sister who was a nurse and had moved in to take care of Mr. Patterson rushed in, and tried to help Patterson senior. She gave him an injection which made him sink into slumber.

"He'll be fine when he wakes up," she assured Mayne. "You look terrible. You should get some rest too. You both can continue your discussion tomorrow," she shooed Mayne out of the room, closing the door firmly behind him.

Mayne's first impulse was to go to Samarah's room. It was night now and she should be back from school. However, his pride would not let him go. If she really wanted to see him, she should come to him. After all, he was in no hurry. He had the rest of his life to make her his. So instead of going to find her, he turned into his room and fell across his bed. It was only then that he realized how exhausted he was. His eyes closed as he relived his day.

One of his father's foremen had been waiting for him at the docks for

several days, because ships hardly made it on time, so several days were
necessary to wait for a ship to sail into the port. Mayne's heart had soared
with joy and excitement when he had caught a glimpse of the Victoria
port. Finally, after over two months at sea, he was home, and what
was more, he would see the people he loved and had missed for so long.

"Welcome Massa." The foreman had given him a toothless grin as he
packed part of Mayne's luggage into the jeep. The rest would follow in
a cart. Mayne embraced the man.

"Jombi, I am so glad to see you. How's everyone, and my father?" The
man quickly pulled away as his eyes darted round. Several people had
halted in their tracks to watch them. Jombi grinned again. The young
master had not changed at all. That was good. Everyone on the planta-
tion had been scared that he would return acting more stuck up, like the
other masters, but this gesture had put his mind at ease.

"Couldn't my father make it here?" Mayne asked as he took the car
keys from Jombi and got into the driver's seat, asking Jombi to get into
the passenger's seat.

"Ya papa no well. e no be fit kam."

When they had driven into the gate about six hours later, most of
the workers had been there to meet him. He had shaken hands and
embraced those he had known when growing up. His eyes had searched
for Samarah in the crowd in vain. How he had longed to catch just a
glimpse of her. Maybe that would calm the roaring in his heart. No
Samarah. She was one stubborn girl!

*

Bessem smiled at Samarah as she poured tea into a tea flask. Both
girls were in the kitchen getting breakfast ready. Samarah asked
after Mr. Patterson's health and Bessem told her he had another
attack the night before. Bessem handed the flask to Samarah and
asked her to take it to the dining room. When Samarah entered

the room, she saw Mayne and the two friends – Mark and Eustace Smith, who had come to check on him last time, at table. It was easy to tell that these two were twins, what with their identical sandy hair, aquiline noses, gray eyes, and lanky body build. Mayne was smearing jam onto a piece of bread. She started and almost dropped the tray which contained the flask. However, bracing herself, she walked up to them, her eyes lowered.

"Good morning Sirs." Her voice was barely audible as she tried to set the tray down. It clattered as it touched the table. She studiously avoided looking up from the table.

"Good morning, Samarah. Where were you yesterday?" She could hear the amusement in Mayne's voice and felt butterflies in her stomach.

"In church, Sir, trying to keep from ..." she stopped herself just in time, stepped back and would have left but Mayne said, "sit down, and have some breakfast with us." Three pairs of astounded eyes flew up to Mayne's face, but he was interested only in one pair.

"Ex…excuse me?" she stammered.

His smile spread across his face.

"That got you to look at me. Like what you see?" he teased. Samarah shot daggers at him with her eyes and his smile widened.

"There isn't much to see. May I go now, *Sir*?" she said through her teeth. He continued to grin and nodded. Samarah stormed out of the room, and the laughter of the three young men followed her.

"Stunning girl," Eustace said.

"Yes, sassy too," Mark added.

"And extremely stubborn," Mayne concluded.

Eustace winked as he said, "you must be having the time of your life."

"How so?" Mayne inquired.

"She is so ripe for the plucking, and no one could mistake the vibes surrounding you both. So, can I get a go at her after you are through?"

"Don't leave me out. I want a piece of her too," Mark added. Mayne knew he shouldn't get angry. This was just boy talk, but he found himself fighting down his ire.

"No such luck, boys. She is all mine."

The other two looked at him.

"Alright, hands off, but what a shame. If you ever change your mind…" Eustace started to say,

"Don't push it," Mayne cut in. There was something in Mayne's voice that made Eustace say, "you don't have to sound so protective, Mayne. She is just a native." Mayne was about to retort but then he thought better of it. Instead, he forced a smile.

"Sorry. What's been going on while I've been away?"

Samarah stormed into the kitchen.

"Why didn't you tell me Mr. High-and-mighty was already in the dining room?"

"Isn't it obvious?" Bessem gave her the kind of look one would give an extremely slow toddler. "I knew you wouldn't go in there if you knew, and he practically begged me to make you come."

"Why would he do that? Can't he just leave me alone?" Bessem shrugged.

"He asked after you yesterday."

At Samarah's surprised look, Bessem laughed and her eyes twinkled. "I think he is interested in you. The last time he was here, he pestered me with questions about you."

"Humph!" Samarah frowned.

"I think you are as attracted to him as he is to you," Bessem peered at her.

"Me?" Samarah scoffed as she averted her gaze. "Attracted to him? He's white, Bess. Please give me some credit!"

When Mayne's friends left he went in to see how his father was doing. Mr. Patterson was lying in bed with his eyes closed, but they fluttered open when Mayne walked to the bed.

"How are you feeling now Papa? I checked on you earlier but you were asleep." He sat down beside his father. Mr. Patterson's wrinkled flesh stretched into a lopsided smile.

"Look… son… about yesterday …"

"Let's not talk about it. I'm sorry I brought it up when you are so sick. I shouldn't have sprung it up on you like that."

"No, son…" Mr. Patterson's words were coming out in gasps of air. "You did the right thing." His voice came out so weak that Mayne had to lean closer to hear what he was saying. "Remember, my boy… this land has been… and is your home, you and the children you'll have… with Samarah." Mayne drew in and held his breath, afraid to let it out. "I must admit… that the possibility had never crossed my mind. She wouldn't be my first choice, or any of my choices… but… she is a good person, Mayne… she will make you a good wife." Mayne dimpled as he beamed at his father.

"How can I ever thank you, Father? I have your blessing, then?" Mr. Patterson nodded.

"Now, I think I need to rest." He croaked. He smiled at his son and then closed his eyes. "I'm proud of you, and love you, son." He murmured. Then he gave a faint chuckle, "I would love to see you try to win her hand… Hahaha, now that would be a sight I would like to see." Mayne joined in the laughter. Everyone knew his Sam. Mayne was strangely elated. He knew that his father adored him, but that was the first time Patterson had actually said the words to him.

When Mayne was sure his father was asleep, he tiptoed out of the room and headed straight for the kitchen, where he knew Samarah should be, but she wasn't there. Bessem told him she had gone to the local market but would be back any minute, since it had been a while since she left. While he sat there chatting with Bessem and looking out of the window every few seconds. The frantic sound of a bell interrupted their conversation.

"Father!" Mayne dashed out of the kitchen and up the stairs with Bessem at his heels. They raced into Mr. Patterson's room. One look from the nurse's face to the bed and Mayne rushed to his father. He clutched the old man's fragile hand in his and let go. It fell lifelessly to the bed. With a sob, Mayne held the frail body to his chest, and rocked it, never letting go. He let out heartrending sobs. His father was gone, and he was all alone.

When it had really dawned on Mayne that his father was no more, he knew that it was his responsibility to see to the burial arrangements. First of all he asked for Jombi, whom he sent to tell Father Vincent and the Smiths. Jombi took along the nurse in the jeep. Mayne also sent Bessem to tell the foremen to call all the workers back from the fields.

Thirty minutes later Dr. Ryan's jeep sped into the courtyard, and he ran into the house with one of the nurses. When he found Mayne upstairs in Old Patterson's room, Ryan asked Mayne to give them some time to prepare the body for burial.

As Mayne left the room and descended the stairs, he heard another jeep arrive. Father Vincent came in. After shaking Mayne's hand and extending his condolences he asked Mayne if there was anything he could do to help.

"Yes, Father. I know that my father was not a religious man. Before we came to Cameroon we belonged to the Lutheran church but since my mother died, he stopped going to church. I know this may sound absurd but I would feel so much better if you said a mass for him." Father Vincent said he would do it pointing out that God was one, even if a lot of religions had sprung up to celebrate Him. Mayne told him how grateful he was and just then he saw Mark and Eustace drive in, so he excused himself and went out to meet them.

Samarah heard the news in the market and immediately rushed

back. After asking Bessem where Mayne was, she ran to the living room to see him, but most of their white neighbors were there, so she retreated into the kitchen.

In the late afternoon, Fr. Vincent said the funeral mass in the courtyard. Mayne sat in front of the coffin Dr. Ryan had brought, with the Smiths. The workers sat all around them. It was a solemn occasion.

Samarah sat with Bessem in the crowd behind Mayne. All through mass she prayed that he would be alright. She also felt sad at Mr. Patterson's passing. True, he had not been a very warm employer but at the same time he had been fairer to the workers than Mr. Wakerman ever was. She found herself praying for his soul with all her heart.

When the mass ended, a procession to the grave started. Eight workers carried the coffin towards the back of the left side of the house where Mr. Patterson's grave had been dug. Fr. Vincent followed them, while Mayne and the other white people followed him, then Bessem, Samarah, Jombi and the other labourers came. After Fr. Vincent had sprinkled the coffin with Holy Water and declared, "you are dust, and unto dust you shall return."

Mayne approached, stood silent staring at the coffin that held his father's remains in the ground, and trying his hardest not to break down and cry. Finally all he said was, "rest in peace, Father," and then he took some earth and threw it unto the coffin. Ten male workers then began the task of covering it up with earth.

Throughout the funeral ceremony, Samarah looked at Mayne's face and felt his pain all the way to her heart. She wished there was something she could do to make him feel better. She thought she understood just what he was going through. She had felt that kind of pain before.

By evening the guests began to leave and by eight p.m. the house was empty of all the guests. Mayne lay down on his bed, staring up at the ceiling, his eyes mostly unblinking. He felt a void building, and growing in his chest, threatening to devour him. He could not believe it. His father was gone... just like that. He thought of all the time he had spent away from home and wished he had been obstinate and refused to go to England. Now, all he could do was wish.

There was a knock on the door and Samarah came in with a plate of fruits and a glass of milk.

"Go out!" Mayne said without opening his eyes. She did just the opposite and set the plate and glass on his table.

"Eat something. You've starved yourself the whole day."

At the sound of her voice, he opened his eyes. He heaved a sigh.

"Well, what do you know? It takes my father's death to bring her to see me. Have you come to laugh at me? Well, we are even now – see? A white man's world is crumbling at his feet," he sniffed. Samarah looked directly into his eyes and her gaze did not waver as she replied,

"I know what it means to lose a loved one. I'm sorry."

Mayne held her gaze for a moment, then nodded, and turned his face away.

"Thanks for the concern. Please, I need to be alone now," he said. Samarah hesitated. Knowing that she would probably kick herself later, but willing to take the kick anyway, she leaned forward and took his right hand in both of hers. Mayne was startled by the gesture.

"Life goes on," she whispered. She let go of his hand, turned and walked towards the door. When she reached it she looked back over her shoulder, "please, Mayne, eat something."

She opened the door and walked out of the room. Mayne stared at the hand she had touched.

"Life goes on," he repeated.

The next day Mayne composed a letter to his maternal

grandparents in London telling them about his father's death. He also wrote a letter to Carl. These he gave one of the young boys on the plantation to give to Fr. Vincent who would be going to Victoria the day after.

For a week Mayne was hardly seen outside of the house. He stayed in his room lying on his bed and staring into space. Bessem and Samarah tried to get him to come out and take a stroll but they succeeded only twice. They also had to force him to eat everyday by threatening to feed him if he did not eat by himself.

One day when Samarah knocked on his door and got no answer, she became worried so she opened the door and went in. Mayne was lying on the bed with his eyes closed.

"Mayne," she said, "you have to pull yourself together. Believe me I understand what you are going through, but it is time for you to concentrate on the living. Mourn your father by continuing the work which he started. This plantation needs you, we all need you." He opened his eyes to see her retreating back as she went out of the room and closed the door. "Life goes on," he repeated to himself again.

Two days later, Mayne gathered all his workers together to hear their complaints and see into their problems. After that he asked the foremen to follow him into the house for a meeting. The men were stunned. Mr. Patterson had never let any of them step on the veranda, let alone enter the house. At their hesitation, Mayne smiled and told them he would be honored to have them in his house.

In single file the men walked up the steps, and removed their shoes before entering the house. They entered the house with their heads bowed and their backs bent, the way they usually entered the palace of a great chief. They murmured in awe when they saw the set of comfortable sofas and settees arranged round huge carpets. Flowers, both artificial and natural were everywhere. There were paintings on the wall, of Indian, English, Native American and

African origin.

When Mayne asked them to sit down, they were so baffled that they stammered that they preferred to stand. After failing, to convince them, Mayne started the meeting. He thanked them for having been loyal to his father all these years and for all their hard work. He then proceeded to ask them what their problems were.

The spokesperson of the foremen, Pa Ateh, explained in broken English that the first problem was that of wages. They would be grateful if their wages were increased. The next issue was housing. The houses they had on the plantation needed repairs and more houses were needed as the population kept increasing with the birth of their children. A third problem was that they needed more foremen, and another was that they needed new machetes, hoes and other tools used on the plantation. He concluded by saying that the last thing they needed was to be able to ask for and obtain permission when absolutely necessary.

Mayne listened and then thanked him. He promised to address the issues that Pa Ateh had raised. At the end, they were served food and drinks. Mayne added a bottle of whisky for them. They thanked him and said they would eat and drink outside.

When they went out, the group of workers who had gathered round when they had heard that the foremen had gone into the house, engulfed them and fired questions. How did the house look inside? What had they seen? Was it true that many, many steps linked the top floor to the one below? Every one wanted to get firsthand information and description of the house, so as to narrate it to the others who were not fortunate to be there.

The foremen, who had found themselves the center of attention, told them all that had happened, and how they were now the proud owners of the white man's *'Fire Mimbo'*. Only a very few had ever tasted whisky before. The best news of all, however, was the revelation that they would earn better salaries. Everybody rejoiced, proclaiming the new master to be a good man.

When Samarah returned from school that evening, Bessem told her all that had happened.

"Did he really do all these things?" Samarah was filled with wonder. Bessem nodded.

"Aren't we lucky to be working here?"

"I did misjudge him, didn't I?" Samarah pondered. She had never heard a negative word about Mayne on the estate – well, except that before he went to England, all the girls had liked him, and he had liked most back.

Like a flash, she remembered what he had told her before leaving; *One day, I'll come back for you.* Did he even remember? What had he meant? She shrugged. It was really none of her business, but she found herself smiling the whole day. She even went as far as serving him supper, smiling all through, and answering his inquiries about her day monosyllabically, but pleasantly enough. When she asked him how his own day went, he gave her a quizzical look.

"Are you sure you are alright?" He placed a cool palm against her forehead. This made her burst into laughter. He too broke into a grin – the first since his father had passed away.

"I'm fine, Mayne, now do you want to help me carry these to the kitchen?"

"With pleasure, ma'am. After you," he laughed.

CHAPTER EIGHT

JULY – EARLY AUGUST 1919

Carl reached the coast of Cameroon at the Victoria port. Mayne waved frantically from the crowd. Carl waved back and hurried form the ship. They embraced each other in a bear hug.

"How was your journey?" Mayne asked.

"Very interesting. Sorry about your dad, buddy. It must have been hard."

"It still is, but easier to bear now than before. It sure is good to see you!"

"And it wasn't difficult to spot you. I mean, you stand out, being white and all."

"There are other white men here, Carl," Mayne laughed. "Come, let's get your stuff into my jeep."

As they made their way through the crowd, each carrying some luggage, Mayne spotted the medical doctor of his area, Dr. Ryan, with some others. After they had put their luggage in the back of the jeep, Mayne took Carl to meet the doctor. As they approached, Dr. Ryan saw them and grinned.

"Finally, your friend has arrived. It's nice to have you here." He shook hands with Carl. "I hope you'll enjoy your holiday."

"I am already. This place is swell – a real, exotic jungle." This response drew a laugh from Dr. Ryan.

"Just beware the mosquitoes," he cautioned, "or they'll make your life here miserable." They were joined by the Commissioner, the Banker and the Magistrate of Victoria and its environs. Mayne introduced Carl to them. Then Mayne led Carl to the jeep. As he drove off Carl said, "did you notice the look in the Magistrate's eyes? Hahaha, I can imagine what the poor man must be saying to the others now: 'A negro! It's a good thing Old Patterson is not here to witness the scandal. He'd probably have a fatal heart attack all over again.' I like Dr. Ryan though. He looks like a pretty decent chap to me."

"Hmmmpf! The things you say Carl," Mayne laughed. As he sped along past the crowded streets to the less crowded, less travelled road that led to the plantation, Carl's head spun from side to side as he tried to take it all in, like a camel would drink from an oasis after a couple of days in the heart of the Sahara desert. As he looked around, he commented on Mayne's appearance: Mayne was evenly tanned, his shirt buttons were open, his hair was so much longer, and, goodness, Mayne looked like a rogue! Grinning at Carl's words, Mayne replied that in a day or two Carl would have gotten rid of all his ties and coats. It was far warmer in Africa than Europe or America, even though it was the rainy season.

After observing passersby for a while, Carl asked, "say, most of the women we've passed have only loincloths tied on their bodies. Are clothes very expensive here? Can't they afford them?"

"Some can, others can't. However, it is the tradition for women to dress like that."

"Mm, and does your Samarah dress like that too?" Carl was hoping for a smile from Mayne and he was not disappointed.

"Come to think of it, I've never seen her in anything else."

"Doesn't she have dresses?" Mayne chuckled at Carl's question.

"I bet she does. She's just too stubborn to wear them, probably seeing them as a mark of colonialism." Something in Mayne's voice as he spoke the last words caused Carl to glance at him sharply.

"Has she turned you down?" Mayne concentrated on the road.

"I haven't asked her yet. I'm waiting for the right moment. She can be a real spit fire. That girl has a fiery temper and a sharp tongue, but she has a heart of gold." Mayne raised his eyes heaven wards. Carl threw back his head and laughed.

"Mayne Patterson is about to lose his war like the Germans."

"The Treaty of Versailles was too harsh on them, don't you think? June 28 must have been a very sad day for them."

"What about Wilson's fourteen points? I guess those made sense. At least the points gave the Germans a sense of security and showed that their surrender would not be humiliating. If you ask me, that was what contributed to the German military leaders putting pressure on their government to end the war." Carl said.

"Well, yeah, but didn't those points sound a little too idealistic? A utopian world is not one that comes that easily. It will be a while. Anyway thanks to him, the League of Nations is on its way to being born." Mayne responded. Carl sighed and said he just hoped that the world would be at peace now.

They reached the estate in the pouring rain about three hours later. Bessem was waiting for them with towels when they dashed from the jeep to the veranda.

"Hi, you must be Samarah. I have heard so much about you." Carl breathed as he took Bessem's hand and kissed it before taking the towel she extended to him. Bessem was disconcerted at Carl's surprise kiss, and neither knew what to say nor where to look. Mayne stepped in and said,

"Bess, meet my friend, Carl White." Bessem's smile was timid as she dropped her eyes and said, "welcome, Sir. My name is Bessem and I work here."

"Work?" Mayne snorted. "You practically own and run this house. And you don't need to call him 'Sir'. He doesn't deserve it." His joke helped to remove some of the tension Bessem had felt and she gave him a grateful smile.

"I will see to your bath."

The smile she gave Carl was shy and then she turned and all but ran into the house. Mayne and Carl followed her in.

"I'm not Samarah. My name is Bessem. It's nice to meet you, Carl."

About an hour later, they had taken a bath and had a hot supper of rice and stew. Mayne asked Bessem where Samarah was and she replied that she had complained of a head ache and gone to bed before they arrived. Mayne would have gone to Samarah's room to see her but Bessem explained that it wouldn't do Samarah's head any good to wake her up.

It was past ten the next morning when Carl came downstairs and sauntered into the kitchen. Mayne was sitting on a stool drinking a cup of coffee, while Bessem peeled yellow yams she would cook for lunch.

"Someone slept like a log," Mayne commented as Carl took the stool opposite him, saying good morning. Carl stifled a yawn and smiled before demanding,

"The suspense is killing me. Where is Samarah?" Bessem raised an eyebrow and looked at Mayne, who grinned.

"Gone to the market. Get some breakfast and then I'll show you around."

Much later, Carl realized that 'showing around' entailed going round the whole estate. Mayne drove him first to the church to greet to the priest, and then to the neighboring estates. Many people offered them fruits as well as food. Carl was enjoying himself so much that when Mayne suggested that it was getting late and they should go home, Carl glanced at his watch in surprise.

"Six p.m. already! Okay, man, just give me a minute to drain my cup of palm wine. This stuff tastes really good. I can't believe it is natural. You know, I believe I have just found the love of my life – Palmwine!" Carl had almost finished a keg alone. They were in one of the elderly natives' compounds.

The old man, who Mayne referred to as Pa Matuteh, smiled, exposing his almost toothless gums. Mayne had told Carl on their way to this old man's compound that he had been the closest thing to a butler they had had when Mayne was much younger, and had often served as a father figure to him when his own father had travelled, or was too busy to pay him any mind.

Now, Pa Matuteh beckoned to his three wives and seven grand-children, who had been regarding and grinning at Mayne and Carl from a safe distance every time the men glanced in their direction. His grown up children had left the compound, the ten sons to look for work, and the three daughters to live with their husbands.

The women and children approached with halting steps, not sure of just how far it would be proper to stand in front of a white man. Even though they had watched Pa Matuteh leave every morning to work at Mr. Patterson's, and return every evening before his retirement five years before, they had not had a chance to see the inside of the house themselves. The new master visiting them was a novelty in itself, talk less of a black man who spoke and acted like a white man and had come from the white man's land. Wonders would never end!

"Massa wan go?"

"Yes, Pa," Mayne replied. The old man asked his oldest grandson to put another keg of palm wine in the jeep, along with one of the chickens which happened to be strolling round the compound just then. Mayne thanked him and they took their leave.

It was close to seven p.m. when they arrived home. Samarah was not home. Bessem said she had gone to see Father Vincent. Mayne excused himself, explaining to Carl that he had to go and get her. Carl asked him to take all the time he needed.

As Mayne drove up the path to the Parish House, he saw the

priest and Samarah walk out. His heart lurched when he saw her.
It had been a week since he had last seen her. She was saying
something to the priest and finally gave him a hug just as Mayne
drove into sight. Mayne usually thought of himself as a reasonably
God-fearing Christian. He had never felt like throttling a priest
before but at that moment, the feeling was almost uncontrollable.
His hands gripped the steering. What business did he have hugging
Samarah? Mayne jammed the car to a halt, jumped out, and strode
towards them. The Father saw him first. He smiled and welcomed
him. Mayne said good evening. When Samarah turned and saw
Mayne, her face lit up in a smile.

"Mayne! Welcome back. How was your trip?" She asked. He
glared at her.

"If you really wanted to know, you should have asked before
now... but hey, wait, yeah, you haven't been around since we came
back!" At his tone, a surprised Samarah turned to look at Father
Vincent, and then back at Mayne. He looked like he wanted to
strangle somebody, and she guessed that that person was her. What
could have made him that angry? What had she done?

"What are you doing out so late?" He gritted. Samarah's mouth
fell open. Clearly he was spoiling for a fight.

"It's not that late. I had to see Father."

"Ok, let's go." Samarah's confused eyes sought out the priest's.
He was grinning from ear to ear!

"But I..." She did not complete her sentence because Mayne's
hand was round her elbow as he spared a glance for the priest,
and explained that it was late and he wanted to take her home.
The priest waved off his explanation, saying he was glad Mayne
had come for Samarah because he could see rain clouds gathering. Mayne nodded, said good night and tried to lead Samarah
away, but she hung back. Her nostrils flared and she knotted her
eyebrows together.

"Stop this immediately, and stop pushing me around. I am not your slave."

"No, you are not. You are just one hell of a virago. Now be quiet." Samarah spun round to look at the priest, who was watching them with his hands folded in front of him, and that smile on his face. What could amuse him so?

"Father," she almost whispered.

"Let him take you home. I'll see you in church on Sunday. I think I hear the first drops of rain," said the priest.

"Allow me," Mayne murmured, and the next thing she knew, he had caught hold of her wrist and was pulling her towards the jeep.

She did not say a word as he opened the door for her and closed it when she got in. He went round to his own seat. On the veranda of the parish house, Fr. Vincent continued smiling.

After driving for a few meters, Mayne parked the car by the side of the road, and turned in his seat to look at Samarah, who in turn stared straight ahead.

"I don't want you moving about alone, especially at night. It is dangerous."

"Yes, *Sir*." Mayne's sigh was exasperated.

"What's up with the 'Sir' again? You stopped calling me that about five months ago."

"You stopped yelling at me about five months ago." She fired back. Mayne drew in a deep breath and exhaled slowly.

"I'm sorry, Sam. I've behaved terribly. It's just that since I came back with Carl, you've been avoiding me."

"I was not very well last night and this morning when I got back from the market and asked after you two, Bessem said you'd gone out and then I had to see Father Vincent... I don't even know why I am explaining this to you." How could she tell him that she had gone to the market that morning to buy spices which were used to cook stew just the way he liked it? Could she say she had taken all afternoon to cook for him and his friend? No. She couldn't, because she did not understand why she sought to please him.

The raindrops had increased a trifle, but they sounded rather loud because of the pregnant silence in the jeep. She glanced at him. It was already dark but she could see his face, and for a few minutes she forgot he was white. All she saw was a man. He was one of the most considerate and simple people she knew, and yet he was so complex, or rather her reaction to him was complex. She knew just what would make him smile, and what got him angry. He seldom got angry. For the past months, she had seen him angry just once, and that was because an old couple, Pa Wase and his wife, had been evicted from their house on the estate by one of the foremen, because they had grown old, their children had left home, and so the husband and wife could not work on the estate anymore. When they'd been evicted, without Mayne's knowledge, they had come to plead with him to give them a few weeks to get a place to move in to. Mayne had lost his temper with the foreman. These people had been loyal workers on the Patterson estate for as long as he could remember. He gave them back the house and assigned two girls to assist them in the house. He told them that if they ever needed anything, they should let him know. Mayne had yelled at the foreman and told him to bring matters like that to him first. He sent the foreman home with a warning that if it repeated itself again, he would be fired.

Samarah continued to look at him. She might be attracted to him. Samarah started. Was she insane? How could she possibly be attracted to a white man? Love? She wouldn't think about it. She could not love him; she just could not let that happen.

Mayne watched her from the corner of his eye. He saw the emotions flicker in her eyes. He could kick himself! Surely the best way to recommend himself to the lady he wished to marry was not to drag her all over the place against her will. He had to admit that he had completely lost it when he had seen her with the priest. It was over half a year since he had returned to Cameroon, and with each passing day, he got caught in her spell more and more.

"Sam?" He looked at her directly in her eyes. His palm came to cup hers where it lay against her knee. "Please marry me." He blurted out. Samarah's eyes opened wide and her breath caught in her throat, causing her to choke.

"Wh…what did you just s…say?" she stuttered.

"I love you so much. My heart hasn't found any peace since we met for the first time in the woods. You are whom I've been looking for all my life. I want to grow old with you, to have babies with you, to care for you and to share my life with you. Please, I need you because… well, because I love you." Samarah stared at him, at a loss of words.

"Please Sam, won't you say something?" She opened her mouth but no words came out. Finally, she shook her head from side to side.

"You can't love me," she finally uttered.

"I do. I love you with all my heart," Mayne whispered as he raised her palm to kiss it.

"It's not right." Her voice sounded far away, as if she was lost in thought. "Blacks and whites do not fall in love with each other. They can't marry each other."

"Why ever not? It happens all the time… Look Sam, I'm not rushing you. I've waited a long time to tell you this. Please do not give me an answer now. Let me just enjoy the fact that I have finally told you what's in my heart. I can wait a while longer. You can give me an answer when you've given this some thought."

"But… but I am betrothed."

She breathed. She was finding it hard to think with his thumb stroking her palm ever so gently.

"I know. Bessem told me. That was done when you were still a baby. It was done without your permission."

"But I care about Bintum, and I know he will come back for me."

"Samarah, look at me," Mayne's thumb and index finger held her chin and tilted her face up.

"I love you. You are very important to me. I'm ready to fight for you. I just need to know that you feel something for me… However, if you decide to wait for him," He almost choked on the last word but forced himself to go on, "I'll love you enough to let you go to him, if it will make you happy. All I ask is that you give me a chance to prove to you that we are meant for each other. I know you feel this too." They kept on looking at each other until they heard the rain drops increase to a downpour.

"I'd better get you home before you catch a cold," Mayne whispered. He let go of her palm and started the jeep.

All the way home, neither one spoke. Both concentrated on their thoughts. When they pulled up in front of the house, Mayne reached over and took and umbrella from the back seat. He went out and walked round to open her door. She clutched her loincloth to her body as he put an arm around her and they hurried unto the veranda. The front door opened and Carl stood there.

"You didn't tell me Carl's black!" Samarah whispered.

"Is he? I hadn't noticed!" Mayne grinned at her. "I'm full of surprises, aren't I?" Carl was already engulfing her in a bear hug and proclaiming how happy he was to finally see her. He pulled her into the house and whistled as he looked at her.

"You had every right to talk my ear out about Miss Fantasy, Mayne. Samarah, for a year now, Mayne rarely talks of anything else but you, and now I know why he's got it so bad for you."

Samarah looked at Mayne, who winked at her.

*

On Sunday, Samarah wore a knee-length white dress, the first dress she had worn since her mother died. She had bought it about two months before in the market, but had not wanted to wear it till this day. She looked at herself and laughed. She looked strange, and she felt different.

She was already seated in church when Mayne and Carl entered. During offertory, her eyes followed Mayne as he made his way to the alms basket in front of the church. The night he had proposed to her, she had found it rather difficult to sleep. Since then she felt pretty awkward in his presence, not quite sure what to do or say. However, whenever she thought of him or saw him, her heart raced and she always felt the desire to go close to him. Was it because Bintum might never come back to her, or was she falling in love with Mayne for real? She had fought this 'thing' she felt for him for over a year, but it simply would not go away.

The sound of the bell at consecration pierced through her thoughts, forcing her back to reality. She prayed to God with all her heart that she would make the right decision – whether to wait for Bintum whom she still missed terribly, or give in to her powerful feelings for Mayne.

After mass, she left before Mayne and Carl came out of the church. She hurried home and assisted Bessem to make lunch. She knew everyone would want to invite Mayne's new friend home, and so Mayne and Carl wouldn't be back till much later. After they'd finished cooking, she said she had a head ache and didn't wish to be disturbed, then went to her room to sleep.

Mayne stood at his window towards dusk, lost in thought. The object of his thoughts hurried from the compound. He looked at his watch and frowned. It was six thirty p.m. Where was she going all alone? Without another thought, he strode out of his room. This woman would always keep him on his toes!

Unaware of being followed, Samarah wandered into the woods

nearby. She followed a bush track and moved on, lost in thought. Of one thing she was finally sure. She was dangerously on her way to falling for Mayne Patterson. She found a fallen tree trunk and sat on it. '*I have to move on, Bwan. You and Baa and Bintum will always have a place in my heart. I will never forget the love and strength you gave me. Maybe it's time for me to let go of the past, to lay it to rest… I've waited so long for Bintum, and I am certain I've lost him forever. Now there's Mayne, whom I care so much about. He has come to mean so much to me that it scares me. Everyone I love, I end up losing. People always leave. I don't know what to do.*'

She heard a footstep behind her and spun round. When she saw Mayne she relaxed. He came to sit beside her and cradled her face in his palms. She did not pull away.

"What are you doing?" he asked.

"Thinking. Why did you follow me?"

"To prevent you from coming to any harm. It's almost totally dark now."

"I'm not afraid of the night. I've lived in these parts for at least three years." Mayne let his hands drop to his knees, and she was surprised at the feeling of loss that engulfed her.

"I know. It's just that I need to know you are safe. I wasn't here to protect you before, but now I am, and that's exactly what I intend to do." A sharp scream pierced the silence around them. Instinctively, Samarah reached for Mayne, as he moved to draw her closer to him. They heard the scream again. The voice sounded like a woman's.

"Stay here. Hide behind that tree. No one will see you there." Mayne ordered as he started to move in the direction of the scream. Samarah clung to him,

"I can't let you go alone. I'll come with you."

"No, I'll feel better knowing you are safe here. The main path isn't far away. If I don't return in a few minutes, run home and get help."

He strode away. Samarah let him go a couple of steps, and then tiptoed behind him.

Mayne quickened his pace and heard grunting and hard breathing ahead. He burst into a clearing with a thatched hut in the middle. He ran to the window and peered in. What he saw caused his blood to boil. A white man was shredding the clothes off a native woman, who tried to fight him off. He pushed her unto a grass heap.

"Massa, I beg, no do dis ting," she cried.

Mayne could feel the anger rising in him like bile, and without any thought, he exploded through the door into the hut. The other man rolled over, startled by the sudden intrusion. When his eyes focused on Mayne in the fading light, he relaxed.

"Here. The bitch won't mind us two. Let's have fun."

Mayne lunged at him and landed a blow on his cheek.

"What the –." The man returned the blow and in a matter of seconds, the two were rolling all about the floor in a cat-dog fight.

It was then that Samarah ran in to help the woman off the floor. As she helped the woman towards the door, she saw something flash in the twilight from the man's pocket.

"Mayne, look out!" she screamed. Too late! The man had plunged his knife into Mayne's side, quite close to his heart. Mayne yelled in pain and rolled back. At his scream, Samarah ran to him as the other man dashed out of the hut and ran into the night. Mayne lay on his back with Samarah crouched over him. She cradled his head in her arms. Blood was gushing out of the wound and she sobbed as she felt the blood wash over her hand. She tried to tug his shirt off, but it would not budge.

"Hurry, go to Mr. Patterson's. You know his house, don't you?" The woman nodded as she trembled.

"Go get help, please. Hurry. Tell them the Master has been wounded." The woman ran out.

Left alone with Mayne, Samarah tore off part of her gown and tried to use the torn bit to stifle the blood. In a matter of seconds, it was soaking wet and still more blood oozed out.

"That hurts," Mayne gasped. He had a feeling the roof was floating. Samarah supported his head in her laps. He raised his eyes to hers and with an effort, lifted his right hand to caress her cheek.

"Naughty girl... I told... you to ... to hide!" Samarah caught his hand in hers and squeezed it.

"I couldn't let you wander off alone. I had to protect you." She tried to smile, but failed.

"You followed me... that means you must... care a little." His hand went limp and Samarah lowered it to the ground. She smoothed his hair from his damp face covered with sweat. She looked at the wound. He had lost too much blood. Where, oh where was the woman? What would happen if help did not come soon? No, she could not lose him too. Not Mayne. She would fight to keep him. She loved him too much.

"You are crying... my darling." He panted. Her sobs increased.

"That's because I love you." She heard herself say, "I love you so much it hurts, and I couldn't bear to lose you. I don't want you to ever leave me. If you still want me, I'll marry you."

"Oh Sam... I ... love you so!"

After what seemed to Samarah like hours, Carl, the woman and most labourers from the estate came. Mayne was lifted unto a stretcher and carried outside. Carl looked from Samarah's tear-stained face to her hand gripping Mayne's firmly.

"He'll be alright, Sam. We already sent for Dr. Ryan." Samarah nodded her thanks. They took Mayne to the main path where the jeep waited. Carl drove him home.

Two hours later, Samarah, Carl and Bessem waited outside Mayne's bedroom. The door opened and Dr. Ryan was greeted by three pairs of anxious eyes. He looked tired and weary, but he smiled.

"He lost a lot of blood, but he'll be alright. I stitched up the wound. He was lucky the wound didn't reach his heart." He saw relief mirrored in all the eyes.

"He's awake now, but weak. I've given him a sedative, so he'll be asleep in a few seconds. However he keeps muttering 'Sam', so if you could find this Sam, it would do Mayne a lot of good. You can see him now but I recommend one person at a time." They all thanked the doctor as he took his leave.

"Go to him, Sam." Carl said gently and nudged her towards the door. She nodded and went in.

The nurse glanced disapprovingly at her dress, and went out as Samarah went closer to the bed. It was only then she thought she must look a state. She still had on the bloody dress. In fact she had not left that door since Mayne had been brought through it. Mayne's half-shut eyes opened a little wider when she walked close to the bed. His smile was as sleepy as his look. The sedative was already working. She entwined her fingers in his as he breathed,

"What I heard in the hut... did you really say it?"

She could feel the tension behind those words.

"I did." She smiled.

"Thank God. I always have to have a crisis... for you to let down your... guard," he joked. Her smile spread as he continued, "I'll probably have a heart attack before you agree to bear my child. My darling... we'll have children... lots of babies." The last words were slurred. He was fast asleep. She smoothed the hair from his forehead and her heart soared.

"Yes, Mayne, lots and lots of babies."

*

Two weeks after Mayne was stabbed, he was healing nicely. Samarah hardly left his bedside except when she had to go to school. All the workers usually gathered in front of the porch in the evenings to get news about the master's health. Samarah had not told anyone about their engagement, and had begged him not to say a word, even though he had been bursting to tell everyone within earshot. However they had decided to tell Bessem and Carl.

Samarah sat in the kitchen, grinding spices on a pepper stone. Bessem was stirring a pot of *Mbongo* sauce.

"There's something I want to tell you," Samarah said.

"I am listening."

"I'm getting married," Samarah announced.

"You are?" Bessem raised her eyebrows. Samarah could see the teasing in her friend's eyes, "You? The girl who's famous for turning all men down? Miss heart-of-stone? The girl who wouldn't look at any other man if his name's not Bintum? The girl who has nothing to do with men?" Samarah shrugged.

"That's about to change. You haven't asked to whom I'll be joined in happy matrimony." Bessem turned to look at Samarah more closely.

"You are serious! Who is the man?"

"Mayne."

"Mayne?" Samarah watched Bessem as the information sank in. "Mayne?!" Bessem cried out. "Gods of our fathers!" She sank into a nearby chair. She asked Samarah if she was very sure about what she was saying, and Samarah elucidated that her feelings for Mayne had undergone a tremendous change the past months and that she was sure she wanted to spend her life with him. "Do you think he cares for me?" Samarah asked.

"Cares for you? Samarah, the man would die for you! Oh Samarah, I'm so happy for you… but what about Bintum?" Samarah's face clouded over at the mention of Bintum's name.

"He's gone, Bess. Bintum is not coming back. It's been so long. He is gone from this world. Maybe we just weren't meant to be… I think about him everyday, but it's no use. I need to be happy… I deserve to be happy, don't I?" Samarah looked like she would burst into tears any minute.

"Of course you do dear. You won't regret it. Mayne is a good person. He will make a wonderful husband."

"Thanks. Here are the spices. Let me check on him. He may have woken already."

Samarah went to his room and knocked on the door. Carl opened it. When he saw Samarah, he pulled her into a hug, saying she had made his friend a very happy man, and wishing them both joy in their decision to tie the knot. Samarah glanced at Mayne on the bed. Their eyes met, and locked. For both of them, time seemed to stand still. Carl glanced from one to the other, muttered something about his siesta, and left the room, shutting the door behind him.

Samarah sat at the side of Mayne's bed. Mayne pouted, "No kiss for your fiancé?" His eyes twinkled. Samarah felt the heat creeping up her neck. "Just one teensy-weensy kiss." Mayne coaxed. She leaned over him to kiss his forehead. When she would have retreated, he wrapped his arms around her and pulled her down, pinning her to him. She landed on him and her feet dangled in the air.

"Mayne, stop it. I might hurt you."

"Nah! See, my nurse is one talented witch. I'm healing nicely thanks to her." Samarah had been his nurse ever since Dr. Ryan had stitched the wound. The hospital was short on staff, so the nurse had had to go back and Dr. Ryan had trusted the student nurse to take care of the patient.

Mayne's hand came up to cup the back of her head as the other one pulled her closer to him. Now she was half-lying on top of him, with her head dangerously close to his. His eyelids came lower and lower until his eyes became slits.

"I want you to move into the house," he said.

"Mayne, we are not married yet."

"We'll be in two weeks."

"The others will talk."

"Let them. You'll be my wife soon. I need to be able to be with you at any time of the day… or night."

He bit his lower lip after the last word and smiled. Samarah's heart did a flip.

"I'll stay in my room until we get married," she insisted.

"Then we'll get married tomorrow."

"You can't be serious."

"I am. I want you in my house, by my side as soon as possible. I want to go to bed every night with you in my arms. I need to see you every morning as soon as I wake up… Where do you want us to go for our honey moon?" Samarah said she had not thought of that. Mayne asked her if they could go to the coast, specifically to Victoria. Samarah was very pleased with the idea. She said she really had to go to the kitchen and assist Bessem.

"I'll walk you," he offered.

"And have the whole house talking? I don't think so – not until I have your ring on my finger." He chuckled at her words and promised to see the priest the next day for the bans to be read in church.

That Sunday, the banns were read. Samarah and Mayne would be married on the 14th of August, 1919. That was seventeen days from the present day. The outburst of murmurs that greeted the announcement was remarkable. Mayne could feel the tension which the announcement had caused, in the air. He also saw how the two white men and their wives, one of the couples being the Smiths – parents to Mark and Eustace, stared at him with mouths agape. He was glad Eustace and Mark were not at mass. They had just come back from England the day before and his guess was that they would be sleeping. He glanced backwards, hoping to catch Samarah's eye and offer her solace just by his look. When he finally saw her, he saw the way she looked at the priest, sitting as stiffly as a stone, and he could only imagine what she must be feeling.

Samarah wished she could sink into the soil and disappear as she felt the gazes of those who knew her burning on her, with incredulity shining in their eyes.

The black girl sitting to Samarah's left, shifted farther away from Samarah as if she did not want to be scalded by the brewing scandal that would surely erupt at any time. Bessem, who was sitting to her right took Samarah's hand in hers and squeezed. Samarah held on as if for dear life. She looked straight ahead, thankful that banns usually came just before the end of mass. She dared not glance around even though she desperately wanted to look at Mayne, who was sitting right in front with Carl.

As soon as mass ended, She grabbed Bessem's hand and the two of them sped out of the church. They were however not fast enough because Mayne and Carl were right behind them.

"Samarah, Bessem, wait," Mayne called. When the men had caught up with them, Samarah said almost in a whisper,

"I don't think we should be seen together right now, Mayne. No one is saying anything but look, they are all staring at us. We'll just hurry off and you can meet us in the house."

"Nonsense!" Mayne said. "We are going to be man and wife. It does not matter what anybody says or thinks. The sooner they get used to seeing us together, the better. Come on, let us go home." Just then the Smiths sped passed by in their jeep and did not so much as glance at Mayne. All four of them noticed this snob.

"Mayne, I am already causing trouble for you. Please let us wait, push the wedding forward." Samarah pleaded. Mayne grasped both her hands in his and said,

"You are going to be my wife. I am going to swear to love and protect you above anyone else. I intend to start now. Let me get the jeep. Sam, we are in this together."

Mayne smiled, and after squeezing her hand, he left to bring the car to them.

Carl gave Samarah a sympathetic look.

"Listen Samarah, people will always judge us by their standards. Don't let that get to you. It is your life not theirs. I have had a lot of experience in the department of not being wanted, or of being regarded as a plague, and so I have developed a thick skin and am a proficient in the art of ignoring. Take it from someone who knows: it may not get easier, but you can choose not to let it bring you down. If you want I can give you some lessons in ignoring people," he finished. This made Samarah and Bessem laugh as he had intended for them to do. He bowed and said, "the jeep is waiting. After you, girls." As they went towards the jeep, Samarah wondered how she would go through the coming seventeen days.

Two weeks later Samarah knocked on Mayne's bedroom door and opened it. Mayne smiled when he saw her but then the smile disappeared as he took in her taut expression. Before he could ask her what was wrong, she burst out,

"I can't do this!"

"Do what?" Mayne came to take her hand and guide her to sit on the bed. He sat next to her.

"This marriage, being with you, all of it. Have you noticed the way everyone on this plantation treats me now? When I am not being looked at and shunned like a leper, I am supplicated from every angle by people with requests for you. People hardly talk to me anymore as they used to, and as I go about my chores I feel eyes watching me, judging me. I don't like this attention. Just now I was on my way to talk to Bessem in the kitchen when I came across the new girl, Awung. She curtsied! To me! And then she wouldn't meet my eyes as she called me 'Madam' and asked if I needed anything."

"Sam, calm down," Mayne said when she paused for breath. His palm covered hers where it lay against the blanket. "You are going to be mistress of this place soon. It is just natural that people will not treat you the same, whether you want them to or not."

"But Mayne, it is not just about me. I saw the way the other plantation owners looked at you, and don't you think I have noticed that your friends, the twins, have not been to see you as often as they used to? Their parents probably told them to stay away. What if other people shun you because of me? I would not want to be the source of your unhappiness."

"Sam, it is my decision to make. If we are together, we can overcome anything. It will not be easy but we will make it if we stick together. I would be far more unhappy if I didn't have you."

"Mayne —"

"Shh. Now I am going to walk you to the kitchen, or your room, or anywhere you want to go. I intend to stick to you till everyone on this plantation understands that you are mine." He pulled her up from the bed as she gave a reluctant smile, and dragged her out of the room.

The Patterson plantation was very busy for the weeks before the wedding. Bessem was in charge of planning and directing the preparations for the wedding. She shared the workers into groups, each with a specific task to fulfill. One male group was in charge of slaughtering goats, plucking chickens, and slaughtering the cow which Mayne had bought for the occasion. Another male group was in charge of building shades and making plank chairs for the occasion. A group of teenage girls saw to watering and sweeping the courtyard, getting flowers to decorate the trees and shrubs. There were three women's groups set up to take charge of the cooking.

Now Samarah thought the workers were slowly accepting the idea that marriage between Mayne and her was not a dream. True, some people still avoided her and she almost always saw people looking at her or pointing their extended lips in her direction. She knew she was the talk of the plantation. However, many more people were talking to her but it was never the same as before, except for Bessem of course.

Two nights before the wedding, as Samarah made her way to her room, she overheard Bessem and Eposi, an older woman who usually cleaned the house, talking.

"It will come to no good," the woman was saying to Bessem. "I'm telling you. White people never ever marry blacks. He is probably planning to use her, and then leave her for some pretty, sweet white girl."

"Don't say that," Bessem responded. "Mayne is different and you know it. You are just jealous."

"Hehehe, me jealous? Have you seen how much Samarah has changed? These days she goes around with her head held high and as if her feet do not touch the ground. She hardly has time for us anymore. Now she thinks that she is better than us simply because a white man wants her to warm his bed for a few nights." Samarah heard Bessem gasp and respond, "you and I know that you are the one who has been avoiding her since that Sunday when the banns were read for the first time. The master will not hurt Samarah. He loves her." Eposi shrugged and then shook her head slowly from side to side, "I tell you, it will not work! Time will tell, won't it? Pregnancy does not hide."

Samarah tried to shake off the feeling that the woman's words had evoked in her. She told herself that Mayne would never hurt her, that he loved her. Once again, she vowed to herself that she would not let him go. She had lost one love, life had given her another shot at happiness and by all that she held sacred, she would do all in her power to protect this love.

CHAPTER NINE

AUGUST, 1919

The morning of the wedding found Samarah groaning. Her stomach felt like twenty knots had been tied inside. She felt dizzy and lightheaded. She had hardly slept a wink the night before. It was drizzling outside and she wondered if this was an omen. When Bessem and another girl, Sonneh, who assisted in the house, came to dress her up. Samarah was fretful, sulky and totally frightened.

"I can't do it!" she wailed. The other two exchanged smiles..

"All brides-to-be say that. Don't worry, everything will be alright." Bessem said.

"I'm scared," Samarah cried.

"Most women are on their wedding day. My mother told me she was dragged to the ceremonial ground on her wedding day, but today she cannot imagine life without my father," Sonneh said.

"What if I don't make a good wife? What if Mayne does not show up in church?"

"Samarah, he loves you, and you'll do just fine," Bessem assured her.

The girls finally convinced her to take a bath. Her white gown was long, covering the whole length of her slim body. It fitted her body closely from the top to the waist, where it billowed all the way to her feet. The arms were short and embroidered with lace. Mayne had ordered the dress from England a while before, and had kept it safe in a trunk. When Samarah, amazed at that, had asked him what he would have done with the gown if she had not agreed to marry him. He had laughed and said he would have kept it till she said yes. He told her he had not wanted to take any chances of her changing her mind because of the length of time it would take for a dress to reach Cameroon from England. Samarah did not trust this answer entirely, but she had smiled and thanked him. She ran her fingers through her hair, which was not in braids this time. It was combed out and tied at the nape of her neck with a big, white ribbon. Her eyes sparkled and her full lips glistened.

"You look really beautiful," Bessem complimented her. She managed a weak smile as Bessem handed her a bouquet of wild flowers, and tucked one of the flowers into her hair.

While Bessem and Sonneh left her room to get ready, Samarah sat on her bed as if frozen to the spot, her hands clenching and unclenching in her lap. When Bessem returned, she squatted in front of Samarah and noticed that she was crying. Bessem took both of Samarah's hands in hers.

"Mayne is the man for you. You have nothing to fear. He loves you."

"I know he does. I love him too. It's just that I would have wanted so much for my mother to see this day. We had talked a lot about it when I was growing up. It's just so sad she is not here today to share it with me," Samarah sobbed.

"Oh, but she is. Right in here," Bessem touched Samarah's heart.

"And I'm so scared. I've never been this afraid."

"That's because you've never been married, silly!" Bessem's comment made Samarah smile. "You love Mayne, don't you?" Samarah nodded. "Do you want him to see your puffy eyes and guess that you've been crying?" Samarah said no. Just then, they heard the hooting of the jeep. Carl had come to drive them to church, where Dr. Ryan had already driven Mayne. Samarah turned terrified eyes to Bessem.

"I can't do it!"

"Sure you can. Take a deep breath. Good. As soon as you see Mayne, everything will be just fine."

*

The church was packed full by the time Carl arrived with Samarah and Bessem. The windows were crowded with lots of people. Samarah felt giddy as Carl assisted her out of the car and into the church building. As soon as she went in, the ceremony started.

Father Vincent and the mass servants came down the aisle. Samarah peeped out of the sacristy and saw Mayne and Carl standing on the altar. They both were dressed in black suits. The choir sang on:

Father within thy house today
We wait thy kindly love to see
Since thou hast said in truth that they
Who dwell in love are one with thee
Bless those who for thy blessing wait
Their love accept and consecrate!

Samarah felt a wave of nausea hit her and she staggered. Bessem held her hand.

"You can do this." She whispered. Samarah nodded, took a deep breath, and walked down the aisle. She could see Mayne's back as he stood in front. His black suit fitted him like it had been sewn solely for him. His long, dark hair glistened. She was thankful for the veil that covered her face as she walked on with Bessem right behind her. It was the longest walk she had ever done in her life, this short walk to the front of the altar where her life would change forever. When she reached the front, Mayne turned to look at her. She saw his eyes light up. When he smiled, a dimple appeared on his cheek. Her heart rate increased and she gave him her brightest smile. At that moment, she understood what Bessem had said. All at once, everything was alright, and the churning in her stomach stopped.

"Dearly beloved, we are gathered here today to witness the marriage between Samarah waa Yenla and Mayne Arnold Patterson Junior…," began Father Vincent.

All through mass, Mayne thought he was dreaming and prayed that if that was the case, he should never wake up. Time and again, he would take a glance at his wife to be and each time he did, his heart soared with love for her. He had never thought it possible to love a woman this much. When he slipped the simple gold ring unto her finger, and gave her a chaste peck on the lips, his joy was complete. She was finally his and he would never ever let her go. The whole world was witness to the fact that he had branded her his forever. The whole church cheered as Father Vincent pronounced them man and wife. Some people were genuinely happy for them. Others had come to witness for themselves this marriage between a white man and a black woman. Most land owners however had made up one excuse or another not to attend.

After mass, the guests and all who could make it trooped to the Patterson plantation. Many canopies had been erected and music boomed from a gramophone. Even though it was the heart of the rainy season, they were blessed with good weather. It did not rain, as Samarah had feared, and there was no bright sunshine. It was just calm. People sat down, drank, ate and danced. Samarah and Mayne sat on the veranda to participate in the festivities.

A group of dancing women proceeded into the compound singing and ululating:

Why did you go there?
Why did you go there?
Why did you go to the market and see her?
Why did you come here?
Why did you come here?
Why did you come here and see him?

They pulled Samarah into the group and she danced with them. She turned and beckoned to Mayne. He followed her and the shouts were deafening as he swooped her into his arms and whirled her round and round.

After lunch, while the festivities were still going on, Mayne whispered into Samarah's ear, and she nodded. She went to her room and changed into one of the dresses Mayne had ordered for her. This one was white with blue and pink flowers on it. She held back her hair with a pink ribbon. The dress emphasized her slender waist and made her look slightly taller than her 1.65meter frame. Before walking out, she looked around her room and felt her eyes mist over. She knew she wouldn't be sleeping there any longer. This had been her home for almost four years.

When she went back to the celebration, Mayne too had changed into khaki trousers and a tee shirt. Their suitcases were already in the jeep, and Mayne was leaning against it. Carl and Bessem were talking with him as she walked to them.

"I'm ready." She beamed. She hugged Bessem and Carl kissed her cheek and opened the door for her while Mayne hugged Bessem. The whole crowd cheered and waved as they drove out of the compound. Samarah put her head out of the window and waved back until everyone was out of sight.

She turned an excited face to Mayne. He glanced at her and back at the road.

"I love you," he smiled.

"Mmhmm," she nodded, her eyes downcast. Mayne thought her shyness was very alluring and his smile widened.

"It is perfectly alright to say you love me too, you know," he teased. She smiled, but still would not meet his eyes as she answered,

"Me too," she said.

He burst out laughing. Samarah smiled and looked around her. As she took the scenes, the people, the sights all in, she felt giddy and carefree. In a matter of minutes, as they sped along, she commented about anything and everything, and Mayne loved every minute of it.

"I've never seen you this carefree," he observed when she paused to catch her breath.

"I've never been married before!" she laughed. "For the first time in my life, I actually believe that everything will be fine."

"I'm going to make sure of it, my dear," Mayne promised.

Not long after that, Samarah yawned and leaned back against her seat. It was about three hours since they had left and she was feeling the strain of the past days taking its toll. She stifled another yawn. He glanced at her, smiling, and told her that in an hour or two they would be there. He told her to go ahead and sleep and that he would wake her up when they got there. He said Bessem had packed a picnic basket in case she was hungry. She said she was not the least bit hungry.

"You, on the other hand, must be starving," she said.

"Only for you." His eyes left the road and gave her a fleeting look. His hand reached out to squeeze her palm. Samarah felt the heat rising again and the butterflies in the pit of her stomach fluttered. Then Mayne took his hand away and she felt her breath return.

"I'll just watch you drive," she decided and relaxed into her seat, but in two minutes she was fast asleep.

*

"Sam, wake up darling, we're here." Samarah heard someone say. She forced her eyes open. She had been dreaming that she was married to Mayne. Her gaze focused and she saw his face. Oh God! It was all true. She was indeed married to him. Her lips stretched into a smile as she sat up. Then she gasped in surprise when she looked ahead of her. She saw a long and wide expanse of land bordered by water for as far as she could see. The water seemed to unite with the clouds far ahead. There was a moon outside and this was unusual for the month of August, being the heart of the rainy season and all. The rays of the moon reflected on the water. Coconut trees grew here and there, and the sand on the beach looked silvery.

"It's lovely – just like from a dream." She did not realize that she was whispering. Mayne ignited the engine of the jeep.

"I wanted you to see the beach first. In a few minutes we'll reach our destination." Samarah's gaze was fixed on the beach as they drove along.

A couple of minutes later, they stopped in front of a gate made of painted white iron bars, criss-crossed in elaborate designs. It was not very high- just about three meters of crossed irons. She could tell that it was built not so much to serve as protection as to beautify the place. Through the spaces between the bars, she saw a courtyard filled with flowers and carpet grass, and a tarred road leading up to a big hotel, amid coconut and palm trees. She turned to look at Mayne. His grin widened as he hooted.

"Only the best for the most wonderful wife in the whole wide world." At the sound of the hooting, a black gateman threw open the gate. When he saw them, he gaped, unable to close his mouth. What was that girl doing with the white master at this place? This hotel was too expensive. Few white people could even afford to lodge there. White masters usually took their native women to far less costly and exposed places. This one must be very attracted to the girl!

The couple ignored the man's look. Mayne waved to him as they drove in. Samarah was busy taking everything in. As they drove closer to the hotel, she gasped again. The hotel was three storeys high, and looked like it had been built with precious stones, granite and marble. It was painted cream white and light emanated from most of the windows. She could hear soft music playing inside.

As soon as Mayne packed the car in front of the Sunrise hotel, a native boy of about seventeen ran to take their cases. A much older man came to take the car keys from Mayne. Mayne took Samarah's hand and they followed the teenage boy to the receptionist – a petite, pretty brunette girl. Samarah glanced around in awe. Everywhere she could see flowers. A few white men and women sat in plush chairs, sipping coffee and brandy. A door led to the restaurant and another to the back yard. Between the two doors, a gold painted staircase led to the next storey. She thought the whole place smelled of money.

While she looked around, Mayne asked the receptionist for the keys to the honey moon suite reserved for Mr. and Mrs. Patterson. He had made the reservations through Dr. Ryan a week before. The girl glanced uncertainly at Samarah and then Mayne.

"Uh, will your wife be joining you later, Sir?" Mayne's lips lifted at the corners.

"I don't think so. I wouldn't leave her down here for a second – too many a man ready to make a fool of himself when faced with beauty such as hers. I'm taking her up now." Mayne grinned. Then he turned, wrapped an arm around Samarah's waist and drew her closer to him. She immediately lost interest in everything else and leaned into him as he held her gaze.

"You ready to go, wife?" he asked. She nodded. Mayne looked

at the receptionist and quirked an eyebrow, "the keys?"

"Oh... uh, yes." The girl fumbled with some keys on her table and finally handed a pair to him.

"Thanks. Let's go, love." As they climbed the stairs, Samarah commented that Mayne had probably spent a fortune reserving this place for the night. Mayne said it was reserved for two weeks. When they reached their suite, Mayne gave the boy a tip, and asked him to inform the waiters that they would want supper in their room as soon as possible.

Samarah looked around the room as Mayne closed the door. A big window with long, gold drapes was at the east end of the room. In the middle, a family size bed stood, with white and gold sheets, and a blanket which looked part silver, part gold. The carpet on the floor was thick and rich and light brown in colour. Two sofas stood to one side around a table on which was a flower vase, with a bunch of red roses inside. Some of the rose petals had been scattered unto the bed. An exotic fragrance filled the air. One door led to the balcony, and another to the bathroom.

She felt Mayne's arms wrap around her from behind. She shivered as she leaned into him.

"You alright?" he whispered into her ear. The sensation of his breath on her ear sent another shiver down her body especially when he caught her earlobe between his lips and tasted it. "Hmmm, you taste really appetizing." He murmured. He turned her round so that she faced him. She looped her arms around his neck, her fingers finding their way under his thick, long hair.

"I like the feel of your hair," she said. He threw back his head and laughed.

"I've dreamed of this moment for so long, and now it's here. I can't believe that I really have you in my arms and that you are my wife!" He bent his head to hers and very gently placed his lips on hers. For a moment, neither of them moved, and then she felt him pull her closer and felt his lips part hers. As she wondered what she should do, how she should control her body which was longing for more, there was a knock on the door.

"Drat!" Mayne said against her lips and raised his head.

It was the room service. Samarah said she would take a bath first but Mayne advised her to eat first. A few minutes later, Samarah and Mayne sat in companionable silence, eating. She was too nervous to eat, and barely managed to shove food down her throat. Mayne opened the champagne that had accompanied their meal of rice, potato chips, eggs, tomato stew and some bananas, mangoes, oranges and pawpaw. He filled her glass and then his. He raised her glass to her lips. Samarah tentatively took a sip, tried to swallow it and choked, sending the liquid spluttering unto her chin. Mayne smiled and leaning over, he licked the drops of champagne off her chin. Samarah's breath caught in her lungs. Mayne held the glass to her lips again and said,

"Drink it. It'll loosen your nerves. It's okay for you to have bridal jitters, love."

"How... how did you know?"

"I know a lot about the world, sweetness. Now drink up. It'll help you." Samarah sipped a little more, and found that it tasted nice. She gulped down some more and would have drunk the whole glass at once, but Mayne placed a restraining hand on her arm.

"It's sweet, but very potent. Maybe you should have that bath now before you doze off." She giggled and said she would do.

She was taking a bath when she heard the room service take the dishes away. She wrapped a towel around her body and poked her head out of the bathroom door.

"Your turn," she said to Mayne. While he was bathing, Samarah looked in the wardrobe where their bags had been unpacked for her nightgown. Instead of the cotton one she had begged Bessem to pack, she saw a far above the knee almost transparent one. It was red, and when she touched it, it felt like silk. Dazed, she slipped it on. It accentuated her breasts and flared a little at the hips before ending on her laps. *I can't wear this! Where did it come from?* She had never worn something this revealing!

The bathroom door opened and Mayne walked into the room. Samarah froze. When his eyes fell on her, he stopped walking. She looked at him and her eyes widened. She had never seen him like this. He was wearing a singlet and pajama trousers, but he still looked breathtakingly stunning. His wet hair clung to his face and those dark eyes looked darker.

"This… Bessem didn't pack my nightgown… and … uhm…" As she stood there, shifting her weight from one leg to the other and stammering, Mayne walked to her and slipped his arms around her waist. He bent to kiss her forehead.

"You look divine, just like in my dreams. I got the nightgown for you, and it fits you perfectly." She met his gaze and the look she saw in his eyes made her forget her apprehension.

"Thank you." She reached up to kiss his cheek. He tilted his head and his lips met hers. The smell of his aftershave intoxicated her senses and she realized that all she wanted was to be in his arms forever. When his lips parted hers, she tasted his bottom lip and was amused at how sweet it was and how good it felt. She clung to him as he teased her upper lip, and then her lower one. He raised his head to look into her eyes in the candle light.

"With my body, I thee worship, my queen, my love, my wife."

Samarah was convinced that she was in an ethereal world. Her head spun and she felt things she could not quite explain. Mayne held her to him and stroked her body until she forgot all about everything except the kiss and how wonderful it was making her feel. When he released her mouth to kiss her eyes, her forehead, her cheeks and lower to her neck, she murmured "I love you very much, Mayne." He lifted her up and carried her to their bed as he replied, "I love you too."

Samarah was awakened the next morning by a kiss on her nose. Her eyes fluttered open to find Mayne smiling at her. She snuggled close to him and wrapped her arms around him. She asked if it was morning already and he said it was. He felt her relax against him and looked down at her closed eyelids.

"Hey, wake up, sleepy head."

"I didn't get much sleep last night." Samarah stifled a yawn. Mayne's laugh sounded like music in her ears. She reached up a hand to caress his cheek.

"You'll have to stop that if you ever want us to leave this room." He tilted his head to one side and took one of her fingers into his mouth. With his teeth he gently grazed the skin. Samarah was surprised at the thrill that shot through her. Mayne released her finger only to capture her mouth in a soft kiss. When he finally raised his head, he said, "I thought we'd watch the sunrise on the beach this morning, but this is so much better. After all, we have two weeks." Samarah giggled and pulled him down to her. She had never thought it was possible to be this happy.

Mayne and Samarah walked hand in hand along the beach. They had been at the hotel for a week now, and everyday she felt happier. happier. She was quite surprised by the intensity with which she loved Mayne. He had come to mean everything to her, and she did not know how she would cope if anything ever happened to him. *Please God, don't ever let me be separated from Mayne. Don't take him away from me, like everyone else I have ever cared about. Please.*

"Hey, wife, what's wrong?" Mayne looked at her.

"Wrong?"

"Uh-huh." He leaned closer and massaged her forehead. "There, the frown is gone. Are you alright?"

"Yes. I was just telling God how much I love you." She smiled at him.

"And did you tell Him that I love you more than anything or anyone else on earth?"

"I'll let Him know next time." She laughed. Mayne hugged her to him and then a mischievous light glinted in his eyes.

"I'll race you to that rock right there." Laughing, Samarah nodded.

They both took off running. When Samarah noticed that Mayne was ahead of her, she halted with a cry and bent down to examine her toe. At once, he stopped and ran back to kneel down beside her. At that moment, she sprang up and ran with renewed speed, her laughter floating in the wind. Mayne's laughter joined hers as they both reached the rock almost at the same time.

He caught the breathless Samarah in his arms and toppled her unto the sand. He rolled over and lay partially on her, his body pinning her down.

"I won," she gasped.

"You didn't," he countered.

"I got here first," dhe insisted.

"You cheated," he raised and eyebrow.

"Not really. I didn't ask you to stop, did I?" she smirked.

"You knew I would. Anyway, I reached here the same moment as you."

"No way, you toppled me." She laughed.

"I love it when you laugh." His mouth on hers smothered whatever she would have said in reply. Immediately, she held unto him. Mayne raised his head and cocked it to one side.

"Who won this round, wife?"

"You did," her breathless voice conceded.

*

The couple got home at about seven p.m. After a lot of hugging from Carl, Bessem and a few workers who happened to be around, Bessem proceeded to serve food and went to the kitchen to heat up water for their baths. After the meal, Carl suggested that they bathe and rest. Samarah got up from her seat and headed towards the back door, in the direction of her old room.

"Sam, love, the room is this way." She could hear the amusement in Mayne's voice. Bessem and Carl laughed when they saw her flustered face.

"I forgot." Her smile was sheepish. Mayne looked at the other two.

"Well, a pleasant night to you both."

"But it's just seven," Bessem commented.

"Plenty of time then to spend with my wife," Mayne grinned.

"You've had her to yourself for the past two weeks."

"Consider that we are not back from the coast. If anyone should need anything, we are still on honey moon please," Mayne said. Carl laughed as Mayne grabbed Samarah's palm and ran up the stairs with her. When they reached the landing, Mayne swept her up into his arms. She looped her arms around his neck for balance. They heard Carl whistle from the bottom of the stairs and he yelled, "way to go, Mayne!" Mayne laughed and gave Carl a thumbs-up with the hand under Samarah's knees.

"Welcome home, Mrs. Patterson," he said as he carried her along the corridor, and all the way to the master bedroom, which stood ajar. He carried her in, and kicked the door shut behind them. His head reached down the same instant hers reached up. She felt him open another door and then he raised his head.

"Surprise!" He plunged her, clothes and all, into the tub filled with warm water.

"Mayne!" She screamed as the water soaked her gown and under-wear, and hair, and shoes.

"In a moment."

He pulled off his shoes and entered the tub too with all his clothes. Water overlapped unto the concrete floor, but they did not notice. Mayne leaned into her and planted a kiss on her nose. Then he removed her shoes from her feet.

"We are all wet," she said.

"Mmhm."

"I do love you," she giggled as he pulled her to him, unbuttoned her dripping dress, and pulled it over her head. He let the dress fall unto the bathroom floor. Then he spread out his hands, his wet hair falling over one eye.

"Your turn."

"Come here." She bit her lower lip. Her eyes never left his as she leaned forward, smoothed his hair back with her palm, and placed her mouth against his. He tasted sweet and intoxicating, like the champagne she had drunk on their honey moon. He pulled her closer to him and she let him explore her mouth, as she matched him step by step. As they kissed, she eased open his shirt buttons and slipped her hands inside, to feel and caress his flesh. She broke the kiss to take off his shirt. He groaned in protest. A second later, he took off his trousers and dropped them on the floor. She kissed his forehead and nibbled his earlobe.

"Sweetheart," he said the word like a prayer. She giggled when she felt his lips on her neck.

"Are we going to bathe or not?" She could feel his responding smile against her neck and then his teeth slightly grazed her skin. His hand traveled the length of her body and grabbed her right foot.

"Gotcha!" He started to tickle the sole. Samarah squealed with laughter and tried to wriggle free, but he held on.

"You asked for it!" She tickled his sides and armpits. Both of them howled with laughter as they tried to get the better of each other.

Outside, Carl drank palm wine – his newfound best drink – with a few workers around a bonfire.

"Massa di glad plenty," an elderly man commented. Carl smiled. He had never seen Mayne this contented. If this was love, he could hardly wait to feel the same way his friend did.

CHAPTER TEN

OCTOBER – DECEMBER 1919

Carl returned to the United States of America in October. That same month Samarah completed her training and was employed by Dr. Ryan. Dr Ryan employed her as a full time nurse. Mayne concentrated on the plantation and talked to Samarah about traveling to the hinterlands to check out his coffee plantation in Mendankwe. He had not been there since his father died, and thought it was time for him to go.

It was a time of bliss for the couple. The workers on the plantation were getting accustomed to Samarah and Mayne being together but they still encounterd the odd stare and gossip. Mark and Eustace had been to see Mayne once, but Samarah had been in the hospital when they came. They had told Mayne about the gossip among other plantation owners – how Mayne had 'polluted' the race, and disgraced his people, but how they could not totally cut him off because they needed his plantation produce. His friends said they could not understand how Mayne had done such a thing as marry a native, but since he looked happier and it had been his choice, they could do nothing about it. Mr. and Mrs. Smith however, would only offer a stiff good day when they came across Mayne. They never uttered a word to Samarah.

Despite all this, the couple found comfort in each other. Samarah would spend her days in the hospital, while Mayne spent his either overseeing work at the plantation, holding meetings with his foremen and workers, or during weekends, teaching Samarah to drive. In the evenings, Samarah would return home in time to help Bessem cook supper for her husband. The nights she spent in his arms, held close to his heart. The only time she was sad was during the weekends Mayne went to Victoria on business. On such nights she would gather the workers' children in the large courtyard, and tell them stories.

One day, she went to the local market to buy a few provisions for Mayne who would be going to Mendankwe the next day. She saw everyone in an uproar. When she inquired from a trader what was happening, the man cried over his shoulder as he ran with the others towards the market square, that some survivors had returned from the war. Samarah's heart pounded in her chest and she quickened her footsteps, until she was running with the rest of the people.

A thick crowd had already gathered by the time she reached the square. She pushed her way through, all intents to shop fleeing from her mind. Finally, she made it to the front. She saw about thirty men and boys, some about her age, others younger, and others much older. Everyone was talking at once, and jubilating. She looked from one face to another, her heart constricting at the lines etched in the faces. There was a feeling of sadness and pain behind their eyes, she thought. People were shoving her to find their relatives.

She saw someone who had his back to her, dressed in a worn-out dirty green uniform like the other men. Her heart almost stopped as she took in his height and build. Could it be? She took a tentative step towards him, and then another, and another, till she was practically running. She reached him and touched his shoulder from behind.

"Bintum?" she managed to say. The man turned round, and

Samarah gulped. He smiled at her.

"Madam, I fit helep you?" She felt the tears prick her eyelids. It wasn't Bintum.

"Sorry, I check say you be difrent person." She said.

She turned her eyes away and forced her feet to take her away. She walked from the market towards home. What a fool she was! Bintum was gone, and he was not coming back. When she got home, she dropped her empty basket in the sitting room and went upstairs to the bedroom. There, she sat on the bed and burst into tears. Bessem knocked and came in. She was alarmed to see Samarah crying and came to sit by her, asking what the matter was. Samarah buried her face in her arms and wept.

"Talk to me, Samarah. Our people say a problem shared is half-solved. What upset you this much?"

"Where's Mayne?" Samarah sobbed.

"He went to see Dr. Ryan to get some medications for the workers in Mendankwe. Don't you want him to go? Is that why you are crying?" Samarah just stared at Bessem who smiled. "I know it seems like a long time now, but he'll be away just for two weeks. He'll be back before you know it." Samarah nodded at Bessem's words.

"I couldn't buy anything today. Some soldiers came home, so everyone was in an uproar," she explained. Bessem looked at her as something finally dawned on her,

"Oh God, did you get news of Bintum? Is that what has upset you so much?"

"He wasn't there, Bessem, and no one had any news of him." Samarah's eyes filled up again as Bessem hugged her and told her everything would be alright.

Mayne brought a tray of food to the bedroom that evening. Samarah was lying in bed, but her eyes were open. Two candles burnt o the table. Mayne placed the tray beside them. He came to her and placed a palm against her forehead.

"Bess told me you are not well." He sat down on the bed. She sat up, and putting her arms around his waist, laid her head against his chest and clung to him. He smoothed back her hair.

"Love, if you don't feel well, I won't go tomorrow. I'll wait till you are better."

"I'm fine, just tired." She lifted her face to look at him. He noticed her puffy eyes.

"You've been crying." Mayne frowned with concern. "What's wrong?"

"Nothing," She whispered, "now that you are here, I'm fine. Just hurry home as soon as you are done in Mendankwe. Don't be gone too long," she pleaded. Mayne cupped her face in his palms and planted a kiss on her forehead.

"I'll be back before you know it. And now," he rose, bent over and lifted her from the bed. "I'll feed you." He carried her to the table, sat on a chair and placed her on his lap. "Say your grace before meals."

*

Samarah thought she would die of pain. Mayne and Bintum faced each other, both looking angry enough to kill. She stood between them.

"Don't do this," she pleaded, "We can talk about this." The men seemed not to hear her. They continued to glare at each other.

"I had her first." Bintum yelled.

"And you went away. She's mine now. I married her, for crying out loud!" Mayne shouted back. In a flash, Mayne was on Bintum, knocking him down. They scuffled as she screamed,

"Bintum, NO!" Then suddenly, it wasn't Bintum. It was the man Mayne had fought with. Again, she saw him take out a knife, again she screamed for Mayne to be careful. Again, she was too late, but this

time, the man plunged the knife into Mayne's heart.

"No!" Samarah cried as he cradled the dying Mayne in her arms. "You can't leave me. You promised you would never leave me! I love you. I will always love you," she sobbed. He said he would always love her too, and she watched the life ebb out of him. She buried her face in his chest and cried...

Samarah snapped out of her nightmare and instinctively her hand went to the side of the bed, searching for Mayne. He was not there. A chill ran down her spine as she spun her head around, looking for him. Then she noticed the single candle burning on the table, and the door to the balcony open. She got out of bed and tiptoed to the door. She peeped out. Mayne was leaning with his arms on the rail.

"Mayne, are you alright?" She padded over to him and touched his arm. He said nothing. The silence was deafening.

"Mayne?"

"Do you always think of him?" He asked, still staring into the breaking morn.

"Him?"

"Bintum." Mayne turned to face her. What she saw in his eyes made her take a step back. His voice was quiet, but she sensed the fury smoldering beneath his calm demeanor.

"Bintum? Why would you think that?"

"Just answer the question. Is he the one you were crying for yesterday?" Samarah bent her head. He swept past her into the room. She followed. He was already removing his clothes to take a bath.

"Mayne, I love you."

"Question is: do you love him too?" Samarah looked into his eyes.

"I can't lie and say I don't care about Bintum. I always will. He was always my best friend." Mayne walked into the bathroom, and she followed him in. "I married you, Mayne. I would not do that if I did not love you. You are my husband."

"Then why would you tell him you loved him?" His voice rose slightly. Samarah was more confused than ever.

"What?"

"I heard you in your sleep." The fury was in his voice. "I woke up early to watch your face so I could have something to hold on to while I'm away. Imagine my shock when my wife murmurs her ex-boyfriend's name in her sleep and vows to love him forever!" Mayne exploded. The nightmare came flooding back to her.

"Mayne, if you'd just listen…"

"I have nothing to say to you," he glared at her. "Go back to bed. Go back to your dream."

She felt her temper flare at his words.

"Look, I'll explain this when you are rational enough to listen."

"Then try that when I come back," he snapped over his shoulder.

"I had a nightmare!" she burst out. "You and Bintum were fighting, but all of a sudden, it wasn't Bintum. It was that man who pierced you, only this time, he found your heart." The feeling of loss she had felt in the dream rushed through her again, and she shivered with tears in her eyes. "I held you in my arms, and it was to you that I swore love, it was you I begged to stay with me. If that doesn't mean I love you so much, then I don't know what it means!"

At her words, Mayne stopped filling the tub and looked at her. He walked to her. She turned her back to him. They stood in silence. Then slowly, she felt him put his arms around her, and then he turned her round to face him.

"I've been so jealous, thinking you still pine for him," he said. "I can make you happy Sam. I will make you happy if you let me, but I can't compete with a shadow. I can't compete with a memory especially one that is so important to you. I am so sorry. I guess I just don't know what I would do if I lost you."

"You won't lose me. You have all of me, Mayne."

His eyes searched hers, and he must have found whatever he was looking for in them, because out of the blue, he grinned.

"What about a morning bath with your husband, Mrs. Patterson?" e cocked an eyebrow.

"I wouldn't want anything more, husband." She grinned back. As she joined him, a small voice inside her wondered what she would have done, if the man in the market place had been Bintum.

*

While Mayne was away, Samarah continued with her usual activities. She went to work at the hospital from morning to late afternoon, came home and helped Bessem with cleaning and dusting. She also went out to see how the other workers were.

Ever since her marriage to Mayne, Samarah had found herself the centre of attention. Even though being seen with Mayne was becoming normal, she still felt like she had lost a large part of her relationship with the labourers. She had noticed, for instance, that often, if women or men stood in a group and she approached, the conversation would stop abruptly and the people would scatter in various directions as if she was a taskmaster come to force them to work. This hurt her all the time. Bessem had told her to ignore them, but even though she tried not to show that it mattered, it did matter, deep in her heart. The pain used to be worse on those weekends when Mayne had to travel. Most nights she would cry herself to sleep. But never in all this did she regret having married Mayne. She just wished that Mayne had been black or she white, then everything would be so much easier.

One night when the feelings of rejection were heightened by a comment she had overheard about how she was now a white woman in black skin who had betrayed her own kind for a life of comfort, she left the house and went to the room she had stayed in as a servant. She found comfort in the familiar surroundings and slept there. As time went on, it became a habit to sleep in that room when Mayne was away. It gave her some measure of peace.

There were times when some of the workers told her they did not understand why she insisted to work. She was the woman of the house now. She always replied that her mother and life had taught her to work, and she could not bring herself to be idle.

While some people said that she had not changed and they were glad about that, others, Eposi included, insisted that Samarah now thought herself better than everyone else because she was married to a white master, and worked with another. They never said this to Samarah's face but gossip had a way of stealing itself right back to the one involved in it.

Every night though, when she retired to the bedroom, she prayed for the days to go by quickly so Mayne would return soon.

It had been twenty-one days after Mayne had traveled. Samarah had spent two extra anxious nights, waiting till long after midnight before going to bed. On this night she decided to sleep in her old room and gathering a blanket around her body, she went there, lit a candle, and lay on her small bed. How different her life was now, she mused. Nothing was ever certain. She would never have imagined that her life would turn out like this, being married to a white man, being mistress of the house where she had served as a servant for years, being disowned and shunned by her own kind because she had followed her heart, feeling like a stranger in her own country.

She was lost in thought when she heard a light knock on her door and when it opened, there stood Mayne.

"Now why would my baby decide to catch a cold on the night I hurry back to keep her warm?" he drawled.

"Mayne!" Samarah sprang up from the bed and he engulfed her in a bone-crushing embrace.

"Just one question: what on earth are you doing here?" he asked as he steered her round and led her towards the door. She indicated the candle which he extinguished using his forefinger and thumb. They walked to the back door of the main house and went in.

"Let me heat up some food for you. You must be starving," she said as she started walking towards the kitchen, but Mayne's hand on her wrist held her back.

"Only for you," he whispered and gave her a quick kiss on the lips. Samarah knew that she should be used to his small displays of affection but she still found herself surprised and shy every time he did them. Before the fight with the Germans that had turned her village upside down, she had never seen her father and mother, or any other couple in Chefwa, embrace or even link their hands together in public, except on days when the couple got married. Since Samarah married Mayne, she had wondered what the rules of intimacy were for the Chefwa people and how the women had got pregnant. At the thought of pregnancy, Samarah's hand unconsciously patted her belly. Mayne's eyes followed her movement and his palm covered hers.

"Sam, we will have our own children."

"But when? It's been two months already."

"Just two months, Love. Don't worry, we'll work on it. What do you say we start now?" He enfolded her in his arms.

"Now would be perfect," she agreed.

*

It was mid December. Samarah and Dr. Ryan were sorting out some medications when they were summoned to the Emergency Ward. A man lay there with blood oozing out of his leg.

"First Aid at once!" Dr. Ryan yelled as he ran out. Samarah set to work immediately. She cleaned away the blood with cotton dipped in spirit. Dr. Ryan returned with an injection of anesthesia, which he gave to the man. He examined the wound and told Samarah that they would have to stitch the wound. Samarah swallowed and nodded. She had never really been a fan of blood. One look at her face and Dr. Ryan asked if she was sure she wouldn't faint. She assured him that she would be fine. The doctor proceeded to stitch the wound with her help. Her insides churned, but she steeled herself not to give in to the feeling of throwing up. Mercifully the man lost consciousness.

When the doctor was through, he turned to one of the men who had brought in the man and asked what had happened. They learnt that the man had been wounded in an inter-tribal battle where a cutlass had sliced into the man's leg. Samarah looked at the unconscious man. He was somebody's son, possibly somebody's husband or father. Would people never learn? Why the intertribal fighting? Why did people fight amongst themselves? It was a common saying among her people that when the house was not clean, an enemy could drop his faeces therein. Wasn't that what was happening? The natives were not united, and so the foreigners could take over. Unity was strength, didn't they know that? If her own people were so divided, how did they plan to stand up to the colonial masters? She did not consider her husband a colonial master. Mayne was always fair and compassionate in the treatment of their workers. He worked with them, and he paid them adequately for the work they did. He did not treat them as different. If only the other colonialists could be like that.

Dr. Ryan put an arm around her shoulders and guided her out. They had almost reached the exit when another man was rushed in. This time, the injured man had been shot in the chest. Blood was flowing out nonstop. Dr. Ryan tried all he could but there was no remedy. The man died.

Mayne was standing in the waiting room when Ryan escorted

a shivering Samarah out of the Emergency Ward. He had come to take her out on a picnic. When he saw her, he enfolded her in his arms while his eyes posed a question to the doctor.

"He just died, Mayne. One minute he was alive, and the next, he… he …" She broke down and sobbed. Mayne pressed her closer to him. The doctor told him that Samarah had seen a lot of blood that day and advised Mayne to take her away.

Mayne guided her to the jeep. He drove to one of the pools on the Patterson plantation. He held the picnic basket in one hand, with a mat under his arm, and used the other hand to support her around the waist.

"I'll spread out the mat." When he had done so and put the basket on it, he sat down, asking her to do same. She obeyed. Mayne made her lie down with her head on his lap. She reached up and tugged her fingers into his dark hair. They maintained a companionable silence. She closed her eyes.

"Mayne?"

"Mmm?"

"Why do people fight?" He stroked her arm as he answered,

"I wish I could answer that." He reached into the basket and removed fried potatoes and eggs. Samarah sat up as her stomach rumbled at the smell of food. It was then she realized that she was rather hungry. She had not had any breakfast that morning and it was almost 2 p.m. Mayne picked up a potato chip and held it to her mouth. She bit into it and chewed. Her stomach started to churn again.

"Oh God!" she moaned as she jumped up, ran into the nearby grass, and threw up. Mayne ran to her and held her as she retched. When she was through, her eyes were red and she could hardly stand. She could feel her head spinning.

"I feel so dizzy," her words were slurred. Mayne cradled her close to him as they made their way to the car.

"It must be all that blood you saw. We are going home right now. I will get Dr. Ryan to come see you at home." Once she was in the jeep, he sped all the way home and after putting her in bed he went to the hospital to get the doctor. Dr Ryan's was still busy so he gave Mayne some tablets to take to her. He instructed Mayne to tell Samarah to avoid starving herself and to get enough rest. Mayne said he would make sure she did just as the doctor asked.

CHAPTER ELEVEN

JANUARY, 1920

It was the first weekend of January, 1920. Mayne was about to leave for coast. Before departing, he kissed his wife, and bent his head to look into her eyes. For a week or two now, he thought she had been looking especially splendid – ravishing actually! After their goodbyes, he got into the jeep and drove away. Samarah waved after the jeep until it was out of sight. Then as she turned to go into the house, she felt nauseous. It had been this way most mornings since the day she had thrown up near the pool. She reached out and clung to one of the pillars of the house. Bessem saw her through the window and hurried outside. She inquired if Samarah was ill as she helped her into the house. Samarah said she was feeling better already. Bessem chided her for letting Mayne go when she was not feeling well and insisted that Samarah go back to bed.

When Samarah was safely tucked in bed, Bessem told her to get some sleep and went out. About two hours later, Samarah woke up feeling refreshed and much like her old self. The first thing she thought about after opening her eyes was food. She bounced into the kitchen, demanding what was for lunch. Bessem asked her what she was doing out of bed, muttering that Mayne would never forgive her if she let anything happen to Samarah. Samarah assured her that she was fine and was actually very hungry. She tried to snatch pieces of carrots from the chop board. Bessem tapped her fingers with a spoon.

"It's not even 11a.m. yet. Honestly, Samarah, are you alright?" Samarah just grinned and proceeded to eat a banana she took from the fruit basket which stood on the table in the kitchen. Bessem observed her.

"When did you last have the monthly weeping?"

"The monthly... Oh, that. Well that was..." Samarah stopped chewing and frowned as she tried to remember. "That was... hey, I'm expecting it tomorrow."

"My guess is, you will be dry this time." Bessem smiled. Samarah's eyes widened.

"You don't... I ... we'll see tomorrow. Oh Bess, I hope you are right!"

On Monday, Samarah rushed to the hospital. She had waited and waited all week end, but still no blood. She told herself it was her anxiety that was causing havoc to her system and willed herself to relax. Her heart beat fast as she went to see Dr. Ryan. He told her they would do a pregnancy test the next day. Samarah was simply ecstatic. She hardly slept that night. She said all the prayers she could and called on the saints she knew to intercede for her. She wanted so much to be a mother. She imagined the look on Mayne's face when she would get the results and tell him that she was carrying his baby. Finally, her eyelids grew too heavy for her to open them, and she fell asleep.

It was almost midnight when Mayne came home. He tiptoed into the room and lit the candle, which usually stood at the side of the bed. In the soft light he looked down at his wife's sleeping form and thought he was the luckiest man on earth. He shrugged out of his clothes, had a rub down and put on his pajamas. Then he climbed into bed. He leaned over and kissed her temple. She stirred and her eyelids fluttered open.

"You're back," she murmured as she shifted into his arms. He held her close to his chest.

"I love you. Good night," he whispered.

"Mmm," she was already fast asleep.

The next morning Samarah got up and made Mayne breakfast while he still slept. She carried it into the room.

"Good morning, Mayne." He did not stir.

"Wake up, sleepyhead. It's past ten." He still did not move a muscle. She deposited the tray containing the food on the table, and walked to lean over his sleeping form.

"Mr. Patterson – Oh!" His arms came round her and pulled her down to him. She lay sprawled on him. His eyes shot open and he grinned.

"I heard you the first time. I've got some news." He kissed her soundly. Then he rolled over so that she lay beneath him. "I've missed you." He kissed her thoroughly. She laughed.

"You can tell me all about it while you have breakfast."

"Alright." Mayne rolled away and pulled her up. He told her that the Commissioner had organized a party at his house that evening. They had an invitation. Even though it was abrupt, it was the perfect opportunity to meet other plantation owners, and explore new avenues for business. At this news, Samarah stared at him. He asked her what the matter was and she explained that she could not go, that she was different. She had realized that most of the land owners had kept away from Mayne since their marriage. Mayne took both of her hands in his and told her she was his wife, and he could not wait to show her off. She had as much right as any of the others to attend the party. Samarah said she would go only if that was what Mayne wanted, and he replied that indeed it was.

"I have a present for you." He rummaged through his bag and pulled out a wrapping, which he tossed to her. "For the evening." He smiled.

"Thanks!" She hugged him.

As soon as Mayne drove off after dropping her off at the hospital, Samarah rushed to Dr. Ryan's office and after a hasty greeting, asked about the results. The smiling doctor offered his congratulations. She just gaped at him. Then she sprang up from her seat and hugged him, all the time not quite believing the news.

An ecstatic Samarah came home that day. She was bursting to share the news with Bessem but she thought she owed it to Mayne to tell him first. She prayed for him to come home quickly.

By 6:30 p.m. she took a bath and wore the long, red dress, Mayne had given to her that morning. It fit her perfectly, accentuating her slenderness. She pulled her hair into a pony tail at the nape of her neck, and tied it with a red ribbon. She stood in front of their bedroom mirror and placed her left palm over her stomach. She rubbed it slowly as she fingered her mother's necklace around her neck.

"I look so normal. No one can guess that there's life growing inside me. God, you are great! I am pregnant! I am carrying Mayne's baby." Her eyes misted over. This was her parents' first grandchild and they were not there to celebrate with her. She remembered all the rituals of childbirth in her village. Now, her baby would not have those, but her baby would have both of its parents, to love and care for it always.

She was still standing in front of the mirror when Mayne rushed in. He stopped short at the sight of her.

"You are gorgeous," he complimented her. She flung herself into his arms.

"Oh Mayne, I am so, so happy today. I got the results of the lab test."

"Test? Were you sick when I was away?" His brow furrowed as he looked at her. She laughed.

"No. I am pregnant!" Mayne looked like he had been hit on the head with a fufu stick. He gazed at her until the news registered in his brain.

"Oh God, sweetheart!" He swept her off her feet and swirled her round the chamber. He scattered kisses all over her face, and then bent to kiss her stomach.

"A baby, we are going to have a baby, Sam, and I didn't even need to get a heart attack first!" He was beside himself with joy. "What did I ever do to deserve you?" he asked as he set her down on her feet and kissed her.

"You've got to get ready dearest. We shouldn't be late."

"I'd rather stay here with you and our baby." He placed a palm across her stomach. She giggled.

"We have the rest of our lives for that. I want my husband to win as many contracts and create as many links as he can this evening. Who knows? We could always decide to come home early."

Minutes later, Mayne emerged in a black suit, deep blue shirt and silver tie.

As they drove off, Samarah felt her apprehension rising again. It would be the first time she was attending a function with white people, at which she was not a servant. She squeezed her palms together in her lap. Mayne's took his hand off the steering to rest on hers, and he assured her that everything would be just fine.

The Commissioner's lawn was packed full with jeeps by the time they drove in through the gate. Samarah looked at the house. It was almost as big as theirs but built out of solid concrete and stone. She thought the building looked very imposing. Classical music wafted to her ears from inside and she felt her stomach clench. Mayne found some packing space, packed the jeep, and came round to open the door for her. He held her hand and smiled at her.

"Hold your head up high, Mrs. Patterson." He bent his head and kissed the back of her palm. He held his elbow out to her and she looped her arm through it. They walked up the steps to the open front door, where a black butler stood and bowed as they approached.

"Good evening, Sah, Madam."

"Good evening," the couple replied. Samarah moved closer to Mayne and clutched his arm with her free hand. She had never seen so many white faces together in her whole life. She saw however, a black face or two dotted here and there.

"The warrant chiefs?" she whispered to Mayne. He nodded.

"And their wives," he whispered back, just before the crowd engulfed them. The men shook Mayne's hand and kissed the back of Samarah's, while the women shook Samarah's hand, and Mayne kissed theirs.

Samarah's eyes kept darting about. She saw Dr. Ryan making his way towards them. He joined them, and so did Father Vincent. They chatted for a couple of minutes, then Mayne made excuses and he and Samarah walked on. He presented her to the Commissioner and most people he knew. Samarah was surprised to see everyone so civil to her.

"White people aren't monsters, you know," Mayne teased when he saw the stricken look on her face. She smiled,

"I know. I am married to one!"

Someone cornered Mayne for a chat and Samarah excused herself and went to talk with Father Vincent. As they talked, she watched Mayne. His eye caught hers and he smiled and winked at her. She smiled back. He made his way to her and asked if she wanted to dance. She replied that she did.

He swept her unto the dance floor. As they swayed to the classical music, she felt his palm against her stomach. She smiled. She knew Mayne would make a very dedicated father. As the next song began, Dr. Ryan cut in and asked if he could dance with her. Mayne whispered in her ear to join him in the garden later.

Mayne stood in the shine of the moonlight, amid the beautiful flowers and fruit trees. Why was it taking her so long to come? Maybe he should go in there and take her home. Dr. Ryan had kept her too long. He heard a footstep behind him and his mouth spread into a smile.

"I thought you were never coming," he teased as he turned round. Then his next words stuck in his throat and his eyes went round. Lucy laughed.

"Surprise, surprise!" She ran to him and flung her arms around him, almost knocking him off balance. His hands came around her to steady himself.

"Lu!" he cried out and grinned as he embraced her and held her away from him to have a good look at her. She looked like a blossoming white rose – cool and breathtaking!

"Talk about destiny! So it truly was you I saw the other day. Here I was lounging in the Sunrise Hotel when someone descended the stairs in a great hurry. I could not believe my eyes. I ran after you, but you had already driven off. Father was there with me and when I asked after you, he suggested you might be at this party. Unfortunately, Father couldn't make it, so I'm a guest here. The Commissioner has graciously offered me a bed for the night, unless you want to take me to your house. Gosh, I've missed you!" She flung her arms around his neck again and hugged him.

"Wow!" was all he could say. She commented that he did not look too happy to see her. He assured her he was, and asked what she was doing in Cameroon. She said she had decided to come back and be with her father.

"Ah, we should go in. It's cold outside." He held her arm and tried to steer her back in. She did not move.

"I like it here. If I recall correctly, you always loved the garden – apparently still do."

"Uh, ok. I… well, I hope I will see you again." He made to walk past her, but she took hold of his arm, asking what the hurry was.

Someone cleared their throat behind them. Mayne raised his head, and saw Samarah standing a few meters away looking at them. Mayne pulled his arm away. Lucy followed his gaze and saw a slim, well-dressed black girl looking at them.

"What are you gawking at? Go on, scram. You natives just love to pick up gossip, don't you?"

"Shut up," Mayne interrupted her. His tone made Lucy's eyes widen.

"But they have no right to listen to important conversations."

Something in the other girl's voice made Samarah take a few steps closer. She peered at the girl, who glared back at her. That expression was familiar. It was one Samarah had seen everyday for the worst years of her life. She felt the blood drain from her face. The girl too seemed to recognize her. They stared at each other for a few tense seconds. Mayne looked from one to the other, his heard sinking. He walked to stand by Samarah. Neither of the girls noticed.

"Lucy!" Samarah whispered as recognition dawned on her.

"Samarah!" Lucy cried at the same time. Both of them froze. Mayne put his arm around Samarah's waist. She felt as cold as ice to his touch.

"Sam, let's go in, let's go home."

"Lucy, what are you doing here?" Samarah was oblivious of Mayne. Her voice was so cold he shivered. Lucy stared from one to the other.

"What is the meaning of this?" She demanded.

"What are you doing here with my husband?" The words were very calmly said, but they fell out like ice. Lucy's mouth dropped open.

"Husband? What's this nonsense?" Mayne pulled Samarah closer to him.

"Samarah and I are married."

"No!" Lucy shook her head from side to side. That one word held all the disbelief that was mirrored in her eyes. "It is just not possible. I don't believe you. There's no way she is the one you left me for." At Lucy's words, Samarah turned her icy gaze on Mayne. He gulped.

"You... and Lucy?" Samarah's voice failed her.

"Samarah let's go. I'll explain at home, please," Mayne begged.

"Mayne, how could you do this to me?" Lucy's shock still had her gaping. "Why would you throw away all we had for a nobody like that? You made me yours, you promised to never hurt me!" Samarah pulled out of Mayne's arms.

"Sam, trust me. She is not telling the entire truth," he pleaded.

"When were you planning to tell me about... about..." She could not even bring herself to say Lucy's name. Mayne swallowed.

"It was wrong of me not to tell you, but I swear I was going to. I was just waiting for the right time."

"Well, time has finally caught up with you, hasn't it?" She grated.

"Sam, I love you," he began.

"That's not what you said two days ago at the Sunrise Hotel!" Lucy put in. Samarah felt her heart giving way inside. She felt a headache coming on.

"Good Heavens, Lucy, how can you be this conniving, this heartless?" Mayne exclaimed.

"It's for her own good. No reason why she should expose herself to more hurt. How many times have you touched me Mayne? How many times have we kissed? How often did we make love?" Samarah inhaled as she put her palms over her ears, and tears glistened in her eyes.

"Sam... I met Lucy in England. We had a relationship, but all that changed when I saw you again after meeting you in the woods... I told her I loved someone else. I chose you because it is you I love."

"What about two days ago, Mayne?" Lucy wailed. "Weren't we both at the Sunrise Hotel? Don't you want your *wife* to know?"

The tears welled up in Samarah's eyes but she refused to give Lucy the satisfaction of seeing her cry. Mayne tossed caution to the wind and engulfed her in his arms. Samarah felt the pain all the way to her heart. What a fool she was to still crave his touch, to still try to draw strength from him. She let him hold her for a while and then extricated herself.

Turning to Lucy, Samarah raged "you have caused me enough pain. I won't let you cripple me in those destructive forces any more. You may have had him, but he chose ME. I'll say this just once, Lucy, stay away from MY HUSBAND!" Then she turned to Mayne, "take me home." She walked past Lucy. Mayne followed her but Lucy grabbed his arm.

"I'm doing you a favour, Mayne."

"By lying?" he spat out. She shrugged, "all is fair in love and war. I did not tell a single lie. We had a relationship, we slept in the same hotel, and you did not tell me you were married."

"That's because we didn't even get to talk to each other."

"I didn't say we did, did I? It's not my fault she is so dumb she reads meaning where there isn't any."

Something inside Mayne snapped. He reached for her as his temper exploded and shook her till her teeth chattered. Never before had he felt this overwhelming urge to hit a woman or strangle another human being.

"Get this clear, you witch, if you ever come near me or my family again, I'll kill you, and I'll enjoy doing it!"

"Mayne!" Samarah saw him grab Lucy, "She is not worth it. Let's go."

They walked down the path to the jeep. They got in silently and he ignited the engine. They drove home. Neither one uttered a word. When they went into the house, he attempted to take her hand in his.

"Sam."

"I'll sleep in the guest room tonight." Without even glancing at him, she went upstairs. He followed her. When they reached the guest room, she opened the door.

"I'm so sorry, Sam… I love you." He hugged her. She did not hug him back. When he let go, she turned and went in without a word.

Mayne paced the floor of their bedroom the whole night. In the early hours of the morning, he collapsed unto the bed and stared up at the ceiling. What had he done? He was too close to losing her. He would not let that happen. He had to make her understand that she was his whole world. He glanced at the clock. It was 5:30 a.m. He made up his mind and strode out of his room to the guest room. He tapped on the door. Getting no answer, he tried the handle. The door was not locked. Sending up a prayer of thanks, he tiptoed into the room. He would not wake her if she was asleep.

The bed was empty and looked like it had not been slept in. His heart pounding, Mayne went to the balcony. No Samarah. He checked in all the rooms of the house. She was not in any of them. He rushed to Bessem's room and asked the sleepy Bessem if she had seen Samarah. She had not.

A couple of minutes later, the workers had been mobilized into a search party. The whole of that morning, and afternoon, they searched and combed the whole area, but she was not found. They searched the whole night with no success.

A worn out and worried Mayne drove into the plantation in the early hours of the morning, desperately hoping that Samarah had come home. She had not. Bessem begged him to eat something, saying he needed all his strength to continue the search for Samarah.

After taking a quick bath and a glass of milk, Mayne was once more in the jeep. He went straight to the Commissioner's to report the disappearance of his wife and ask for assistance. He could plainly see from the Commissioner's face that the man thought Mayne was being too paranoid. When Mayne insisted that he would not leave until he had had some help, the Commissioner assigned six natives to help in the search.

When Dr. Ryan and Fr. Vincent heard that Samarah had gone missing, they too tried to help to find her. While Dr. Ryan asked all the patients he received if they had seen a woman with Samarah's physical description, Fr. Vincent pleaded in church that anybody who had any information concerning her should come forward. No one ever came.

A week went by but still there was no news of Samarah. The Commissioner told Mayne that there was nothing more they could do, especially when some members of one of the search parties found pieces of red cloth in the forest not far from the Patterson plantation. There was the general conviction then that a wild animal had devoured her in the bush. Most of the workers gave up the search and returned to work on the plantation.

Mark and Eustace came to see Mayne and the three of them continued the search for another week, but they did not find Samarah. Finally Mayne's two friends advised him to stop. He was only hurting himself. She was no longer in the land of the living. It was time to accept that fact and move on. Mayne lost his temper and yelled, "you never thought she was good enough for me in the first place! Look, I appreciate all the help you have given me and I understand if you want to stop, but I won't. I will search for her till I see her again, or till I have concrete proof that she is dead. Some pieces of torn cloth are not good enough for me. There could be a thousand explanations for that." After exchanging glances, the boys patted Mayne on the back, and said they would take him home to rest. If he wanted to continue the search, then he needed to take better care of himself, they said.

Mayne lost interest in everything else. Every morning after a quick breakfast, he would leave to scour another area of the region. When it became clear to him that Samarah was not there, he made a trip to the coast and spent over a week asking and searching. Nobody had anything to tell him, even though there was a ransom for any information about her. Two people at the coast had actually come forward and claimed to have seen somebody who fitted the description of Samarah. One said he had seen her board a ship with some other black servants of one of the rich white men at the coast, and another said he had seen her but could not remember where she had gone. Mayne knew outright that these men were lying, but still he gave them some money and thanked them.

For two months, the search for Samarah continued. The more he met with failure, the more persistent Mayne became. He vowed to himself that he would search for her until he found her, even if it took the rest of his life.

One day, Mayne was lying on his bed staring at their wedding picture when Bessem informed him that he had two visitors. When he entered the sitting room and saw Mr. Wakerman, and Lucy, his stomach knotted.

"What are you doing here, Lucy? I thought I made myself clear the last time I saw you." He did not even greet them. Courtesy be damned! Mr. Wakerman cleared his throat.

"Now Mayne..."

"I'll think you should stay out of this, Sir," Mayne snapped. Wakerman shut his mouth.

"I've come to say I'm sorry. Honestly, I didn't expect her to be foolish enough to run away," Lucy said.

"You come into my house, and dare to insult my wife in my very presence?!" Mayne yelled.

"I'm sorry," Lucy burst into tears. "I'm going back to England.

I'm so sorry for everything."

"Well, that won't bring her back, will it? Congratulations! You should be very proud of yourself. You've succeeded in ruining my life. Go straight to the devil." Mayne turned on his heels and walked out of the room. Lucy cried harder as her father took her by the shoulders and led her out of the house to his jeep.

As the days and weeks went by and Samarah did not come back, Mayne lost interest in everything he did. He grew more and more reserved and quiet. Everyday, he prayed for a miracle. Deep in his heart, he thought she was out there somewhere, and he would find her. Even when some workmen came home one evening with the shreds of a red dress they had found deep in the forest, Mayne refused to believe that it was Samarah's dress. He would not believe that she was truly gone, because without her, his life as he knew it was over.

PART THREE

CHAPTER TWELVE

JANUARY – APRIL 1920

The night Samarah disappeared she had not planned to run away. She just wanted to have some time to herself to clear her head. Two hours after she went into the guest room, she opened the door and walked out. It was still dark but she did not care. She walked out of the plantation gate and followed one of the narrow paths that led away from the plantation. She did not exactly know where she was going. All she knew was that she had to get away from Mayne. Bitter tears ran down her cheeks. Mayne had betrayed her. He had cheated with Lucy. Lucy of all people! She had always known that Lucy was trouble. If Mayne could do this to her, who could she trust?

When she had left that night, she had been planning to walk around until she had calmed down. Some part of her hoped that Mayne would give her an explanation that she could believe, so that their problems would be over. However, when dawn finally broke, and her mind cleared, she did not recognize where she was and could not trace the way home. She had never ventured this far into the woods.

She trudged on and finally came upon a little hut. It was common to find huts like this one built in the forest to be used by travelers and hunters. She peered through the undergrowth, and noticed that smoke rose from the roof and an open window. The smell of roasting meat filled the air. Her stomach rumbled. As she remained hidden in the grass, a man of about thirty walked out of the hut. He had on a loincloth around his waist and a spear in his hand. A chain of cowries was tied around his neck. He was darker, taller and fatter than she was. He looked around and then in her direction. Instinctively she leaned into the shade, but apparently it was too late. He walked in her direction. She trembled as he approached and parted the leaves with his hands. When he saw her, his eyes registered surprise.

"Ashia, you don loss?" he asked in pidgin. She took a deep breath and nodded. His face broke into a smile. "Come, rest, chop. I go helep you." He parted the grass for her. Samarah walked after him to the hut. She looked down at her red dress. It was torn and some grass and thorns were stuck to it. She was glad that she had at least had the presence of mind to wear leather slippers.

The man indicated a small bamboo stool which she sat on. She looked at the man. He was not dressed like someone from these parts. In a way he reminded her of her people, far away in Chefwa. She glanced about the hut. The room was small and a fire burnt in the fireplace made of three stones. A rat mole roasted on the flames. A calabash stood nearby and the man asked if she wanted some water. At her nod, he handed a calabash to her. They sat in silence while the man concentrated on roasting the rat mole. Samarah's stomach rumbled again and it was only then that she remembered that she was pregnant. Both hands flew to clutch her stomach, and she felt her eyes going wet again. The man's eyes followed the movement of her hands but he did not say a word. He took the mole from the fire and put it on some plantain leaves he had spread on the ground. With a knife, he disjointed it, and invited her to eat. After thanking him, she ate like she had not seen any food in days. This baby was something else! The man smiled as he watched her wolf down the meat, and drink the water in the calabash. They ate in silence.

When she had finished eating the sun had already risen, and the man suggested that she sit in the shade of a nearby baobab tree. He asked to know where she was from so that he could get her back home. She immediately thought of Mayne. He must be worried sick about her. As she opened her mouth to reply, the nausea swept over her and groaning, she dashed into the nearby bush. When she returned, the man's pitying eyes were on her. He asked if she was feeling better and she nodded. Then she remembered Mayne and Lucy the night before and the pain seared through her heart. *Let him worry!* she thought. *I could kill him right now!* She smiled at the man and inquired if he was from these parts. He replied that his name was Nfon and he was a trader all the way from the interior. He was from a place called Tardu. Samarah gasped when she heard that. She exclaimed that she was from Chefwa. Chefwa and Tardu were neighbours. The incredulity in the man's eyes soon gave way to joy. He wanted to know everything about her.

"My name is… Yenla. I've wanted to go home for a long time now. My mother and I were taken to work this way about ten years ago. She's gone now… and it is time for me to go back," she decided. Her mother had taught her to believe in signs and this was one, if she remembered any of those lessons. It was no coincidence that she had been led to Nfon. Maybe it was time for her to face her past, to go back to her roots.

"I'll be delighted to have company. Are you sure you won't be missed here?"

"I assure you, I won't be. Orphans are hardly missed."

"That's fine, then, but first, I think you should go into the hut and use one of my loincloths. Your white woman's dress is ruined. We have to hurry. You see, my wife is heavy with child." He grinned. Samarah's hand went to cup her stomach as she smiled and said they could leave that very moment.

*

Three days later, Samarah wondered for the twentieth time if she had done the right thing to follow her impulse. What would the people she had left behind like Bessem think? What was going on in Mayne's head? She quickly reprimanded herself and told herself that Mayne did not care about her. He loved Lucy instead. Much as it hurt, she knew that she could not go back. There was nothing waiting for her at the plantation except heartache and misery. She had been foolish enough to fall in love with a white man, and see what had happened. Nevertheless, a small voice in her mind, reminded her that Mayne had always been different. She forced herself not to think of him.

She was going home... HOME! She had learned from Nfon that the Chefwa people had long returned and reconstructed the village. The village was now ruled by Kintashe's younger brother, and everyone hoped that one day the old queen and her daughter would return. When he asked her if she had known the princess as a child, she said, "she's the best friend I ever had. I knew her as much as someone could know herself."

As they went along, sometimes they were fortunate to be given lifts on carts or horses. In the evenings, there was always a family which was ready to take them in for the night. Finally, after fifteen days, they came to the outskirts of Tardu. Nfon's footsteps quickened and Samarah had to practically run to keep up with him. At about noon, they entered the village. She saw a house or two with flattened stone roofs. The majority had thatch roofs. People called out greetings to Nfon in their native tongue, which sounded very familiar to Samarah.

They arrived at his compound. It was made of three huts built with mud bricks and thatch roofs. A brown dog lay across the path into the compound. When it saw them, it ran to them, barking and wagging its tail. It rose on its hind legs, putting its fore paws on Nfon's lap and licking his palms. Nfon laughed as he squatted to rub the dog behind the ears. The open door of the hut farthest to the left was occupied by a woman with a protruding stomach. She was fair in complexion and her short dark hair looked disheveled. Smoke made its escape from the hut through the door and window.

When Nfon saw her, his grin widened and he stood up and walked toward her. Her lips broke into a smile and she tried to hurry towards him. When he reached her, they embraced. Samarah smiled from behind.

"Why, my husband, did you take so long to return?" As she spoke, she pulled back to adjust her loincloth over her breasts. Then she noticed Samarah and raised questioning eyes to Nfon.

"This is Yenla of the Chefwa people. I met her near the coast. She was lost." The woman gave her husband an inquiring look, but smiled at Samarah.

"Lost so far from home? Poor girl. You must be very tired. Come, I will get something for you to eat and water for your bath. You will spend the night here." She looped an arm through Samarah's and led her into the kitchen from which she had emerged a few minutes before.

That night, Samarah collapsed unto the bamboo bed she had been given. Her palm rested on her abdomen. As was the case every night, she found her mind riveted to Mayne. As she stared into the darkness, she wondered why life was so unfair. Why was it that she ended up losing all the people she loved? Tears ran down her eyes and that infuriated her. This had been a regular occurrence since she became pregnant. She cried at the least thing. It was embarrassing! This baby was doing strange things to her body, but she would die before she let anyone hurt it. She would not lose her son or daughter. Not after she had lost the child's father.

The next morning, Samarah rose with a fever. Her head ached

continuously and she felt nauseous. Nfon's wife, Ngoneh, ordered her to stay in bed and brewed a concoction of fever grass and pawpaw leaves for her to drink. After drinking, she fell into a deep sleep, and every time she screamed in her nightmare, she would feel a cool cloth pressed to her forehead. She mumbled words and tossed and turned, oblivious of everything and everyone around her.

Finally she opened her eyes and saw a fire glowing. It appeared to be night. She was too weak to keep her eyelids open, so she closed them for a while. In the end she tried to sit up, but hands gently pressed her back.

"Lie still. Thank the gods the fever has broken," Ngoneh said. She heard Ngoneh's footsteps as she walked out of the hut. A few minutes later, she returned with a bowl of pap. She fed the contents to Samarah. Samarah took a spoon or two and then fell asleep. The next day, she felt much better. Ngoneh brought her some food and after she had eaten a little, she thanked the other woman and apologized for putting her through so much trouble. Ngoneh smiled and said she was just a tool in the hands of the gods. She proposed that Samarah should sit with her outside, explaining that the air would do her some good.

When Samarah was finally seated comfortably with her back against the wall of one of the huts, Ngoneh sat next to her on a wooden stool. Samarah asked where Nfon was and was told that he had gone to the palace to see the chief. They sat in silence for a while and then Ngoneh said,

"Our people say that he who asks questions never loses his way. I do not mean to pry, but there is something that is worrying me… are you pregnant?" Samarah started. Then she dropped her eyes and nodded. She felt the tears rising again. She tried to control them as she wondered again what was wrong with her these days. "Is the baby my husband's?" Ngoneh's quiet question shocked Samarah. Her mouth hung open. How could the woman think that? Then she thought that she would probably jump to the same conclusion if Mayne appeared at their doorstep with a pregnant, seemingly single woman after having been away for a while. Another thought struck her. This woman might believe that her husband had been unfaithful with her but Ngoneh had nursed her back to health. This woman had been kind and caring to her. More tears flowed at these thoughts and Samarah's heart almost burst with gratitude. Ngoneh patted her arm and smiled at her. Sadness shone in Ngoneh's eyes. Samarah finally found her voice and replied.

"Your husband has no hand in my pregnancy Ma. He has been a very kind person who has helped me so much I don't know if I can ever repay him. Now that I have seen just how kind his wife is, I think the gods of my father have already rewarded him enough. You have nothing to fear. Your husband loves you very much. He kept telling me about you and how much he missed you all these days. Thank you for being so kind to me, Ma."

Ngoneh smiled, and replied in the native tongue, "he who welcomes a stranger welcomes a god. Thank you for saying that. Now my heart is at peace for I sense that you would not lie to me…You speak like a white woman. You mumbled a lot in the white man's language when you had the fever."

"What did I say?" Samarah felt her heart sinking.

"Oh, you kept talking about someone called Mayen or something like that… you sounded just like a white lady." Samarah was oblivious of the admiration in Ngoneh's voice.

"I hate them," she hissed. "I don't want to be like them in any way." Ngoneh shuddered at Samarah's tone, and said she had to prepare lunch. Then she hurried away to the hut. She returned a couple of minutes later with corn flour which Samarah sieved while she cooked the *bufaneh*. Nfon returned a few minutes before lunch was ready and chated with the two women till it was time to eat.

*

Three days later Samarah thanked the couple and said it was time for her to go home. Ngoneh thought she was not well enough, but Samarah was anxious to see her homeland again. She thanked them for all the kindness they had shown to her and promised Ngoneh she would return around the time when she would give birth. Nfon decided to accompany her.

They set off for Chefwa at dawn the following day. As the sun rose, they stopped to eat the *koki* Ngoneh had wrapped for them. After they had drunk some water and rested, they started off again. It was about 11.00 a.m. when Samarah started to think that she recognized sites around her. Each time she saw a familiar setting, her heart leaped within her chest. As they crossed over the stream which separated Chefwa from Tardu, Samarah remembered how she used to dive in the water and swim with Bintum and their other playmates. There was always a *Nchinda* with them for protection.

As they walked down the dusty path that led to the village, Samarah felt as if she was floating on clouds. She drank in the sights and sounds around her like one who had been lost in the desert for days and then suddenly had come upon an oasis when he had almost given up hope of ever finding one. A few thatch huts came into view, and as they passed by, she called out a greeting in the Chefwa dialect. An old woman greeted back, and waved. She had missed this. She had not spoken her language since her mother passed away. They went on. Samarah's footsteps quickened as she took the path which branched off from the main road towards the site where she remembered the palace to be. Nfon kept up with her.

"I thought we would go to your compound first. Don't you want to see your family before going to the palace to pay your respects?" He asked. She smiled at him and said her home was that way too. As they walked she looked around, and her heart sank at what she saw. Many of the huts looked new and she did not recognize any one. Nfon followed her eyes and explained that the whole village had been burnt down about ten years before, and since a majority of the inhabitants got back only about five years before, the village was still very much under construction.

Samarah looked ahead and saw the kola nut tree which marked the entrance into the palace. She felt as if her heart would explode as she quickened her pace. When she reached the tree, she threw her arms around it. How many times had she sat in its shade and spun stories about heroes of the past? How often had she played under this same tree? She leaned her head against the trunk and murmured to it, as her eyes misted over.

"You have not changed too. You are still here. You waited for me, and now I have returned." Nfon stood a short distance away observing her. Something strange was going on here. From where he stood, it looked like the girl and the tree were somehow connected – like they were one. Samarah finally remembered that she was not alone. She turned to look at Nfon and sniffed back her tears.

"It has been such a long time." She drew in a deep breath. "I have not been completely honest with you. The truth is that Yenla was my mother's name. I am Samarah, waa Yenla, kfweh Kintashe, Princess of Chefwa."

At this news, Nfon gaped at her and was speechless. Samarah maintained eye contact with him. "I'm sorry I did not open up sooner. I had to trust you first. Let us proceed. The courtyard is this way." She walked in front of the still bewildered Nfon, her head held high, her shoulders straight, like she had seen her mother walk when she was little.

The cluster of big huts that formed the palace was surrounded by eucalyptus, kola nut, banana, plantain, mango, pear and guava trees, planted close together. Samarah offered a silent prayer of thanks when she saw that the palace had not been burnt down.

As she walked through the open bamboo gate, she recognized the central building, built from wood and bamboo with markings of masquerades and other symbols on it. This hut had existed for at least four generations, her father used to tell her. To the right of the hut were other small huts, constituting the inner compound, where the Chief and his wives and children lived.

The inner compound had five huts clustered into a circle around the courtyard. Samarah remembered that her father had inhabited one, her mother and herself another, and each of his own father's three wives and their children had lived in the others. According to tradition, her father was supposed to have inherited his father's wives except his birth mother, but he had declined to do so opting to keep Yenla as his only wife. Two of these women had been about Yenla's age. He had wanted to let them marry his brothers or whomever they chose, but they had refused. They had threatened to go back to their compounds, but the Council of Elders and sub chiefs insisted that he keep them, because tradition had to be upheld. As a result they had stayed on in the palace and Kintashe had provided for them like a husband would, but he had reserved his conjugal rights only for Yenla. This arrangement had provoked petty jealousies targeted at Yenla even though the women had ocassionaly lived in relative peace and unity.

Samarah pulled herself out of her thoughts and looked behind the hut which used to be her father's. Sure enough, the sixth hut was still there. This one was for the family masquerade or juju. It was situated behind her father's hut. She remembered that women did not look or go into the juju house. A woman who broke that law could be cursed. She might give birth to a juju, or sprout horns. Only men were allowed into it, and only during festivals or celebrations. It was common knowledge among the Chefwa people that jujus were not people. They were spirits who had come back from the grave to commune with the living. Behind this hut, she could see the coffee farm just a stone's throw away.

To the left of the main decorated reception hall was the shrine where Kintashe had offered sacrifices to the gods on behalf of his people. There was a flat stone about three metres wide. On it was placed a woven mat. On the mat, a monkey skin rug was placed along with a calabash whose tip had been cut off, and a clay pot. The calabash contained sacred water used in cleansing rituals, the clay pot contained kola nuts, cowries and sacred other items needed to offer a sacrifice. Branches of the *nkeng* peace plant were always put in another calabash which hadn't been cut, and which stood behind the other two containers. Also another calabash full of palm wine had to be there. This wine was used to pour libations to the gods and ancestors during a sacrifice. Accompanying these were carved statues of past chiefs and warriors of Chefwa. A hearth had been built close to the shrine. When a sacrifice had to be offered, the Chief would light a fire to summon the whole compound.

Samarah remembered an incident from when she was four years old. She had been sick. Her father had taken her to the shrine and sprinkled the sacred water on her head, calling on the dead ancestors to protect the living.

You the dead, come to our aid
Bokongki, this is you, this is your child
You are the one who will take care of this child
Protect this child and stop her from getting sick

And she had felt better straight away.

As her emotions engulfed her at these memories, Samarah broke into a run in the direction of the hut, which used to be her mother's. People in the other huts stopped talking and watched her. One woman who was pounding cocoyams in a mortar stopped pounding. A few children, who had been playing stopped and looked in her direction. More women and children came out of the other three huts. The two *Nchindas* who stood in front of the main reception hut hurried in her direction as Nfon ran after her.

When she reached the door, she fell on her knees and sobbed as if her heart could not hold in any emotion any more. When the *Nchindas* saw her kneeling, they stopped. A small crowd of women and children was gathering.

"Emeh, emeh, eh nu yeh, Bo Nyo? (who can this be, ye gods?)" The women muttered among themselves. Samarah heard them and raised her face to look at them. One of them gasped.

"Yenla, is that you?" Samarah's gaze followed the voice and she saw an old woman leaning on a walking stick and peering at her. She, like the other women, had tied a loincloth over her breasts, but in addition this woman wore a headscarf. There were lines of age etched into her forehead and her skin looked wrinkled. For all this, she looked graceful. For a moment Samarah looked at her, then as recognition registered in her eyes, she burst into fresh tears, and hurled herself into the woman's arms, almost knocking them both down. The woman was called Yaa by all the children of the royal household, she remembered, and she was the oldest wife of Samarah's grandfather, the one her father had considered as his mother when his birth mother died, the one Samarah considered as her grandmother, the one she had always run to when other members of the royal household had been nasty to her. Samarah finally let go of the puzzled woman long enough to say, "Bwan, it is I, Samarah, Yenla's daughter."

After the initial shock, the old woman held Samarah to her with exclamatory shouts and cries. Her shrill voice which belied her years pierced the air as she tightened her arms around Samarah and tears stood in her eyes. One of the *Nchindas* ran in the direction of the main hut and disappeared inside. The other women and children came to hug Samarah with cries of "welcome, welcome!"

Soon a voice yelled "Bo Ntow!" and all of them squatted. Samarah saw a man, who looked to be about forty-five years old, tall,
dark and lean walking towards her. For an instant, she thought she
was dreaming and reached for Nfon's hand. He clasped her hand
as she clung to his. The approaching man was the splitting image
of her father. The man walked closer and Samarah recognized him.
For a moment she thought she had taken leave of her senses but
now she recognized him. It was not her father, but his younger
brother, Kentaw.

"Baa!" she murmured and bowed low. The man was flanked on
both sides by *Nchindas* with loincloths over their waist. He was
dressed in flowing robes made of animal skin and held a short staff
in his hand. The women raised their eyes to see what was going on.

"You say you are Samarah?" he asked.

"Yes, Baa, I am."

"This can't be right. Yenla and Samarah died long ago, killed by
the Germans."

"Baa, we did not die. We were captured and traveled for several
days to a strange land."

"Hmm." He looked at her again, then shrugged. "You do look
like Yenla, and you talk with the authority of my late brother…
Follow me… and who is this? Your husband?" He pointed at Nfon,
who bowed low. Samarah said he had helped her find her way back
home. The Chief asked him to accompany them. They walked
towards the main hut. As they went into it, she heard the crowd
outside erupt into noise.

It was much darker inside. The room was large and round, with
bamboo chairs lined against the wall all round. Looking at the
room, she felt as if time had stood still for this place. It was exactly
the same way it had been when she had said goodbye to her father
close to ten years before. At the center was a chair carved out of
dark wood. She remembered with a pang that her father used to

sit on that chair. Now, Kentaw sat on the chair and indicated for Samarah and Nfon to sit. Kentaw cleared his throat.

"If you are truly who you say you are, why did you not come home after the wars ended?"

"I did not know how. I was too far away, and I did not know the way back."

"I see. And where is Yenla?"

"My mother joined our ancestors five years ago. She got burnt in a fire." The memory of that day swept across Samarah's mind. Kentaw must have seen the pain because his face softened.

"My child, I just want to be sure you are our daughter. I wish there was some kind of proof." Samarah looked at Nfon who shrugged. She said, "I do not have proof. All I can say is that I am the daughter of Chief Kintashe, brother to Chief Kentaw." As was the case whenever she was nervous, Samarah's hand rose to finger her necklace as she pleaded, "You must believe me. I speak our language well, I look like my mother. I've tried so hard. I've taken weeks to come back here." She remembered the chain she was touching. Without a word, she rose and walked to stand in front of the Chief. Then she removed the necklace and handed it to him with the words, "This was my father's. He once told me that you had helped him to make this for my mother when he was still courting her. He was slain and it was passed on to my mother. She gave it to me on her dying bed." The *Nchindas* leaned forward to see it too. Kentaw examined it, then looked up at Samarah. His face broke into a grin.

"The gods be praised! Our child, my daughter, Princess of Chefwa, welcome home." He clasped both her hands in his and she flung herself into his arms and cried.

*

Two weeks had gone by. Two weeks of feasting and merry-making. News had spread fast and people flocked to the palace to see the long lost princess. Samarah was pestered with questions from both the old and the young about the coast and the south from whence she had come. Her days were spent receiving visitors who came to see her.

Now, she was on her way to see Nfon and Ngoneh. With her were four *Nchindas* carrying bags of corn, beans, groundnuts, and potatoes. One *Nchinda* held two chickens in one hand and pulled a rope tied to a goat's neck in the other. When they entered Tardu, a crowd gathered to see where the princess of Chefwa was going. When Samarah and her entourage entered Nfon's compound, Ngoneh was sitting in front of her hut. She was already very heavy with child and struggled to stand up. Samarah ran to her and squatted in front of her.

"Your Highness," said Ngoneh with a smile. Samarah smiled back. Her hair had been plaited and cowries were attached to it. She wore earrings made from some beads and her mother's chain shone around her neck. Her loincloth was embroidered with beads and cowries, and her ankles were covered with anklets made of beads too. Her arms were adorned with bead bangles. She looked like royalty indeed. Nfon came out to say welcome and assisted the *Nchindas* to put the food in the hut. The animals were kept behind the hut.

"Pray, do not stand, Ngoneh, and please do not address me as highness. Samarah will do." Samarah grinned. After all the things had been packed in, Samarah ordered the *Nchindas* to go back. She had planned to stay there for a week or two. As soon as they left, she dashed into the room her things had been put in, removed all her adornments, and tied a simple loincloth over her breasts.

"Much better," she sighed as she joined Ngoneh outside.

The next night, Nfon and Ngoneh lay in bed, commenting on

how blessed they were to know Samarah. Suddenly she stiffened. He asked what the problem was. She felt it again – a sharp, searing pain. Her eyes widened, she screamed and stared in horror at her husband.

"Oh no, it's the baby!"

"The baby?! But it's past midnight!" Nfon jumped out of bed and stared at his wife with wide open eyes. Ngoneh screamed again that another bout of pain had shot through her. Nfon went to her and held her hand still looking confused. Just then they heard a knock at the door and Samarah's voice inquired,

"Are you alright? I thought I heard someone scream." A second later, Nfon flung the door open and she entered the room.

"It's the baby! What will we do? Ngoneh's mother is not here yet! It's past midnight." Nfon was pacing the floor. Samarah assessed the situation.

"We won't make it to the hospital. Quick, get a fire burning. We need the light. Get me a bowl of warm water, and a cloth. Go!" Nfon sprang into action. Samarah approached the bed and smiled at Ngoneh. "Don't worry. Everything will be fine." She assured Ngoneh, who flinched.

"I'm afraid. My mother is coming in three days' time! This baby is early." She caught her bottom lip between her teeth to keep in a scream.

"I am a trained nurse. I've helped to deliver lots of babies. Now, let's get this baby into the world."

The whole night, Nfon ran in and out of the room. He awakened some female neighbours who came to help Samarah. Samarah shouted out orders to them, and they obeyed. In the early hours of the morning, Ngoneh gave birth to twins – a boy and a girl. Before she fell asleep, she squeezed Samarah's hand. "Thank you." She breathed. As Samarah went out of the room, Nfon held her hand.

"A blessing be on the day I met you in those woods. I will never forget your help, Highness. Thank you." She smiled at him.

"The English say one good turn deserves another. It is you I should thank for giving me my family back."

*

Samarah returned to Chefwa a week later. Ngoneh's mother and Nfon's mother had both come to look after the twins and partake in the birth rites. Two days after she got back, as she walked round the village, she heard a woman wailing. She ran into the farm nearby and saw a woman clutching a small boy to her chest. The woman cried that a snake had bitten her son. She pointed to the spot. At once, Samarah tore a piece of her loincloth and wrapped it tight above the wound. Then she tried to squeeze out the blood. She left the woman to get help. In a matter of minutes three young men helped her to carry the child to the palace where she administered first aid fully.

When the woman narrated how Samarah had saved her child's life, sick people in Chefwa started flocking to the palace. Samarah went to Nfon and gave him some money to buy basic health supplies and medicine from Kimbo, a few miles from Tardu. The British had opened a hospital there. When supplies came, she gave them to the sick, and more and more people came for help. Her uncle, the Chief commented that even though she had been torn away from her people, it was for a greater purpose, and in any situation, the ancestors knew better. She smiled at him, and quoted a Chefwa proverb, "when something spoils, it makes better another!"

CHAPTER THIRTEEN

MAY – JULY 1920

Samarah returned from visiting Bintum's mother one day. It was one of the many times she went to sit with the woman and recount stories of the days she had spent with Bintum in the south. His mother usually listened like it was the last thing she would hear. Sometimes they both cried when they thought of him at war and did not know whether he was alive or dead.

As she came into the palace, she was told that a strange man was waiting for her inside. After greetings had been exchanged and the kola nut broken and chewed, the man stated the purpose of his visit. He had been sent from Kimbo by the medical doctor, Dr. Samuel Worthy to get her. He wanted to talk with her. Chief Kentaw inquired why the doctor wanted to see Samarah, and he replied that the doctor had learnt that Samarah was a trained nurse, and was wondering if he could employ her. The Chief asked Samarah what she thought and she replied that she would like to talk with this doctor. The Chief then asked the man to tell Dr. Worthy that they would be waiting for him the next day.

Towards sundown the next day, a jeep drove into the palace, followed by screaming children with torn clothes, waving and laughing. A white man drove, while the man who had come the day before sat next to him. Most of the palace children hid behind their mothers' loincloths and peeped at the white man. Very few of them had actually seen a white man before. From the window of her room, Samarah studied the doctor. He had brown hair which reached just below the nape of his neck. Mayne's hair was longer, and darker, she thought. The man had a small beard, but no moustache. From his sunburn, she guessed that he had not been in Cameroon for long, probably just a couple of months. He was about 1.75m tall and slender, almost as slender as Mayne. She felt a pang in her heart at the thought of Mayne and her face creased into a frown. She watched as the two men made their way into the main hut. Soon after, a messenger came to inform her that the Chief wanted to see her.

When Samarah went in both men stood up and slightly tilted their heads down. Greetings were exchanged and as was the tradition, the kola nut was broken and shared. Samarah took a piece which she held in her hand and did not eat. She had never liked kola nuts, but she could not refuse to take one. It would mean that she was not in unity with the people who had to share the kola nut. She addressed Dr. Worthy in English.

"I heard that you wished to see me doctor."

"Yes, Princess. I'm sorry about intruding upon you, but I need your help." He went on to explain that since the English had taken over the region, the German doctors had left and it was not easy to get any medical staff. He would be grateful if Samarah would agree to run a small health unit he wished to open in Chefwa, so that the people and those of the neighbouring villages would have quick access to health facilities.

They talked at length and in the end she said yes. The chief granted his blessing and allocated some land near the palace to be used for building the health unit.

That night the village crier went from one end of the village to the other. Every few steps he would stop, play his gong, and announce in a voice that rang out, "people of Chefwa, once again the ancestors have smiled on us. Tomorrow, everyone must come to the palace at sunrise – man, woman and child, none should stay behind."

When everyone had gathered the next day, Chief Kentaw told them about the health unit. He said it was the community which would put in all their efforts for the good of all their people. Next he called the sub chiefs into his palace where they talked and at length, and work was divided among the various 'big' compounds that the sub chiefs controlled. One group was in charge of getting the wood needed, another of getting the grass that would be used to make a thatch roof, a third of clearing the piece of land and leveling it for the building process, a fourth group of molding mud bricks for the building, and the fifth group of making the bamboo beds and other furniture that the health unit would need. The building proper would be done by the whole village.

For the next couple of weeks, the work was intense. The Chefwa people each took their part of the work seriously. The women were in charge of cooking food for the men and carrying stones that were needed for the foundation, to the building location. The children who were above nine years old assisted by carrying stones, and providing water and raffia wine to the workers.

Being the rainy season, the work did not go as fast as had been intended since the rains posed a problem, especially in relation to the mud bricks. The solution was to mold these bricks in some huts and keep fires burning in the hearth at all times. The heat helped to make them dry and firm.

Finally the hard work paid off and two months later, the health unit was ready. It contained an infirmary, a consultation room, a delivery room, and one room with six bamboo and straw beds in it, for critical cases which needed

Samarah soon started her job. She was astounded at the number of people who needed help. She was so engrossed in her work that she was usually surprised when evening came. She referred the more difficult cases to Dr. Worthy's hospital, and trained two girls to assist her in her work. In this way a month rolled by.

One day she was summoned to see the Chief. He was seated with the full Council of Elders. At once, she knew that something was very wrong but she could not figure out what it was. Then she noticed an old man and a young girl standing in the room. She recognized the girl. She was one of her patients. She had treated her for sores on the body. She remembered that the girl had told her she had been beaten by the man her parents had given her to as wife to repay a debt, because she would not let him have intercourse with her. She had explained that the man already had two wives and was old enough to be her grand father. Looking at the man who stood with the girl, Samarah understood the situation immediately.

The man started to complain in a loud voice, "Bo Ntow, the Princess instigated my new wife to be more headstrong. Since she started going to the health unit, she has become more obstinate and she keeps on talking about men and women being equal, quoting the Princess as her reference." The man was so angry, his voice shook and he practically trembled.

"What do you have to say, Samarah?" Kentaw asked.

"Simply that when this child came to me, she had been beaten so much she could barely stand. I said no human being should be treated like this. Women are not the property of men. They are human beings too. I said it was not fair."

"And where did you get the notion that women are equal to men?" one of the elders spat. Samarah said nothing. The man went on, "how can a mere woman who squats to pass out water be the equal of a man? Women are like children. They need to be told what to do because a woman's head is small and she cannot think for herself."

"My fathers," Samarah began, "if given the chance, women can think for themselves. Sometimes they can even do better than some men."

"Soon she will be saying women are needed for more things than giving birth to children and taking care of the house," another elder cut in.

"Who said women should do this and men that? I am asking us all, who said the men should go hunting and do all the hard and intelligent things while the women go to the farm and cook the food, easy things any one can do?" a third elder questioned. "Our ancestors laid down these laws for us. They had done it this way from generation to generation. If they kept it all this time that is because they saw that it was the good thing to do."

"I am not saying women should try to do everything men do, my fathers," Samarah said.

"Then what exactly are you saying?" the last elder to speak spewed out.

"That girls are worth more than repaying debts as wives, or being child bearers, home keepers, and instruments of pleasure."

"You see what happens when a woman is given any little knowledge? She now thinks she knows everything – no doubt she has no husband!" An elder grumbled. The Chief, who had been listening to all cleared his throat. At once the room fell silent. He looked at the young girl, little more than a child. Her head was bent and she dared not lift it up.

"My child, what do you want? Do you want this marriage? Raise your head and talk," he said. At his gentle command, the girl obeyed and stammered "Bo Ntow, my parents forced me to marry Shey Kongbom… they said it was my role to help them in their old age… I did not want to marry him. He is too old for me. He was my grandfather's friend… Please, Your Highness, I want to go back home." The child's voice trembled and Samarah thought she would burst into tears. Chief Kentaw looked at the man.

"If this debt was paid, would you let her go?" Shey Kongbom replied that he would. The chief asked what it was and was told it amounted to ten goats. The Chief nodded, and then turned to Samarah.

"Your job is to cure those who need curing, not meddle in affairs that do not concern you, child. Is that clear?" With a bent head, Samarah said it was. The Chief asked everyone to leave except Samarah. When they were alone together, he explained to her that even if certain aspects of tradition needed to be changed, these changes were not to be rushed; things would change at their own appointed time. He then said he would send a messenger to take the money needed to purchase the goats to the girl's family. Samarah opted to give the money to the messenger. Since she started working at the health unit, Dr. Worthy paid her but she hardly ever spent the money. Her uncle smiled at her and patted her head.

"Everyday, you remind me more of my brother. He too had a lot of radical ideas, and a big heart. Change will come, my child, but it is a gradual process, so please promise me we won't have any more scenes like this and you will keep this keen mind of yours hidden." Smiling, she said she would try.

While work was still going on in the month of June, Samarah's pregnancy began to show. At first, no one had noticed, but as time went on her stomach kept protruding until it became an open secret. People whispered about it.

"Strange," an old woman commented to another. "A daughter of the royal house returns with a pregnancy and no husband."

"Ai! Abomination!" her friend agreed with her. The whisperings became so common that the Chief summoned Samarah.

"I do not know much about what happened when you and your mother were lost to us. I do know that you were betrothed to Bintum. What happened? How come you have a seed in you and no husband?" Teary-eyed, she recounted what had happened to Bintum, how he had been torn away from her and sent to fight she knew not where. She explained how she had been taken to another plantation once her mother had died in the fire. Then she went on to say she had finally married someone else. She could not bring herself to tell her uncle that her husband was white. When he asked her why her husband had not accompanied her back, she was quiet for a couple of minutes and finally said the marriage had not worked out, and it was a mistake. The Chief asked her if she had got pregnant while she was married and she assured him that she had.

"Then it is settled," he said. He sent a messenger to summon the town crier. That night, the whole village was informed that Princess Samarah was a married woman, and it was only a matter of time before her husband showed up. In this way, the gossip was curbed.

July came and Samarah's stomach grew rounder. Every day she would place her palms on her abdomen.

"Our baby grows bigger, Mayne. How I wish you were here with me to enjoy this mystery of love." She wondered if Mayne still thought about her or whether he had married Lucy already. Sometimes she also wondered what her life would have been like now if she had not come back to Chefwa. Would Mayne have asked for forgiveness? Would he have shelved her to one side and been with Lucy? But Mayne loved her. She had been so sure that he loved her. What was love anyway? What did love count for?

One day Ngoneh came to visit. Samarah was not in a good mood. Ngoneh held her hand and asked what was wrong.

"Everything!" Samarah exploded. "I wish my life was different. I wish my parents were still alive. I wish my husband was here with me... no, I take that back! I wish I had never met my husband. I wish my best friend, my first love had never left to fight the war and we had got married instead. I wish... I wish... but they are just wishes," she sobbed.

"What happened to your husband? Did he move on to the land of our ancestors?" Ngoneh asked when Samarah didn't say any more.

"No," Samarah sobbed. "I ran away." Her tears increased.

"Don't upset yourself, Samarah. I am sure you had a good reason. Did he maltreat you?"

"No. He was the best of husbands until... until he fell in love with someone else." She recounted to Ngoneh how she had met her husband and the other woman in a garden. "And what hurts so much is that I truly hated that woman. Why did it have to be her? My husband said she was lying, but she was so forceful about it." Samarah cried into her friend's shoulder.

"Samarah, everything will work out, you'll see."

"How can it work out?" Samarah cried. "I want him near me when I give birth. I want to feel his arms around me. I am scared of having this baby alone... and do you know what hurts most? He didn't even try to look for me. I've been gone for months! How could he have completely forgotten me?"

"Maybe he has looked for you Samarah. You don't know because he hasn't found you yet. It's a long way from the coast to here... You have known your husband and this woman. Who's more trustworthy?"

"My husband," Samarah said without even thinking.

"Then I'd say it's possible he was the truthful one. He might not have cheated on you." Samarah considered Ngoneh's words for some time.

"Even if he did, I've forgiven him already. I just wish he was here with me. I wish I had never left. I wish I had given him a chance to explain." Ngoneh squeezed her hand.

"If he was truly meant for you, you will have him back. The gods do not lie."

*

Samarah had just finished the consultation for the day when one of her assistants poked her head into the room to inform her that a man was looking for her. Samarah said he could come in. A few seconds later, the door opened and a young man walked in. She squinted to get a better look at him. Then her eyes widened as her heartbeat quickened and a choked sound came out of her throat. He smiled and took a step closer.

"Bintum?" She whispered. The next minute, he had reached her and pulled her out of her seat in a giant hug. She clung to him as he spun her round and round, and their laughter mingled and filled the air. She kept on exclaiming that she could not believe he was really there. He finally set her on her feet. She did not know that she was crying until she felt his hands wiping her tears away. She raised her hand to touch his face. Then she was in his arms again. Samarah felt the beating of his heart and felt peace descend on her. He was back. Her Bintum was back.

"I promised I would never leave you." He smiled. Samarah could not seem to take her eyes off his face. His face was a mature version of what it had been before. Only now, she saw how arresting he was, how it would be easy for him to turn any girl's head.

"Where have you been?" she asked.

"We'll talk as I take you home." She called to her assistant and notified them that she was on her way home. Bintum had walked a little distance in front. As she hurried to meet him, she saw his eyes on her stomach. Instinctively, her hand went to cradle it. He noticed and raised his eyes to hers. The expression she saw in his eyes cut through her heart like a hot, sharp knife through rubber. She opened her mouth to speak but no words came out. She stopped walking and bent her head. Would he walk away, or would he ask her questions? She wasn't sure she was ready to handle either of those reactions. She felt her eyes mist over. This pregnancy was really upsetting her hormones.

She did not know for how long she stood there with her head down, when she felt his hand slip into hers. She raised her head to look at him. He smiled. She could tell that his smile was forced, but she was grateful that he smiled all the same.

"I'll take you home, and tomorrow, we will talk." She bit her lower lip and nodded. They walked hand in hand, as they had done since they were children, until they reached the palace. Before she went in, he gave her a quick embrace.

"I've missed you."

"So have I, you don't know how much," she said. He kissed her forehead. They parted after she promised to visit him the next day.

*

"Who did this to you?" Bintum was walking around in a bid to calm his temper. Samarah's gaze followed him. They were in the room he had been given by his uncle, who had replaced his dead father as sub chief and head of the compound.

"If you'd just calm down..." she began.

"Calm down?" he cut in. "I spend close to five years dreaming about you and then I return only to find that someone has made their mark on you, and is nowhere to be found. Who is he?" Bintum exploded. Samarah averted his gaze.

"You've been here a day. Surely you must have heard a thing or two." He paused in mid step and glared at her.

"Yes, I have heard crazy stories about you being married from my mother, but no one bothered to tell me you were with child. Where is this man, your so-called husband?" he roared.

"He... we are not together any more."

"What? The criminal left you with child? What kind of a man would do that to his wife? He should have stuck around to face his actions. What coward did you fall for?"

Samarah sprang to her feet so fast she felt dizzy.

"He did not abandon me. I left him. It's my fault we are not together any more." Bintum's eyes were fixed on her.

"And the idiot didn't think to stop you?" Samarah sighed at his words. She did not quite blame Bintum. What would her own reaction have been if she had returned to find Bintum married to another woman, who was pregnant for him? She felt her heart go out to him and wished there was some way she could comfort him. She was sorry their lives had had to turn out this way. He gave his back to her. She watched how tense he was. She reached out and touched his shoulder from behind.

"I never forgot you," she said. "I waited so long for you, but you were gone… I did no know what had happened to you."

Bintum remained silent. They stood like that for a few more minutes, then Samarah heaved a sigh. "I'll just go," she said softly and turned to leave. His fingers curled around her arm.

"Where are you going?" he asked.

"Home. I can see you are very angry with me and I understand. I'm so sorry our destinies had to be different."

"No, not different," he replied as his arms enfolded her in an embrace which made her heart pump. "Just difficult." He cradled her head on his chest.

"You are mine Samarah. You have always been mine. No matter the difficulties that surround us, we always find each other again."

Samarah's heartbeat quickened at his words. She wrapped her arms around him and held him tight. She had missed him. She had missed talking to him, and laughing with him, and holding him. She had missed how she felt when she was with him. How simple it would be if she had not married Mayne. She sighed. Now they would have no future. It would be wise of her not to entertain hopes that she and Bintum could be together. Bintum deserved so much more after the hard life he had been through, not somebody's left-overs. She heaved another sigh and tried to pull away from the comfort of his arms but he held her firmly in place.

"But I am married, and I am carrying another man's child."

"Which I will accept and love as my own."

When she heard this, she tilted her head back to stare into his eyes.

"Bintum, you don't understand. This child's father...."

"Is a coward for having left you alone. What is there to understand? I love you Samarah. I have always loved you, and I always will. I also know that you loved me once, and if you are honest with yourself, you still do."

When she opened her mouth to speak, he placed a finger across her lips, and continued, "I won't rush you, my Samarah. I will rekindle the flame of our love." Samarah wondered what she had done to deserve this wonderful person, but she could not let him wait for her even though her heart screamed for him to hold her again. She would not be that selfish. She had to let him go because she loved him. She would let him go so he would find happiness with someone else, even though the thought of him with another woman made her feel a little sick. She told him that he should find someone else. She begged him to please leave her to her cursed fate, but he would not hear of it, claiming that there was only one person for him, and she was the one. "And now," he continued, "let me see if my mother has finished cooking the food."

"Where did you go? What was it like?" Samarah asked Bintum three evenings later as they sat in the shade of a kola nut tree. He bent his head and was silent for a while. Then he sighed.

"Those are days I do not want to ever remember again." He stared into space as he spoke. "Sometimes things happen to us and we wonder why. We seek some tangible reason, some greater purpose... These past years have made me rethink. Each minute now matters, each second is very precious to me... When you come face to face with death over and over again, then you start viewing the world differently. You are no longer afraid, but at the same time you want to hold on to life any way you can, you just want to live each day fully, enjoying what so many people take for granted. What I saw, Samarah... These eyes saw dreadful things... these hands," he looked down at his open palms, "did unspeakable things to survive." He sighed again and was silent. Samarah saw his shoulder muscles contort and wished she could take away his pain. She looped her arm in the crook of his and leaned her head on his shoulder. They sat like this for some time.

"I was just a boy," he said in a low voice, and the words came out as if they had been wrenched from his body. "We were so young then Samarah. I remember how we both planned to run away and come back home and make our life here, with our people." A wisp of a smile touched his lips at this memory before disappearing so fast that Samarah thought she must have imagined it.

Bintum continued, "after being conscripted into the West African Expeditionary Force, we were sent under the command of Cunliffe... We walked and walked all the way to Garoua. It was so different there. Garoua is hot! It is hotter than Victoria. The heat is dry. It burns you, blackens you, and makes your skin crack. The sand gets blown into your eyes. The heat makes your throat parched and you are thankful for even a drop of water. You could even kill just for a sip of water... In June of 1915, we captured Garoua... We fought and killed. The Germans were ruthless. As we pursued them and they retreated, they wiped out whole villages. It was like if they couldn't have the territory, no one would... It was painful – painful to shoot at our own kind in order to stay alive, while the white men who had the quarrel stayed on horseback and egged us on." He squeezed shut his eyes and rubbed his forehead with his palm.

When he opened his eyes, Samarah saw a far away look in them, and knew that he was not with her. He was reliving the ghosts of his past. She wished she could do something to help, but could think of nothing. So she just sat and listened, telling him by her presence and silence that she was there for him. He continued, "there were times when I wished I could kill our own commander... I remember," he said pensively.

"We had just won a battle on the outskirts of Garoua, and so many people lay dead – fathers, husbands, sons, brothers... As I pulled myself along, these fingers curled around my ankle. They belonged to a boy, a child younger than me. He looked at me as I squatted and raised his head... What did I care if he was on the Germans' side or Cunliffe's? He was a boy like me, his skin was black like mine. He was my brother... and we were slaying each other. I couldn't help. There was nothing I could do... So I held his hand, and watched the light fade from his eyes." Bintum sighed. "I watched his dreams and plans for his future slowly ebb away... and all for what? So our land could pass from one thief to another."

Samarah gathered him in her arms and held him tight as he finally gave in to his emotions and sobbed into her hair. She had a feeling that somewhere along the line he had forgotten how to cry, he had been bottling these emotions in him, being a man, not showing any weakness. She smoothed the back of his head as she held him.

"I'm so sorry you had to go through all these. I'm sorry I was not there to share your pain with you," she said in a soft voice as she stroked his back. He held her for a while longer, then pulled away.

"We have been helpless long enough. We can't let them continue to do this to us. We have to fight for our freedom. If we can fight against each other, then we can rally as one, and fight for our people… and I won't sit back, fold my arms, and watch history change. I will help in shaping history, no matter how long it takes. Even if we die, our children will one day be free," he said.

She recognized that glint in his eyes. He always had it when he was determined to do something, right from when they were children.

They talked about other things. Bintum told her how he had returned to Wakerman's plantation once the war was over and how nobody had known where she was. He had proceeded to Victoria to look for a job in the hope of hearing about her, but all to no avail. After amassing some wealth from working with ship owners, he had decided to come home, because he knew that if she ever got the chance, she would come home too. Samarah told him how she had worked at Mr. Patterson's plantation, got married there, and finally decided to come back home. When he asked her about her husband, a shade crossed her face, and she told him that the past should remain in the past, and that was a part of her life she wanted buried. With Bintum around, Samarah's days were spent in laughter… and her nights were spent in tears.

CHAPTER FOURTEEN

SEPTEMBER, 1920

Bessem knocked on the bedroom door, and Mayne opened it. She told him that his box had been packed into the car. He nodded and thanked her. He was traveling to Mendankwe, to see about the coffee plantation. The foreman had sent word to him that the workers were about to go on strike. He went down the stairs, out through the front door to the jeep. Bessem and the others waved goodbye as he drove out of the compound. 'Nine months!' His mind screamed. Nine months since he had seen his wife. Seven months of pain, and agony and existence. There could not be life if Samarah was truly gone, he decided. As he drove, his mind kept reverting, as it always did, to that night so many months ago. Why, oh why had they gone to the damn party? Everything would have been so different if they had just stayed home.

When it had become clear that Samarah was not coming back, Mayne had thrown himself into his work with an energy that had frightened Bessem. He toiled and toiled, and more often than not, worked in the fields with the labourers. When Bessem expressed concern that he was killing himself, he replied that if that meant being reunited with his wife, then he had no complaints. This answer alarmed Bessem so much that she pleaded with Dr. Ryan to do something. The doctor prescribed tablets for Mayne and told him to ease up a little on the work.

Now, as Mayne drove, he wondered if he would ever again know the happiness and peace he had known with Samarah as his wife.

Mayne and his foreman were sitting in a restaurant in Mendankwe when another man came in. The foreman hailed him to join them. When he came, the foreman introduced him to Mayne as Dr. Worthy. To make polite conversation, Mayne asked him about his work. The doctor replied that it used to be really hectic, but since a unit had been opened in a place called Chefwa things were better. At the mention of Chefwa, Mayne made a guttural sound in his throat. The other two looked at him. His heart raced as he asked the doctor if the Chefwa he had mentioned was near Kimbo. Dr Worthy replied that indeed it was, and said the unit was run by a pregnant nurse, who was a godsend. Mayne felt like a hammer was being hit on his ribcage. Could he dare to hope? But how would Samarah have made it that far on her own? There were lots of tribal wars and resistance to colonial rule going on.

A small voice in his head urged him to get to the root of this. He cleared his throat and asked the doctor how long he had known this nurse and what her name was. A little surprised, Dr. Worthy replied that she was a princess of Chefwa and he had known her for a few months. Before he even said her name Mayne's heart was already singing. Mayne's face went white as milk, and he sagged into his chair, his eyes never leaving the doctor's face.

"Mr. Patterson, are you alright?" His foreman's voice seemed to be coming from a far away place.

"I... I..." Mayne stammered. He tried to pull himself together but his hands shook like he had a fever. Dr Worthy gave him a closer look. Mayne finally found his voice, and asked the doctor when he would be leaving for Kimbo. He replied that he would leave the next day. Mayne explained that he had to get to Chefwa, that the nurse was his long lost wife, and asked if they could leave immediately. The doctor chuckled.

"My dear man, it is almost 10 p.m. Though I sympathize with you, I have to make sure we get there safely, and that means leaving tomorrow at sunrise."

*

Samarah heard a jeep pull up in front of the health unit, and smiled to herself. Dr. Worthy was early today. She heard a knock on her door.

"Come right in, doctor. Just give me a minute." She did not lift up her head as she heard the door open. God, she was so tired these days. She would likely give birth a week from that day, and she wondered how she would cope till then. She felt so heavy!

"Sam," a voice breathed. Samarah froze. That voice! It couldn't be. Mayne couldn't be here. She was suddenly afraid to raise her head. Bracing herself to face the disappointment evoked by her too fertile imagination, she raised her head. Her breath caught in her throat, her heart pounded and she felt wobbly in the knees. Lucky for her that she was sitting down.

"This is not real," she uttered. Mayne could not take his eyes off her even for a second. It was his Sam. He drank her in as he moved closer.

Mayne. Her lips formed the word but no sound came out. She slowly rose from her seat. She was wearing a loose maternity gown, and her long hair had been tied at the nape of her neck.

"My Sam!" Mayne exclaimed as he reached her. For a moment, they just stared at each other, not touching, then he gathered her into his arms, as she wrapped her arms around his neck. They almost squeezed the life out of each other. "My Love! My Sam." Mayne said over and over again. Samarah clung to him, and all she could say was, "Mayne, Mayne, Mayne." Someone cleared their throat and she turned towards the sound and saw Dr. Worthy at the door smiling widely.

"I see there is no one in the wards. In that case, I will just take my own jeep back to Kimbo. I am glad you found your wife, Mayne. See you later, Samarah." He waved and then shut the door behind him. Seconds later, they heard his jeep roar to life. Mayne turned his attention back to Samarah to stare at her face as he said,

"I've looked for you everywhere. I have searched and searched." His tears dropped on her hair as hers wet his shirt. Finally, Mayne pulled away slightly to look her in the eye.

"Don't ever scare me like that again!" he said as he smiled through his tears. She traced the countours of his face with her fingers.

"Mayne, I…"

She had no words, but just pulled him back to her. His laugh was filled with joy and wonder. He told her how he met Dr. Worthy in Mendankwe and he led him to her. He asked her why she had punished him like that. She stepped back and said, "I didn't plan to run away, but I lost my way, and then I thought of you and Lucy, and well, I met someone from Tardu and … here I am."

Mayne grabbed both of her wrists in his hands.

"Nothing happened between Lucy and me once I had married you. I'm so sorry I did not tell you about my relationship with her. I'm so sorry for the pain I caused," he said.

"I've done a lot of thinking these past months. It was wrong of me to leave, but whenever I thought of you and Lucy, well, I decided to leave so that you could have happiness with her."

"Happiness? What kind of happiness can I have without you?" There was a knock on the door, and when it swung open, Bintum came in.

Samarah froze again as both of them turned their heads towards the open door. Bintum stared at the pair in front of him. Who was this who was holding Samarah's hands in his? Then he gave himself a mental shake. Maybe this was a new doctor who had come to see about her pregnancy. Maybe there was something wrong with her. Concern for her drowned the jealousy he felt upon seeing her hands in the man's. He cleared his throat.

"Good day, I came to check on Samarah, but since you are in consultation, I'll just wait outside." Consultation? Both Mayne and Samarah had dubious looks on their faces. Bintum noticed the expressions and his eyes narrowed. "This is not a consultation, is it?" He demanded. Samarah cleared her throat and tried to step away from Mayne, but he instead pulled her into his arms as he spoke,

"You are mistaken."

"So if you are not in consultation, who are you and why are you holding HER?" Samarah suddenly found it easier to study the holes in the floor than to look at either of the men's faces.

"Well excuse me if your sensibilities are insulted, but I did not know there was a law which stopped a man from holding his wife," Mayne said indignantly, surprised at the hostility in the other man's tone.

"Wife?" Bintum's eyes turned to Samarah. "Samarah, who is this? Look at me!" he commanded. Samarah edged her face in his direction.

"This… this is Mayne," she said.

"Her husband, father of her unborn child," Mayne added. Bintum's eyes opened wide.

"You married a white man?!"

"Hey, easy man! Don't upset my wife. And who the hell are you?" Mayne glared at him.

"Mayne," Samarah swallowed, "this is Bintum." At Samarah's words, Mayne's mouth hung open.

"The Bintum?" he asked. She nodded. His arms tightened around her. Bintum moved closer.

"So you are the coward who let a pregnant woman undertake a long and risky journey alone. What kind of a husband were you that your wife ran away?" Samarah moaned as she felt Mayne's muscles tense at Bintum's words.

"Don't meddle in things which are no business of yours," Mayne warned him.

"No business of mine? You took her away from me!"

"Point of correction. She fell in love with me, because you were not man enough to make your way back to her."

"Mayne," Samarah begged.

"Just a minute, Sam." Mayne let her go and turned to face Bintum. Samarah looked at the fury on both men's faces and fear clutched at her heart. "She waited for you." Mayne was saying. "She would not look at any other man because of you. Yet you were too busy with other matters."

"I was in a war!" Bintum roared back. "But you know nothing about fighting and survival, do you, white boy? The only thing that kept me sane was the thought of her, waiting for me." Samarah's insides churned, and she felt some slight discomfort. She leaned against her table. "I searched all over for her. We were betrothed from birth. She is mine, has always been and will always be!"

"Bintum, Mayne!" Samarah gasped.

"What?" Both men yelled and turned to glare at her. Tears stood in her eyes.

"My water just broke," she announced. At once both men lost colour, as their mouths gaped.

"See what you've done?" Mayne accused Bintum as he ran to cradle Samarah in his arms.

"You were the one who shocked her into labour, popping in here quite unexpectedly like an unwanted pimple." Bintum fired back as he held open the door. Mayne helped Samarah out of the room and all the way to his jeep. Bimtum was hot on his heels. Mayne was already on the steering wheel with Samarah lying in the backseat. Bintum jumped into the back and cradled her head in his laps. Mayne took off at top speed as Samarah started to feel the contractions. Bintum smoothed back her hair and she clung to his palm.

About six hours later, some nuns were helping Samarah into the delivery room at the hospital in Kimbo. They had arrived about three hours before and the nurses had been examining her since.

Dr. Worthy accompanied Samarah and one midwife into the delivery room. Before they went in he turned to where Mayne and Bintum stood near the door, and told them to wait there. The door shut firmly behind him. Dr. Worthy smiled at Samarah and told her everything would be fine. She tried to smile back but instead bit her bottom lip as the midwife assisted her unto the bed. A minute later the pain that seared through her was so intense that she screamed for her mother. The pain momentarily subsided. These intervals of pain and relief became more frequent as the minutes passed.

Whenever the doctor asked her to push, she did, and finally she felt something slip out of her. The immediate relief was so intense that she almost sank into slumber. Now she could feel the dampness of the perspiration on her face. Then she heard a sound. It was the sound of her baby crying, and she forced open her eyes. Dr. Worthy was holding up a wriggling pink thing which hardly looked human. The doctor was beaming down at her. Then he leaned down and placed the baby on Samarah's chest. Samarah laughed through her tears. The baby was all wrinkly with wisps of hair on its head.

"It is a boy!" Dr. Worthy announced. The birthing assistant helped her into a sitting position and Samarah examined the baby. He looked all puffy, his eyes were swollen and his lips stretched out rather unnaturally. Despite all this, she thought he looked lovely. She looped her finger into his little palm. Immediately she felt the tiny fingers clutch her finger and she laughed again, filled with

---

wonder. The birthing assistant then took the baby from her as the after birth came out, and she cut the umbilical cord.

"Let's get you cleaned up, and then your husband can see you," Dr. Worthy said.

"Thank you, doctor. Thank you very much," she said.

Outside the delivery room door, when Mayne heard Samarah's screams he tried to open the door but realized that it had been locked from the inside. He and Bintum paced the floor. Both kept glancing at the locked door, both keeping out of the other's way and not talking to each other.

When they heard the baby's cry, both men once more approached the door and stood staring at it. Finally it opened and Dr. Worthy handed the tiny bundle swaddled in a thick little blanket to Mayne saying, "your son."

Mayne received the child gingerly. He had never held a baby this tiny, this fragile before. After looking at the baby whose eyes were closed, Mayne raised worried eyes. "Is Sam alright?" he asked and the doctor nodded. Then Mayne's face broke into a big grin as he thanked the doctor. Unnoticed by him, Bintum looked at the baby, smiled a little wistfully, turned and walked out of the hospital, as Dr. Worthy ushered Mayne towards the ward to wait for Samarah.

*

Samarah stayed in the hospital for three days. Several people visited her including Nfon and Ngoneh. The royal delegation from Chefwa brought greetings from the chief. Everyone who saw the baby went back more confused than they had come. A white child! The princess of Chefwa was married to a white man! Mayne sat by Samarah's side all through, proudly showing off his son to everyone who came. Bintum came to see the baby too. On the day he came, he had been shown to the maternity ward. He had stood at the door to the ward, watching Mayne and Samarah cooing over the baby. When Samarah lifted her head and noticed him, she smiled and beckoned to him to come. At the sight of Bintum, Mayne stiffened but did not say a word.Bintum came in and embraced Samarah, kissed the baby's head, gave Mayne a handshake, and left. He did not come back.

On the third day, the day of a child's naming ceremony in Chefwa, Mayne drove Samarah and the baby to Chefwa. Samarah explained to him on the way what the naming ceremony meant. It was tradition that when a woman gave birth her mother, father, husband's parents, or elderly members of either family would name the child. Out of respect, the oldest member of the family was usally the one to name the child. This person could name the child after a dead member of the family, or after an important event if such an event took place around the time the child was born. Mayne said while he was not opposed to that. The child would at least bear the Patterson name, he thought.

As they approached the palace, they noticed that the whole community had gathered in front of the palace. As soon as the jeep was cited, the crowd erupted into singing, dancing and clapping.

What is more wonderful than a child?
Nothing is more wonderful than a child.

The child's mother got up and screamed 'Ayeeeh!'
The child's mother got up and screamed 'Ayeeeh!'

That her back ached
That her back ached

So she went and went
And came back with a child!

Everyone had come out to see for themselves the white man the princess had married, and the white child she had given birth to. The women wore their most colourful loincloths while the men carried guns ready to be fired at the name-giving ceremony which would take place later that afternoon. Mayne whistled.

"I bet the whole village is here. They must love their princess very much." He smiled at Samarah. She returned the smile and then turned her searching gaze to the crowd. Mayne noticed and his brows knotted in a frown. Was she looking for Bintum? He felt his heart constrict, but before he could say anything, the chief walked into the courtyard with the Council of Elders.

Mayne stopped the jeep and climbed down, but before he reached her side, Samarah had opened the door and come down with the baby in her arms. One of the chief's younger wives, Kibvu, came forward and took the baby and started ululating.

"Our daughter, you are welcome," the chief said. She smiled and nodded. Mayne came to stand close to her. The chief looked at him and then at Samarah.

"So the rumors are true," he lowered his voice for her ears alone. True, her husband did not understand the language, but he did not want any one else to hear. He cleared his throat and with a frown furrowing his eye brows, he nodded to Mayne, who nodded back with a grin. The chief spoke again, for Samarah's ears only, "the naming ceremony and celebration will go on, and then we will talk." Samarah's heart constricted as she nodded. She had always dreaded the day her people would discover that the baby she had been carrying was half-white. She had not known what to expect: would they treat her with understanding and acceptance, or would they too feel that she had betrayed them?

The chief turned to the crowd and they fell silent. He raised up his right arm and pronounced, "let the ceremony begin." The palace women – wives, daughters, old mothers – came forward and started dancing the *njangwan* which was a birth song. Kibvu danced with the baby and led the other women towards Yaa's hut. Next, the chief and the Council of Elders followed, and finally Samarah indicated to Mayne that they should follow. The whole crowd then surged in to have a better look at the ceremony about to take place.

The chief and Council of Elders sat on bamboo chairs that had been put in the shade of a tree next to Yaa's hut. There were two other bamboo chairs against the wall of the hut.

When all the people had gathered in front of Yaa's hut and fallen silent, the old woman walked out. Today she was wearing the *kilanglang*. A row of beads lay against her chest, and she was not holding her walking stick. She smiled at Samarah and beckoned to her to come and sit on one of the two bamboo chairs which had been placed against the mud wall of the hut. Samarah obeyed. Next, Yaa looked at two women who were Yenla's relatives. They moved forward with two calabashes covered by two other calabashes so that they looked round like the moon. They placed them in front of Samarah. Finally, one of the *Nchindas* came forward with a gourd of raffia wine which he placed near the calabashes. Mayne stood in the crowd and looked on, intrigued.

Yaa sat on the other chair, bent and opened the calabashes. In one was cornfufu and in the other chicken roasted and fried in palm oil. Yaa took some of the fufu and a piece of the meat in her palm and put them in Samarah's mouth. Samarah chewed the food and swallowed it. This was repeated three times, and each time Yaa called on their ancestors to cleanse Samarah's womb and send a name for the child. Then water was brought by a small girl for Yaa to wash her hands.

After she had washed them, Kibvu gave the baby to her. Yaa held the baby to her chest, muttering unintelligible sounds. Next she raised him high above her head, and cried out, "this is Kintashe, chief of our people, protector of our tradition, and hero of our songs. This is Kintashe come back to life. His name is Kintashe." Then Yaa turned to Samarah and spoke to her. Samarah looked at Mayne and translated, "Yaa wants to know if you have any other name to add."

Mayne who had stood dumbfounded all through, now found his voice and responded, "Father's name." Samarah nodded and turned back to tell Yaa, who in turn nodded. Then Yaa made her way towards the chief. He rose from his seat as Yaa reached him and stretched the baby out to him. Chief Bornu laid his hand on Kintashe's head and asked the ancestors to bless the child. Then Yaa took the child to Mayne. When Mayne took the baby into his arms, Samarah told him that it was time for him to pronounce the full names of the baby. Mayne was full of smiles as he said in a loud voice: "Arnold Kintashe Patterson." Then he gave the baby to Yaa who took him to Samarah. When Yaa had given Kintashe to Samarah, the chief declared, "let the feasting begin." At once the silent crowd erupted into cheers, and before long the whole palace courtyard was filled with people eating, drinking and laughing.

Samarah and the baby went to the hut which had been Yenla's. Mayne sat with some men and drank raffia wine. In the late afternoon however he departed for Kimbo after going into the hut and holding his son for some time.

The next day in the morning, Samarah was summoned by a *Nchinda* to the chief's presence. She went in and realized that the Council of Elders had assembled too. One of the elders pointed to a bamboo chair on which she sat.

The chief cleared his throat, "our daughter, your father, my brother, was a wise man. He contributed a lot to our community, but he was a trifle too radical. He thought women like men could rule; but that has not been our tradition. We were hoping that you would be delivered of a male child, who would stand a fair chance at the throne once I'm gone, along with my own sons. True, you had a son, but he can never be chief. I know you understand why." Samarah nodded. Her son, being part white would never be considered a true heir to the throne. Actually this was the first time a coloured child had been born in the village, and it was in the palace.

"My fathers," she said, "I know that the well being of this village comes first, and I would never dream of upsetting it. I want you to know that I have never wanted the throne. All I have ever wanted is to live peacefully among my people. But I think that our laws should be re-examined and made to fit the changing times. My son should not be discriminated upon because of the colour of his skin. Royal blood flows through his veins – my blood, the blood of my father and his father before him. I know that you, my fathers are wise, and I see that my village has a wonderful ruler, and that is enough for me. I know one day change will come, but that day is not today. I accept this."

"We hear you my child," one of the elders spoke. "What ever you decide to do, where ever you decide to go, know that you are always welcome here. This is your land, your heritage, and no one can take it away from you. You will always be a princess of Chefwa."

"Now, about Bintum," the chief continued, "betrothal is a serious issue for us. We know that you were separated from each other, but fate has brought you together again."

"But, my father, I am already married to another man."

"Only before the white man's god. In front of our ancestors, Bintum is your husband and will remain so unless he willingly says you are free to go. Go, seek him out, and if you both decide to end this thing, so be it. If you decide to work it out, so be it."

CHAPTER FIFTEEN
OCTOBER 1920 – APRIL 1921

Mayne drove into the palace courtyard. He had been offered a room there but had explained that he would sleep in Kimbo and drive to Chefwa every day because he had sensed that Samarah would not welcome his close presence so soon. So far his efforts were paying, at least with Samarah's people. Now, he always had people waving and shouting out greetings in the native tongue to him, and he had picked up a word or two, "*Be yuh wah* (it is daybreak), *O sao la* (what news)?" He guessed that he was becoming a favourite with most of the sub chiefs especially as he had given them each a bottle of whisky at his son's naming ceremony. Every time he came to the palace, there were always people in the courtyard leaving him with little or no chance to spend time with Samarah alone. He did not seen Bintum in all this time. But Samarah had told him that Bintum had visited thrice since she had been back.

On this day, he noticed the palace was unusally quiet. No one was moving about and there wasn't any sound of a mortar pounding, or children playing. The palace looked deserted. When he parked the car, a door opened in a hut to the left and he saw one of the palace maids smiling at him. She beckoned to him to come. With a smile of his own, he complied. She made way for him to pass in, and then shut the door behind him. Samarah was sitting in the hut, suckling their son. She was dressed like a Chefwa princess with the rich *Kilanglang* cloth of the royal family, and lots of beads. He loved it when she was dressed like that. It was a sight he had seen only here in Chefwa and it suited her. His face split into a grin and his pace quickened. The maid went out, closing the door behind her. Samarah looked up at Mayne and smiled.

He squatted in front of her and ran his had through the baby's hair. "My son!" he muttered. Then his gaze went to Samarah and she saw an uncertainty there that she had never seen before. They looked at each other in silence, the only sound being that of the baby sucking. Finally, he pulled a bamboo chair closer and sat down. "The palace is very quiet," he commented. "Where is the chief?"

"He went with the elders to Kimbo. The British made the Nso Fon a Native Authority, so His Highness had to go to pay taxes. He also has to explain why fewer Chefwa men participated in the road construction this month."

"Oh!" Mayne exclaimed. He knew that when the British had taken over their own fifth of Cameroon, they ruled them as part of their colony in Nigeria. Since they had adopted the policy of Indirect Rule, where they ruled the natives through their local chiefs, they had appointed six influential chiefs as Native Authorities in the region – the Fons of Bali, Kom, Nso, Bangwa, Bimbia and Buea. In other areas where influential chiefs were not found, they had appointed natives whom they thought were responsible enough or subservient enough.

Samarah lifted the baby to her chest and gently rocked him till he burped and a little milk spluttered unto his chin amidst his giggles. Mayne smiled and held out his hands. Samarah placed the baby in them. Mayne cooed, and oohed and aahed, while the baby gave a smile and made baby sounds.

"He grows bigger everyday," Mayne said as he raised his laughing eyes to look at Samarah. He rocked the baby as he spoke to her. "I love you," he said. She swallowed and opened her mouth but no words came out. Finally she said, "here, let me have him." Mayne had not realized that the baby had fallen asleep. Samarah carried him to her bed and laid him between the sheets. Then she stood with her back to Mayne as she gazed at their son, and wondered what to say. She did not hear Mayne move, and almost jumped out of her skin when he spoke close to her ear.

"I never stopped hoping, Sam. Even when everybody said you were dead, I kept on hoping, because my heart told me you would not leave me."

"Mayne..."

"No darling, I need to say this."

His arms circled her waist from behind and he pulled her closer so that her back rested against his chest. He had loved to hold her that way. The memory made her heart tightened. How she had missed being held like that! She leaned into him and closed her eyes as he continued talking.

"These past months have been hell without you. I am so sorry I hurt you. Please, come back to me, Sam, come back home."

He turned her round to look into her eyes.

"I am home," she said with a sigh. "I have had time to think these past months. It was wrong of me to run off without listening to your own side of the story, and it was wrong of me to deprive you of the chance to see our baby growing in me. For those, I am sorry, but I came home. I came back to my roots... My life with you was a dream, a totally fulfilling, beautiful dream."

"And the dream can go on." His arms tightened around her. She shook her head.

"That's what you don't understand, Mayne. People wake up from dreams. I guess my time to wake up was due. I am needed here, among my people. God gave me the gift of you, and for that I will always be grateful, but I have to remain here. This is where I belong," she finished.

"Ok, Sam," he pleaded, "that's no problem. I'll move here. We can live here and I'll get someone to take care of the plantations at the coast."

"Mayne, I couldn't ask you to do that. I know what the plantations mean to you. You… you'll have to go back, without me." He let her go and turned his back to her as he absorbed her words. Then suddenly he whirled round to face her.

"It's him, isn't it? You are staying for him too." Samarah did not need to ask who.

"Mayne, you are missing the point."

"It's you who are missing the point here, wife. I married you. I pledged to love you for life. I vowed never to let you go. Surely, if there is one thing you've learnt about me, it is that I keep my promises."

"Mayne…"

"I'm not letting you go without a fight. I love you, and I know that you love me. Sweetheart…" He grabbed her right hand and placed it on his beating heart.

"Feel this! Every beat says I love you." He pulled her against his chest and held her tight. "I feel your heartbeat too. It tells me that you love me. How else do you want me to make you see the truth?" Samarah's body was already growing weak, and she was feeling the familiar stirring again. It was such a long time since she had felt that way and she realized that she had missed that too. A lot. Of their own volition, her arms wrapped around his neck as her body swayed closer to his.

"See, Sam?" he smiled and dimples appeared in his cheeks "your body and your heart are united in this." His gaze dropped to her lips. "And your lips tremble. I want to kiss you so much," he whispered and bent his head towards hers until his breath caressed her face. Samarah drew in her breath and her upper teeth grazed her lower lip. Her eyelids closed as she tilted her head up a fraction. Mayne bent his head and kissed the left side of her mouth as he inhaled her scent. She smelled fresh, and her mouth tasted so tempting. His right hand at the back of her neck pulled her head back so he could brush his lips against her throat. She let out a small moan and her fingers dug into his hair. His mouth covered hers in a kiss that touched her all the way to her soul. She had missed this. She had missed him. She clung to him and kissed him back with all the hunger she felt inside.

Amid the fog that clouded her mind, she heard a sound far off. It took some time for her to realize that their son had awakened. Mayne realized it too, and lifted his head and grinned. "Worst timing!" he said.

Samarah drew in a deep breath to steady herself as she reached for her son. She told Mayne it was okay if he left without looking at the baby. For a moment, she thought he would not budge, but then he came forward, bent down, kissed his son on the forehead, and told her he would be back the next day. Then with a piercing look in her direction he turned and walked out. Samarah's eyes filled with tears.

"Bwan, where are you when I really need you?" she murmured.

*

Samarah gazed at the setting sun as her mind wandered. Mayne would be leaving Kimbo the next day for the coast. Once again he had begged her to go with him but she had said no. He had kissed his son and promised to be back in a couple of months to see him. After he had left, Samarah had cried herself to sleep that night. Choosing to stay was one of the most painful decisions she had ever had to make in her life. But her people needed her, and she had found Bintum again.

"I know you love both men," Ngoneh said when she had come

to see Samarah. "I can't choose for you, but what I'd like to say is that you should follow your instincts." Now, as she looked at the sky, Samarah suddenly knew what she must do, what would make her truly happy. She had to find Bintum! She desperately had to see him. A smile spread across her face as she raced to his mother's house. After exchanging greetings with her, Samarah asked where Bintum was. His mother bent her head and in a sad voice told Samarah that Bintum was gone.

"Gone? What do you mean, gone?"

"He left this morning. After locking himself up for a week, he has finally left this morning." When she asked if Bintum had said where he was going, she was told that he had said he would return when he would return. At this news, Samarah sank to her knees as tears spilled over her eyes.

*

"Mr. Patterson, your luggage has already been packed in your jeep," one of the waiters in the Rest - House where Mayne was staying informed him.

"Thank you." Mayne glanced round the room. The time was ten a.m. and he had waited all morning, and an extra hour, hoping that she would come. She had not and he had to accept the fact that he had lost her. At least he knew she was alive. He would still be a part of her life and their son's. It was far more than he had hoped for when everyone had been convinced that she was dead. Heaving a sigh, he picked up his car keys from a table and with one last look around, went out.

He got into the jeep and tried to start the car, but his fingers trembled. "Darn!" he cursed and hit the steering. Then he bent his head unto the steering and tried to keep the tears from spilling out.

"Why, Mr. Patterson, are you leaving your wife and your son

behind?" A voice drawled. His head snapped up and he saw Samarah smiling at him from the veranda of the Rest – House. Mayne
looked like he had been struck by lightning. She walked to the
jeep with two *Nchindas* carrying her luggage. Mayne still had that
stricken look on his face when she climbed into the jeep. The
Nchindas put the luggage in the back, next to Mayne's. They bowed
good bye to Samarah, and walked away. Mayne took a deep breath.
Samarah smiled at him. "Marriage is a life-long issue, and I intend
to stick to you till the end of my days." A smile started to form
around his lips at her words, but he still looked at her like she was
a figment of his imagination.

"If you keep on looking at me like that, I might think you don't
want me any more, and then I'll just go." She made to open the
door. In a flash, Mayne's hand held her shoulder.

"Go where?" he pulled her close as he leaned over, "back home?"

"Everywhere is home as long as I'm with you," she smiled.

"Oh Sam, I do love you." He grinned and kissed her.

*

A couple of months after their return, Bessem came into the
bedroom and handed an envelope to Samarah. "Letter for you
Samarah," she said.

"Thanks, Bess. Maybe it's from Dr. Worthy, telling me how the
health unit has been functioning since the other nurse took over, or
Mayne telling me he'll be another week at the coast." She ripped
open the letter. Bessem left the room to go give Kintashe a bath.
Samarah glanced down at the letter, and then gasped. It was the
first time she had heard anything about Bintum in months. Her
mind flew back to the evening she had gone to tell him that she
had decided to go back to Mayne, only to find him gone. Now he
had contacted her. With shaky hands she concentrated on the letter.

April, 1921

Dear Samarah,

I don't know where to start. I am sorry I left without telling you. You must understand that it was a shock to see you with a white baby. However, I hope he is fine.

I gathered that you are back with your husband. When I saw you both at the hospital, I knew that I had lost you. I also knew that you would stick to me if I put pressure on you, but I wanted you to be happy, and I guess you are.

I won't lie and say that I am alright. You see, I still love you. I love you so much so that I am happy to let you go if you will be happy away from me. So I release you of our betrothal. You are free.

I beg you to destroy this letter after you read it, because of what I am about to write now. The secret of the owls must not be made known in daylight. I have met up with some people here in the coast. We are planning to free our people, and our nation from colonial rule. I cannot reveal their names because that would endanger them. We are working with some of our brothers in French Cameroon. I ask you not to worry about me, not to fear for me.

I have always had two loves in my life – you and our people. I have lost one. I won't lose the other. We will be free, no matter how long it takes. I do not know my future. I have chosen the rocky path, but I know our ancestors will see me through. When you think of me, think not of one who sacrificed himself for a foolish cause, but of one, who loved so much his life meant so little.

I can do this with one heart now, my Samarah, because I know that husband of yours will take care of you. He loves you and I know he will make you happy. So take care of yourself, and know that even though I was hurt because of you, I bear you no ill will. I will always love you. May the ancestors protect you.

Always,

Bintum

She did not realize that she was weeping until the tears dropped on the letter. She read it over and over again, then went to the hearth in the kitchen. After reading it one last time, she dropped it into the embers. As she watched it burn, she prayed for Bintum. Then she heard the hooting of the jeep and a few seconds later, she heard Mayne's footsteps racing through the living room and up the stairs to the nursery. When she heard him shout in delight, she knew he had swept their son up in his arms. With one last look at the fireplace, she smiled and walked out of the kitchen. When she reached the nursery, Mayne looked at her with Kintashe in his arms, and smiled. He extended one hand to her. She ran to him and embraced them both. As she raised her head to receive his kiss, she wished fervently that her country, and Bintum, would one day have their own fairytale.

ABOUT THE AUTHOR

Kefen Budji is a freelance writer, poet, teacher and storyteller residing in Bamenda, Cameroon. Her works have been published in 100% Youths! and other national magazines. She holds a BA in English and a diploma in Journalism and Mass Communication. When she is not busy teaching English and Literature to secondary school students, she volunteers as a counsellor to raise awareness about HIV/AIDS and reproductive health among youths. She enjoys listening to music, dancing, reading, acting, and documentary film-making. Boundless is her début novel.

Printed in the United States
By Bookmasters